Fire on the Altar

Doris M. Dorwart

AuthorHouse™ LLC
1663 Liberty Drive
Bloomington, IN 47403
www.authorhouse.com
Phone: 1-800-839-8640

This book is ripped from headlines over a period of years. It is not based on any particular cult, religion, or actual people living or dead. The characters in the book represent an amalgamation of the people that live only in the author's imagination.

Published by AuthorHouse 07/24/2014

ISBN: 978-1-4969-2939-6 (sc)
ISBN: 978-1-4969-2938-9 (e)

Library of Congress Control Number: 2014914160

This book is printed on acid-free paper.

CONTENTS

Part Three: Lockdown

Part Four: Sweet Revenge

ACKNOWLEDGEMENTS

When stories hit the headlines, especially those that seem bizarre, I find myself thinking, *"What if...."* As a result, some of the scenes in this book are taken from such headlines, but they also include all fictional characters. As you will find, the cult in this book has never really existed. It is only real in my mind. As any storyteller will verify, nothing excites writers more than when they hear or read about a strange happening. Immediately, their minds begin to create completely different characters and events. Just a bit scary!

My two editors, Jane Lloyd and Mary Jeanne deGroot, have helped me take my imagination and bring it to the written page. Their astuteness, while editing my manuscript, and their probing questions about the characters and events in the story have made my work come alive—thank you, ladies.

Even before I wrote the last page of *Fire on the Altar*, my imagination began taking me to my next book. Imagination can be both frightening and rewarding—it just depends on how authors react to the characters running through their minds.

PART ONE

THE TRIAL

Of a truth, God will not do wickedly, and the Almighty will not pervert justice. Job 34:12

CHAPTER 1

(The Trial: Day 1)

It was a hot, muggy, mid-September day in 1973 and the packed courtroom was like an oven. The fifth-floor windows of the old courthouse had been opened wide in a vain attempt to catch some air. Shiny chrome electric floor fans, strategically placed around the jury box and the witness stand, were creating a steady, monotonous, high-pitched hum that only added to the discomfort of the restless spectators.

The Valley River, one block west of the courthouse, and usually a charming showplace for the city of New Valley, the capital city, was hardly moving at all and had taken on a dark and dreary surface. The ominous-looking water appeared to be waiting for the heavens to provide a breeze to carry the accumulated debris away. The leaves on the trees, which lined the banks of the waterway, were motionless. Benches along the shaded bike paths were filled with senior citizens, trying to get some relief from the unbearable heat of their center city apartments. The concrete steps around the front of the courthouse, ordinarily filled with people watchers, were deserted since no one apparently had the stamina or the desire to sit in the direct rays of the sun. Even the stately cement lion that was perched on a five-foot pillar on the right side of the entrance was bathed in such brilliant sunlight that his facial features looked as if they had disappeared.

But the oppressive heat did not deter people from flocking to the courtroom in record numbers. Even Pete Forster, New Valley's most recognized reporter, had arrived early and had managed to claim a seat in the second row. Bodies were jammed together on the hard, wooden benches and tempers were easily frayed. Even the four rows in the stifling balcony were filled to overflowing, and some spectators stood in the niches that, at one time, held statues of famous New Valley politicians. However, one man, who was seated in the first row of the balcony, appeared to be oblivious to the environmental conditions. His small, dark eyes were fixated on the back of the male defendant's head with a steady unfaltering gaze. Completely unaware of the beads of sweat that were slowly rolling down his scraggy face and into the corners of his mouth, the gray-haired man remained stoic as if frozen in his seat.

Judge William Calder tugged incessantly at the collar of his heavy black robe and kept wiping the sweat from his neck with his white, monogrammed handkerchief. Heaving a noticeable sigh, he leaned toward the jury and, in an almost disinterested tone, said, "Ladies and gentlemen, before we begin, I must caution you not to discuss this case with anyone or among yourselves, prior to receiving all the testimony. If anyone should approach you about this case, you must report it to me immediately. I also caution you not to draw any conclusions about the guilt or innocence of the defendants until all the testimony has been presented, and you have carefully weighed the facts."

The jurors, seven Protestants, three Catholics and two Jews, had been chosen to examine the evidence presented by the prosecution against the defendants, Ayden and Sarah Ash, operators of a small, private religious school, who were on trial for statutory rape, indecent assault, and corruption of a minor child. Most of the jurors were taking advantage of colorful paper fans that had been donated to the city by Nelson Funeral Home and were moving them back and forth rapidly, desperately trying to create some respite from the unusual September heat. In fact, jurors on either end of the jury box were moving their fans in perfect synchronization as they waved the scenic cardboard from side to side in front of their faces. One juror, a rotund man, cupped his right ear with his hand in an apparent attempt to hear over the steady whine of the metal fans, while waving the fan with his left hand so hard that his hair was standing up. Every so often, he would stop fanning and begin pushing his wire-rimmed glasses up the bridge of his long, thick nose. He looked frustrated and annoyed.

New Valley was sandwiched between steel mills to the south and farming communities to the north. Its people were known for their strong religious beliefs and even stronger work ethic. Some had demonstrated their outrage by writing letters to the editor of *The New Valley Press*, accusing the defendants of besmirching the reputation of their city by committing such repulsive crimes and recommending that the Ashes receive stiff sentences for their transgressions.

Ayden Ash was a small man with an almost mole-like appearance. His face, a little on the cherubic side, seemed even larger since he was almost bald. His small hazel eyes, set close together under bushy eyebrows, kept darting back and forth as he scrutinized the people who would soon have his fate in their hands. A beige-colored short-sleeve shirt and matching trousers only helped to make him more unappealing.

Ayden's wife, Sarah, looked more like a teen-ager. Her shimmering chestnut-colored hair hung loosely and cascaded down to her waist. A silver clip above each ear kept the wavy tresses from falling into her eyes. Her thin, sharp face bore no signs of makeup and her skin was smooth and shiny. A widow's peak softened her features and made her almost pretty. She was wearing a simple, dark cotton full skirt, a plain white blouse, and a flowered print scarf wrapped around her tiny waist.

"All right, ladies and gentlemen. I think we will begin at this time. Are the attorneys ready to make their opening remarks?" Judge Calder asked as he looked first to his right and then to his left.

Assistant District Attorney, Ray Barber, was the first to begin. He paced back and forth in front of the jury and did not stop in one place for any length of time. A rather tall man in his early fifties, his appearance was a little disheveled. His lightweight suit hung much too loosely on his lanky frame. A large Adam's apple kept bobbing up and down behind the collar of his oversized shirt, adding an almost comical feature to his appearance. However, surprisingly, when he spoke he commanded attention with his eloquence.

When Barber began to admonish the jury about their duties, Ayden's attorney, Claude Wilson, jumped up and said, "May it please the Court, I must object to the Prosecution giving instructions to the jury at the opening of the case."

Ayden smiled broadly as Judge Calder turned to Barber and said, "That is more proper in your closing remarks. Furthermore, I will instruct the jury on their duties anyhow."

Concentrating on the jurors one by one, Ayden immediately felt a unique connection to a woman in the center of the front row. With his piercing eyes, he began to stare at her, not moving a muscle. Slowly, the woman began to shift in her seat and, sure enough, she turned her head and met his gaze. Quietly, Ayden said confidently, "*Gotcha*." With an ever-so-slight smile and with a nod of his head, he dismissed her.

Next, he chose the young man two seats from his first conquest. Shy, nervous, of low self-esteem, and not too bright—was Ayden's quick analysis of the skinny red-headed man. Fixing his stare on his next target, Ayden was beginning to feel more exhilarated than he had in weeks. The *gift* was still his. The power to select those around him whom he could dominate and control was as strong as ever. The juror began to stir, hesitating only a moment before he looked toward Ayden, parting his lips slightly, as if he were going to speak. Ayden bestowed a slight smile on his victim and quickly added another juror to his mental tally sheet.

Ayden then turned his attention to the women at either end of the front row and decided that they both would be trouble. Their chins looked like they had been set in concrete, and they seemed to have permanent scowls etched on their wrinkled faces. Ayden surmised that they had been reared under strict rules that discouraged people from even talking about sex let alone participating in the act. He was certain they would be tough eggs to crack.

Ray Barber was now questioning the detective who had filed the charges against the defendants. Detective Robert Nonnenmocher testified that he had interviewed Amanda Hoffman at the request of the First Assistant District Attorney, and that he had taken her to the doctor for examination. Ayden could not have cared less what the detective was saying and turned his head to look at the spectators. With his peripheral vision he saw that Amanda's mother, Margaret Hoffman, and her lover John Murray, were seated in the audience. Ayden despised John for several reasons. First, he didn't trust him. On top of that, Ayden felt that John was a scheming, no-account black sonofabitch. He kept staring at John and when the black man met his stare, Ayden mouthed, "*motherfucker*." Ayden hated everything about John. He disliked the way John talked and walked—rather limped down the street. John's right leg was shorter than his left—a fact he tried unsuccessfully to conceal by constantly walking on his toes. Ayden didn't care that John was black. It wasn't his blackness that bothered him. John could have been any color and Ayden would have still hated the man. There were some black people Ayden could tolerate—not many though.

Finally, Barber was finished questioning Detective Nonnenmocher. It was now Claude Wilson's turn. Wilson, a handsome attorney with a great deal of courtroom experience, wore a tailored suit that fit his muscular frame perfectly, and, despite the intense heat, the man did not appear to sweat. Blonde hair, perfectly styled, complimented his exquisite green eyes. He was almost movie-picture perfect as he stood before the detective who was soaking wet and constantly mopping his forehead.

"Detective Nonnenmocher, when you questioned Amanda, at any time did she change her story from the one that she had originally told the First Assistant District Attorney?" Wilson asked with a dramatic flair.

"No, sir," Nonnenmocher responded to the high-priced attorney from out of town.

Wilson did not give up. He rephrased the question two more times, trying to get the detective to admit that in some way Amanda had told several, different versions of her story. When this tactic failed, he finally got the detective to admit that when he questioned Amanda later, however, she had not told the truth about little insignificant details. Wilson took advantage of this admission and spent considerable time going over and over the differences and used the word *lies* several times.

Ayden was glad that he had chosen Wilson as his attorney. He was good. The jury would probably not remember that these little details were meaningless bits of information, but they would recall that again and again the detective had responded that her story had differed at times. Ayden had to remember this strategy. This was good. He had picked a local attorney, Wally Berman, to represent Sarah. He had rationalized this choice by telling Sarah that, since Berman was a local attorney, jurors would be more likely to hold him in higher esteem and side with him. But Ayden knew that *he* was the one who really needed the quick mind and the vast courtroom experience that Wilson possessed. After all, he could only afford one good attorney.

Suddenly, Ayden felt eyes on him so he turned his attention back to the jury—somber faces in a sea of stifling heat. The woman he had focused on earlier was looking directly at him. He could feel the electric vibrations between the two of them, flowing across the courtroom floor, creeping up his leg and into his groin. He returned her stare and for a few minutes nothing else existed. Ayden shuddered as he experienced a powerful sexual feeling, a soft flowing of energy through his body. He closed his eyes and allowed the tingling to run rampant.

"Detective, is it not true that both Mr. and Mrs. Ash came to your office voluntarily?"

"Yes, sir, they did."

Ayden leaned back in his chair—*voluntarily*? Yeah, you could call it that. Originally, when he had had his first opportunity to tell his side of the story, he thought Amanda's accusations would not be believed—but he had been wrong. During the questioning period, Ayden had been irritated greatly by the detective's lack of organization when he had to constantly rifle through paperwork to find what he needed. Ayden believed that good organization meant a good mind. As a result, he had always been methodical about everything, making lists, not only for himself, but for all those who worked in the school.

He jumped when Amanda was called to the stand. Tall and extremely thin, with blonde hair that hung close to the sides of her face, almost concealing her baby-like features, she looked frightened. Her narrow lips were painted in a garish red color, which reminded Ayden of one of those kewpie dolls used as prizes at the county fair. She kept rubbing her hands together with such a strong force that it appeared she was attempting to keep herself warm. Her short skirt revealed bony knee caps and long, painfully thin legs. Amanda was not attractive yet, but, if one looked closely, one could see a beautiful woman trying to escape the prison of a child's body.

Barber approached the girl and said reassuringly, "Now, Amanda, don't be nervous. We just have a few questions to ask you. All you have to do is tell the truth and—"

"Your Honor," screeched Wilson. "I must object. I feel that my honored colleague should not..."

"Objection sustained. Mr. Barber, please get to your questions." Judge Calder said forcefully.

"Amanda, until last May, what school were you attending?"

"I was in the ninth grade at The Church of True Believers School."

"And where is the school located?"

"In New Valley," replied the nervous girl.

"No, my dear, I meant what is the address of the school?" Barber corrected.

"Oh...I'm sorry," Amanda said in a low voice. "It's at the corner of Commerce and Jackson."

Barber then went through a series of questions regarding the school. As the young girl would answer each query, Barber would repeat her answer almost word for word.

"Amanda, let me get something clarified. Mr. Ash permitted you to attend the school without paying any money?"

"I think so," Amanda responded. "He said he felt sorry for me."

"Amanda, how many other students attended Mr. Ash's school?" Barber asked as he turned to look directly at Ayden.

"About ten or twelve—it changed from time to time."

Barber then switched to ask questions about the teachers at the school.

"Well, we had a couple, mostly Jake and Rebekah," Amanda hesitated and then added, "and sometimes Ayden."

"You mentioned Jake. Who is he, Amanda?" Barber asked.

"Jake Mnbonu. He was like the principal. You know, he sort of was in charge and stuff like that. Ayden brought him over here from Africa because he felt sorry for him and..."

"Objection!" both Berman and Wilson shouted.

"Seems like Mr. Ash was sorry for a lot of people," Barber added before Judge Calder could even rule on the objection.

"Your Honor," Wilson said, "I must object to these personal opinions of—"

"Sustained. Mr. Barber, you know better than that. Now please proceed," an agitated Calder said.

Ayden was annoyed. The mere mention of Jake's name made him livid. The bastard had run off the very night that he and Sarah had been arrested and hadn't been seen since. After all that he had done for him, the black ingrate couldn't stick around to support him.

"Amanda, you mentioned Rebekah. Do you mean Rebekah Montgomery?"

"Yeah, she was like a .... Mother Superior."

"Mother Superior?" Barber repeated.

"Yeah., she... well, she gave us heck when we were bad, and she would check up on us and stuff like that. She was nice. Not like that stuck-up Melody Baker," the young witness stated firmly.

"Was Ms. Montgomery the school disciplinarian?" Barber asked.

"She didn't punish us all the time. She was good to us. She gave us advice and listened to our problems and helped us with... with...," Amanda began to stare straight ahead and appeared to lose her train of thought.

Both Rebekah Montgomery and Melody Baker were sitting in the upper balcony of the courtroom. Oblivious to the heat, Rebekah was wearing a yellow linen suit with long sleeves and a blouse that buttoned up to her neck. Little rows of ruffles stuck out around the collar in a pristine fashion. She also wore a small straw hat, white lace gloves, and white leather heels—the picture of a matronly woman unconcerned about fashion statements.

Melody, however, was much more fashionable. Her polyester slack suit, in hues of pink and rose, and sporting the new wide pants legs, was very flattering to her figure. Dark brown sandals revealed toenails perfectly manicured and painted in a bright shade of pink. Melody certainly could not be considered pretty by any stretch of the imagination. She had a plain face that was dominated by a nose too large for her other features, but she took advantage of her alluring figure and carried herself with a great deal of confidence. As she stretched forward to get a better look at the spectators below, it was obvious that she was not wearing a bra. Her hair was pulled back into a ponytail that was held in place with a large pink barrette. The two women, though bonded together through their involvement with the defendants, were complete opposites in their outward appearance. One looked like a spinster while the other represented a free spirit.

"Amanda, did Ms. Montgomery serve as the school counselor?" Barber asked.

"Well, sort of. I remember one time when I had some trouble with a boy I knew, I told Ms. Montgomery, and she helped to get him off my back," Amanda proudly replied. "But Melody…well, she just made fun of me."

Amanda could not see that when she said this, Melody held her head high and giggled.

"Do you mean Melody Baker, the school's secretary?" Barber asked.

"She was not a secretary. She was a trouble maker who was jealous of me because Ayden liked me the best. She's an ugly-looking…"

"Objection," Wilson shouted one more time.

"Sustained. Amanda, I must caution you to answer the questions and do not add your personal opinions. Now, Mr. Barber, please proceed and let's stick to relevant matters," Judge Calder directed.

"Amanda, will you please describe the school for the jurors?" Barber asked.

Amanda took a deep breath, turned toward the ever-fanning jurors and said, "It's a big, red brick building that has—let's see, four floors. The church was on the second floor and there was a little door on Jackson Street that people used to get there. Ayden's private library was also on the second floor. No kids were allowed to go in there. Our school was on the first floor in the rear near the kitchen and the store was in the front, facing Commerce Street. There were four bedrooms on the third floor, and we also had a clinic and storage rooms down the hall. The top floor was like an attic, filled with old junk and stuff. We used to play up there at times. I think at one time it had been a factory."

Barber went on at length, questioning Amanda about the school, focusing specifically on the bedrooms. Amanda explained that Ayden and Sarah had one bedroom, while Rebekah and Melody each had their own quarters; Jake occupied the fourth one.

"Amanda," Barber said, "did any of the children stay overnight at the school?"

"Just a few times—oh, and when we had the hurricane, we did," she replied.

Barber then shifted his questioning to the bookstore that was on the first floor of the building.

"Now, Amanda, can you tell the jury more about what kind of items were offered for sale in Mr. Ash's bookstore?" Barber asked as he once again looked directly at Ayden.

"Mostly dirty stuff," Amanda replied in an accusatory tone.

"Objection, calls for an opinion," an exasperated Berman said.

"Sustained. Amanda, just tell the jury what was for sale in the store. Don't offer opinions," Judge Calder directed in a grandfatherly manner. "Do you understand, my dear?"

"I think so."

Barber paused, took a deep breath and proceeded. "Amanda, let's try that question again. What kind of items did Mr. Ash sell in his store?"

"Mostly books and pictures."

"What kind of books and pictures?"

"Oh, real old stuff like history books. Some were so old that the covers were missing. Most of them were printed a long time ago, before I was born. Some have stuff about presidents and religion and, well, *you know....*"

"What is *you know*?"

"Like sex and stuff."

"Did you say *sex*?" emphasized Barber.

"Yeah, Ayden kept that stuff in the Adult Room and only certain people were allowed to go in there."

"How did you find out what was in that room, Amanda?"

"I snuck in there one day to look around. Ayden found me and he was really pissed off at me," Amanda replied.

"Amanda, you stated that Mr. Ash sold pictures in his store. Can you tell me what kind of pictures?"

"Some were nice like ships and stuff like that. But most were pictures of naked people," Amanda responded, keeping her head down, not looking at Ayden or Sarah.

"Amanda, were some of the pictures erotic in nature?"

"Your Honor, the witness already answered that question." Berman stated.

"Overruled. The witness may answer," Judge Calder said as he began to fan more rapidly.

Barber smiled and, as he walked slowly and deliberately toward Amanda, he said, "The pictures—the ones that were for sale in Mr. Ash's bookstore, Amanda, were they the type that tended to arouse sexual feelings?"

"I don't know what you mean," the young girl said, wiping tears from her eyes.

"Were they the type of pictures that would encourage people, or motivate people, to get involved in sexual activities?" Barber explained.

"Well, I guess so. Most were pictures of many people all having sex together, or sometimes, all by themselves."

"By themselves?" Barber asked incredulously.

"Yeah, like women using things. Sarah said that was okay," Amanda protested.

Several members of the jury just shook their heads in utter disbelief. Others seemed stunned. Ayden was gripping the edge of the table and casting hateful looks at the pitiful young girl.

"Did Mr. Ash sell photographs in his bookstore?" Barber asked.

"I don't think so."

"Did Mr. Ash ever ask you to pose for pictures that he took?" questioned Barber as he turned toward the spectators.

Amanda hung her head and began to swing her foot back and forth.

"Amanda, did you ever pose for pictures for Mr. Ash?" Barber asked again.

"Well, he did take some class pictures," the girl said as if she just remembered.

"Did he ever take pictures of you without your clothes?"

Amanda, without raising her head, began to cry softly. Barber repositioned himself so that he stood between the girl and her view of Ayden and asked again. "Did Mr. Ash ever ask you to pose for pictures that required you to remove your clothes?"

"Well—I—but..."

"Did he ever take those kinds of pictures of you?" Barber asked, using his finest elocution.

Keeping her head down and swinging her foot even faster, she replied very faintly, "Yes."

"Amanda, speak up. The ladies and gentlemen of the jury cannot hear you over the noise in this room. Now, please, one more time, did Mr. Ash ever take pictures of you without your clothes on?"

Finally, Amada lifted her head. "Yes, he did."

The two women jurors, who had been fanning themselves profusely, both stopped and let their fans become still in mid-air. The courtroom became very quiet. The only noise was the constant whining of the fans. Barber took full advantage of the stillness as he slowly sauntered toward the defense table, pausing directly in front of Ayden.

Casting a backwards look at Ayden, and in a rather triumphant tone, Barber asked, "Amanda, were you alone in these pictures?"

"Some I was and some I wasn't," the girl said defensively.

Barber honestly felt sorry for the young girl on the witness stand. He wished that he didn't have to put her through all of this, but he had to win this case. He had to get this slime off the streets. Barber permitted the jury time to let Amanda's words sink in before he posed his next question, "Who else was in those pictures with you, Amanda?"

Now Amanda looked frightened. "Some girl, but I don't remember her name. She was younger than me," she answered softly. "I think her name was Barbara."

"What happened to those pictures, Amanda?"

"I don't know. I don't have them," Amanda replied defensively.

"Did Mr. Ash sell your photographs in his bookstore?" Barber pursued.

"No," Amanda shouted. "He wouldn't do that. He loved me. He said so."

"Oh, but he did take those kinds of pictures of you, didn't he, Amanda?' Barber challenged.

"That's not true," shouted Ayden.

Judge Calder rapped his gavel soundly and said, "Mr. Ash, you will have an opportunity to speak for yourself later, but I will not tolerate any interruptions. Mr. Wilson, please advise your client that drastic measures will be taken if this type of conduct continues. Mr. Barber, please proceed."

Ray Barber then asked Amanda to describe the room that she had referred to as the clinic. "Amanda, can you describe the clinic? Were any medications administered in this room?"

Amanda turned her thin face toward the jury, bit her lower lip and replied, "The only pills I ever got there were for headaches. But the clinic was where the girls would sometimes get examined—like—there was this table—like the kind the doctors use and stuff—we had to get examined to be sure that we were still sanctified."

"Sanctified?" Barber asked, seemingly astounded at this news.

"Sometimes Sarah or Ayden would tell us girls that they had to check our insides to be sure that we had not defiled our bodies that we had already given to the Lord. Must I talk about this with all these people here?" Amanda asked as she pointed to the spectators, many of whom represented the press.

"We explained all of this to you before, Amanda. It will be all right. Just relax. Now go on, dear," Barber explained.

Amanda's lips began to tremble. "Where do you want me to start?"

"You were telling us that Ayden and Sarah would require the girls to be examined to see if they were sanctified. Then what happened, Amanda?"

"Well, one time, I had to—well, they made me—I can't tell you that," the young girl said as she began to weep uncontrollably.

Amanda's mother was weeping openly as John Murray tried to console her. One hand clung to her well-worn pocketbook, while the other was clutching John's arm. She sniffled loudly as she tried to fight back the tears that streamed down her pudgy, round face. The rolls of fat around her waist jiggled up and down as she struggled to catch her breath. Ayden merely glanced over his shoulder and smirked.

After giving the young girl time to regain control of herself, Barber asked, "Amanda, did there come a time when Mr. Ash asked you to leave the school?"

"Yeah, he found out that I had a boyfriend. He got real mad at me and threw me out of the school and told me not to come back," the girl said as she began to pout.

"But you did go back, Amanda, didn't you?" questioned Barber.

"Sure. I had to. I couldn't tell my mom. I couldn't. So I went back, and after I had told Ayden that I was sorry, he said that I could come back to school. After that time, he didn't come near me again and he even took back his ring. He said that I wasn't pure any more and that he didn't want to get some dumb disease from a girl like me. I ain't that type of girl. Ayden was the only one ever. After all, I was one of his wives," Amanda responded as she too began to cry.

A loud gasp could be heard in the courtroom. Spectators were bumping one another and holding private conversations about what they had just heard. Several jurors were now shaking their heads. It appeared that the only person who was pleased to hear this shocking statement was Barber who had a slight smile on his face as he looked at Ayden.

"One of his wives—but, Amanda, how can that be when Mr. Ash is already married? That's his wife sitting right over there," Barber said as he pointed to Sarah.

"He gave me a ring, and he said it meant that I was one of his brides and that the Lord told him that it was okay."

"Amanda, do you know if Mr. Ash had sex with any of the other girls?" quizzed Barber.

"Your Honor, my learned colleague knows better than to ask such a question," Wally Berman, Sarah's attorney, said disgustedly.

"Mr. Barber," Judge Calder said. "Please pursue another line of questioning. I would also like to suggest that as soon as you are finished with this witness that court be adjourned. The heat is becoming unbearable."

"I'm willing to finish my questioning now if I may have the option of recalling this witness later, if necessary, Your Honor," Barber replied.

"Very well then," and with a loud bang of the gavel, Judge Calder said, "Court is adjourned until nine tomorrow morning."

The deputies placed handcuffs on the two defendants and escorted them out of the courtroom, down the elevator, and across the street to the New Valley jail.

Long after everyone else had left the courtroom, a lone figure returned and climbed the steps leading to the balcony. He stood up and slowly said to the empty courtroom, "You sonofabitch. You lying bastard. If this damned court doesn't get you, I will, you little perverted weasel. I swear to almighty God that I will!"

The man moved back to the stairway but stopped in his tracks. Looking to his right, his interest was piqued when he saw a long, narrow hall that appeared deserted. Slowly, he followed the well-worn, linoleum-covered floor and spotted a chain dangling from the ceiling. As he tugged on it, the ceiling panels parted and a small ladder appeared. Making sure that no one was around, he climbed up and found himself in a small attic. It was even hotter there than it had been in the courtroom. He inched himself half way into the opening. Sunlight was streaming in through a dirt-streaked window that apparently faced the front of the building. For several minutes, he remained still. *This is it! This is the way I can kill that bastard. I will get my revenge after all.*

CHAPTER 2

(Twenty months earlier)

Ayden leaned back in his well-worn, brown leather chair, placed his hands behind his head, and watched the snow flakes hit the big front window of his bookstore. It was beginning to look serious out there. The storm, although it had been predicted more than a day ago, had caught many passers-by unprepared since they were trudging along without snow boots. Ayden chuckled as he watched one young woman, in open-toed high-heeled shoes, trying to avoid the snow. How like a woman! If she would rather have her toes exposed to frost bite than to cover them properly, then she deserved whatever she got.

With a wide grin on his face, he turned his attention to the finished manuscript that he had stacked neatly in the middle of the large desk. It was done. This would be only the first of his historical publications. There would be many more. The book was good—he knew that. He had researched the county extensively. He had always found the best information at the State Library, where he had been able to gain access to books, documents and old county maps. And that is where he also had found Melody. How easy it had all been. But then, it had always been easy for him. Women have a tendency to let their vulnerability show, and he was smart enough to take advantage of their weaknesses.

One dreary day, when Ayden had been researching in the State Library, he needed to locate some old county maps. He had gone to the reference desk to seek help. The young woman's face had been partially concealed by her long hair. But as soon as she had raised her head, Ayden had found himself looking into eyes that were cool and refreshing. After a few more visits, Ayden had been able to convince Melody to join him for dinner—from there on it had been elementary. While Melody had been an eager sexual partner, she also had brains. When a position had opened up in a section of the Department of Education, responsible for funding outside contracts, Melody quickly applied. It proved to be a profitable move for Ayden since Melody then knew before any announcements were made what type of projects would receive priority for funding.

Ayden knew that he would not win a prize for his looks. That was a fact that he could not deny. His small frame only carried about 145 pounds and his head was almost completely bald. He had always wanted to be taller—to occupy space in a more commanding manner, but that had only been a dream. Perhaps it would happen in his next life. His mind had always been his most powerful weapon, a weapon as lethal as any that a soldier had ever carried onto a battlefield. He knew how to use his intellect to get the things that he wanted. And he could mesmerize people with his eyes. When one looked directly into his eyes, glints of gold would actually appear, captivating people, especially women, allowing him to use this phenomenon to get into their minds, almost spell-like.

He was proud that he had developed his own unique religious beliefs that gave him more solace than he had ever experienced. He no longer followed the morality code of others. He was convinced that society was filled with individuals who had lost their sense of belonging—they had gotten hung up with the rules and regulations that prevented creativity, love, and understanding of sexuality from being realized. *What right does anyone have to judge another's sexual preference? Our bodies are our own to do with what we please, to make ourselves and others happy—to join in perfect harmony with God.* Ayden's ex-wife had resented his newly found freedom and her jealousy still surfaced whenever the two of them had an occasion to meet. She had been part of a society which was filled with so many rules and regulations that true resourcefulness, true love, and total understanding could never be achieved.

He pulled the center desk drawer open and removed the big, black checkbook. The balance indicated that his current available cash would carry the school until the end of next month. And, by that time he would have received his final payment from the Department of Education for completing his book on the history of Benton County. A nice little sum, which when added to what the women earned in their jobs, would make his financial picture brighter than it had been in a long time.

Ayden hoped that when he was finished with his appointment this afternoon he would have time to stop in at the State Library once again. He loved working in that archaic, august building. When he was roaming through the stacks, looking for materials for his books, he was the happiest—becoming one with the recorded words and images. In his imagination, he would place himself in sundry time periods, and daydream about what he would have done differently than those who actually lived at that time. And, what thrilled him the most was that *his* written words would soon be available to others like himself, tucked among the thousands of works held on the overloaded library shelves. The words in his books and documents would not only influence current society, but they would even shape and mold what people in the future do and believe. *He loved the power of the written word. Unlike women who may desert men, or be unfaithful to the rulings of his church, words do not forsake their creator. Words are power. Words are constant—not unreliable.*

As the antiquated grandfather clock chimed twice, Ayden realized that he had to get moving or he would be late. He had submitted a new proposal to the Department of Education to produce some movies for the New Valley School District. He had developed a script to create a series of films, aimed at teaching children about the dangers of running away from home. And Dr. Mark Jenson, who worked for the State, had indicated that he might be interested in providing the fiscal support needed to produce the films if he could get approval of Ayden's storyboard and script. The only problem Ayden had with this arrangement was that it would require him to deal, once again, with Jenson. It annoyed Ayden that he had to call Jenson *Doctor*! After all, Ayden knew that he was much smarter than this clown even though he did not have a formal education like Jenson. Truly educated people realize that life is the proper school—not some group of buildings run by professors who couldn't think their way out of a paper bag. Life is the teacher—if people would only pay attention.

Ayden had identified Jake Mnbonu, a black man from Africa, as the one who would do the actual filming. Ayden had met Jake through a local association that was connected to an international group concerned with helping people of Third World countries to better understand the United States. Ayden had been offered the opportunity to participate in the program by providing a home and a job to one candidate; Jake was his choice. The idea was that the immigrants would be exposed to a new environment by living and working with American families. In this way, the foreigners would then be able to return to their respective countries with a better understanding of America and the American way of life. However, Ayden hadn't gotten involved until he had given the whole idea a great deal of thought. He had screened the applicants carefully before making his final selection. And a wise one it had been. Jake had indeed proved to be of help to Ayden in many ways. First, Ayden had been able to prove to the Department of Education that a minority was involved in the school and the business—a requirement for getting lucrative contracts from the State. Second, he had trained Jake as a typesetter for the church's printing press—a very *cheap* typesetter. Jake had willingly worked long hours to meet the demands that Ayden had placed on him. While Jake had been a good worker, Ayden made certain that the association ended there. No socializing with blacks for him.

As he drove through the snow storm toward the city, he began to reflect on his success with establishing a church school within just one year after marrying Sarah. With a small band of friends and fellow believers, and four children from the neighborhood, The Church of True Believers School had been founded last spring. According to state law, their little private school had not been required to have state-certificated teachers. However, Rebekah Montgomery held a valid teaching degree—a fact that Ayden felt added to the status of the school even though he personally did not feel certified teachers were better teachers than he, in spite of their formal education.

It often disturbed him that he had married Sarah. She contributed very little to the actual operation of the school. However, just like Melody, she worked every day and brought her paycheck directly to him every two weeks. Ayden provided his staff with small stipends on a monthly basis. If they wanted personal items, they had to make a request to him for money to cover these expenses. Sarah was more like a puppy dog, always hanging around, begging for attention. She accepted unquestionably anything Ayden ordered her to do—even when he brought other women into their bed.

Melody, on the other hand, was like a breath of fresh air. She came to him as open and as free-willed as the first time they had shared their love. She did not question his teachings, but, unlike Sarah, she had a genuine desire to learn more about the teachings of the church and often probed for further clarification, always soaking up Ayden's explanations about his religious dogma. Her eyes would widen with excitement when she sat at Ayden's feet, listening to him philosophizing about all types of subjects. When she called him brilliant, his soul soared.

The building in which the church school was housed was his, free and clear—an inheritance from his father—the only good thing that his father ever did for him. Ayden had few good memories of his father. *A father does not beat his child. A father does not steal his little boy's money. A father helps his son obtain his rightful place in the world and demonstrates to the entire world that his son is bright, and strong, and forceful. A father does not make fun of his son's small stature and lack of good looks.* Ayden now thought of himself as a man who did not have a father. He had built a fortress around himself that blocked out the pain, the emptiness, the hurt. However, one particular old wound, which simply would not go away, still haunted him. Ayden had won a bonus of ten dollars for doubling the number of newspaper subscriptions on his paper route. As soon as Ayden had gotten home, he had shared the news of his good fortune with his parents. His father immediately had taken the money and had not allowed Ayden to question where it had gone.

As the windshield wiper swished back and forth, Ayden thought about the many times that, as a boy, he had eagerly taken sanctuary from the cold damp nights in the warm State Library. He loved sitting on the high-backed wooden chairs as he perused one volume after another. What a safe, wonderful place it had been. He used to stroll throughout the three floors, which held all kinds of marvels tucked between different colored bindings. He had read constantly, often keeping a dictionary close by his side to look up words that he hadn't understood. From the time he was little, he had prepared a list of words each week—important sounding words, words that his father would not understand—and had made a point of using one new word each day. He loved seeing the expression on people's faces when he spewed out his newly found knowledge. Most had been too embarrassed to ask him what the words meant. They had been afraid of his ability—too frightened to admit that they had not understood. Those experiences had given him ownership of the words. And, he had found the power he needed to survive.

As he drove his car through the falling snow across the North Bridge, he began to concentrate on the presentation he would be making shortly to Jenson about the films he wanted to make for school districts across the state. Melody had discovered that only one other proposal had been submitted and that the amount being requested was three times the budget that was in Ayden's proposal. It was almost a certainty that the funds would be awarded to Ayden. Tonight there might be a celebration—a time for rejoicing with the Lord.

After parking the car, Ayden took the elevator to the third floor and headed for Jenson's office. Every time he came to the Department of Education, he had always made certain that he steered clear of Melody. No one knew of her affiliation with him, and Ayden wanted to keep it that way. And, since Sarah worked at the State Library two blocks away, he didn't have to worry about bumping into her. The State had an unusual arrangement in that the State Library came under the jurisdiction of the Department of Education. Lucky for Ayden, that meant that he had tremendous access to information regarding all kinds of available grant money.

The meeting went just as Ayden had predicted. Jenson told him that he would get his contract in a few weeks, and that if the Department liked the end products, they would contract with him to produce other films. As Ayden drove home, his sense of power grew even stronger. He was getting his book published. He was getting contracts from the State. His private school was growing in size. His star was indeed rising.

CHAPTER 3

(The Trial: Day 2)

After an all-night torrential rain, the unusual heat wave finally broke. The weather was picture-perfect. Amid a flurry of anticipation, the second day of the Ashes' trial was about to begin. Representatives from both the press and local television stations were in their glory—they had a sensational trial to perk up their ratings. Much had been made about Amanda's testimony the day before, and it seemed that everyone had developed their own suppositions as to what actually happened in the little church school.

Lines were also being drawn in the Department of Education. People, who had worked with Sarah at the State Library, were standing by her adamantly, while others, who had only known her superficially, were certain of her guilt. The Secretary of Education had encouraged his employees within the Department, as well as those working in the State Library, to remain silent and not to grant any interviews. Suddenly, most State employees had remained aloof and refused to comment on anything, including the granting of lucrative contracts. A cone of silence, while strictly denied by staff members, had quietly been put into place. However, the press had been able to get a few statements from neighbors about Ayden—none of which were favorable.

As Sarah was led into the courtroom, she appeared to be more ill at ease than she had been the day before. Dark circles were visible under her eyes. She was wearing the same outfit as the day before, but she had added a little, cropped jacket. Her hair still glistened like diamonds in the early morning sun. Her demeanor, however, indicated that she was feeling very depressed. As she took her seat, she closed her eyes and silently put words to her thoughts. *How can I possibly love a man and hate him at the same time? What kind of woman am I? All I know is that I cannot live without him. His love is all I have. I cannot raise our little Alice alone. How I wish there were no other women in his life. Why can I not just accept the teachings of our church? Tell me, Ayden, that I am all you need—I beg you—then I can survive.*

Ayden, on the other hand, was a picture of strength, bordering on open arrogance. He strutted into the courtroom as if he were the presiding judge rather than a defendant. He carefully looked over the spectators and, when he spotted his friend Pete Forster, a reporter for the local newspaper, he waved and became a bit agitated when Pete did not acknowledge his greeting.

Pete was talking with another reporter, and they were exchanging thoughts and suppositions about the up-coming, cross-examination of Amanda that would obviously take place as soon as Judge Calder convened today's session. All the benches were filling rapidly. Additional metal folding chairs had been placed around the perimeter of the room to accommodate even more people than were in the courtroom yesterday. The banner of the early edition of the newspaper had labeled the trial as "*the hottest case in years.*" Last night's edition had carried a quote from Margaret Hoffman saying, "*He's as guilty as sin. The devil will get him for what he did to my Amanda.*" All of this made good press and had contributed significantly to increased sales for the newspapers.

As Judge Calder entered, a hush came over the courtroom. His countenance was a bit more pleasant than it had been yesterday. As he took his place behind the bench, he even smiled at the court reporter. With a loud rap of the gavel, Calder called the court to order.

After Amanda was called, Claude Wilson began his cross-examination. "Amanda, yesterday you testified that Rebekah Montgomery was a friend of yours. Is that correct?"

"Yeah," the girl answered sullenly.

"You testified that she gave you advice. Is that correct?" Wilson patiently asked.

"I guess so," Amanda responded in an unconcerned manner.

"You also said that she gave you advice when a boyfriend started getting on your back. Is that correct?"

Amanda rolled her eyes toward the ceiling before answering in a surly manner, "Sure."

"What did you mean when you said your boyfriend was getting on your back, Amanda?"

"You know—giving me grief. He was bossy and stuff like that," Amanda said, showing her annoyance by sighing.

Wilson paused briefly, then asked, "Amanda, were you sexually active with your boyfriend?"

"Objection," shouted Barber. "Your Honor, please." Barber stood up and placed his hands on his hips. "Learned Counsel knows better than to ask such a question. Amanda is not on trial here."

"Where is this going, Mr. Wilson?" questioned the judge.

"I am trying to establish previous behavior patterns, Your Honor," Wilson explained to the exasperated judge.

"You are treading on dangerous ground, Mr. Wilson. You may proceed but keep in mind the age of this young witness," cautioned Judge Calder.

Pounding away at the young girl about the number of boyfriends she may have had, Wilson demonstrated no mercy. The child no sooner answered one question when Wilson would almost shout another at her, giving her little time to think or compose her thoughts. Amanda no longer looked like a bratty teen-ager; she was visibly shaken. Even though Barber voiced numerous objections, Wilson would just rephrase his questions and come right back at the young girl.

"You said you went for walks in the woods, but you want us to believe that you did not have sex with any of your many boyfriends on any of these so-called walks," Wilson challenged.

"Your Honor, this is too much! I strongly object," an angry Barber said.

"Mr. Wilson, I will not warn you again," Judge Calder stated firmly.

"I apologize, Your Honor," Wilson said. Then, turning back to Amanda, he asked, "Amanda, who was the boy you claimed was bothering you?"

"Charlie. Charlie Foreman," Amanda said rather proudly.

"Charlie Foreman—wasn't he last year's outstanding football player from New Valley High School?" Wilson inquired, feigning interest.

"Yeah, you bet," Amanda boasted.

"Didn't Charlie Foreman graduate this year?" Wilson asked, placing his hand under his chin.

"Sure. Why?" Amanda said as she once again demonstrated impertinence.

"Was your mother in the habit of allowing you to date older boys like Charlie Foreman?" Wilson asked as he took on a look of amazement.

"Objection," Barber shouted once again.

"Sustained. Mr. Wilson, please get on with it."

"Your Honor, Amanda's dating habits are a vital part of my client's defense," Wilson argued.

"Mr. Wilson, the objection was sustained, and I will again advise you to move on."

Wilson moved closer to Amanda. "Amanda, isn't Charlie Foreman black?"

Barber jumped to his feet. "Objection. I must strongly object to Mr. Wilson's line of questioning. I think—"

"Sustained. Will the attorneys please come forward for a side bar?" Judge Calder demanded. "Mr. Wilson, I have cautioned you several times about your questioning of this underage witness. I do not want you to start a riot in this courtroom by making race an issue in this case when it is not. I understand your desire to defend your client, but you must not cross over the line of common decency while doing it. Perhaps that is the way things are done in the big city, but they are not handled that way in my courtroom."

"Judge Calder, I have proof that this girl has had several sexual encounters with boys from the local area," Wilson pleaded.

"That may well be, Mr. Wilson, but her sexual conduct is not on trial here. Mr. Ash's is and I will not allow you to proceed in this manner. Is that clear? Now, let's move ahead."

"Amanda, do you recall telling Ms. Montgomery about the time a man tried to kill you in your bedroom?" Wilson asked in an amiable tone of voice.

"She wasn't supposed to tell anyone that," Amanda shouted.

"Is that because the incident never happened?" Wilson asked.

"It did happen. I didn't make up a story about that," Amanda replied.

"Oh, I see. Strange things seem to happen to you when no one else is around. Tell the jury what happened to you the night before school was to begin," Wilson instructed, not even trying to remove the smirk on his face.

Amanda started pouting and glared at the attorney who was standing directly in front of her. "Well, I woke up and I saw a shadow. A man came into my bedroom." She paused and then continued slowly. "Just as I tried to get up, he threw my bathrobe over my face and tried to smother me. I managed to get free and he ran away."

Frowning, Wilson asked, "Amanda, where was your mother at the time of this peculiar incident?"

Amanda kept her head down. "She was downstairs ironing."

"And she didn't hear any of this?" Wilson asked.

"No." Amanda snapped.

"Did you run down the stairs after this attack and tell your mother what had just happened?"

Amanda pursed her lips and glared at Wilson for a few seconds. Then, very loudly, she said, "No!"

"A man just tried to kill you and you did not bother to tell your own mother. Why, Amanda?" Wilson asked as he extended his hands, palms held upward in a gesture of disbelief.

"Just 'cause. I don't tell my mom everything."

Ayden was keenly watching the jurors. He saw their reaction to Amanda's testimony. The little old ladies on either end of the jury box sat immobilized with their mouths hanging open. The red-headed young man looked stunned, and the little pudgy man with the wire-rimmed glasses shrugged his shoulder.

"Let's talk about another odd incident, Amanda. How about the time when you were riding your bicycle near the woods and a man tried to grab you? Did you ever tell your mother about that?" Wilson was obviously enjoying shocking the spectators, many of whom were now sitting on the edge of their seats, waiting for the next bombshell to explode.

"Ms. Montgomery wasn't supposed to tell anybody about that either. She had promised. I thought I could tell her secrets and she wouldn't tell," sobbed Amanda.

Rebekah Montgomery shifted in her seat. She didn't usually repeat what her students had told her in confidence, but this situation was different. Her loyalty was to Ayden, no one else. She did not like that some people were looking at her because she hated being the center of attention at any time. She clasped her hands together and started to pray that the questions would shift away from her.

"Secrets—or lies, Amanda?" Wilson said with skepticism.

"Your Honor!" Barber was on his feet again.

"That's all I have for this witness," Wilson said as he confidently moved back to the defense table, not waiting for the judge's ruling.

"Mr. Berman?" Calder stated.

"I have no questions for this witness at this time," Berman said.

"Mr. Barber, please call your next witness," Judge Calder said.

"Your Honor, the Prosecution calls John Murray."

John moved slowly toward the witness box. As he passed the defense table, he turned his head ever so slightly and looked at Ayden. Just as he rounded the step to enter the small confined space, he tripped and stumbled into the chair. Barber rushed over, but before he could be of any assistance, John had managed to right himself. Ayden laughed sarcastically.

"Mr. Murray, is it true that you live with Margaret Hoffman and her daughter?" Barber asked.

"Yes, I do. I treat Amanda as my own." John said sincerely.

Ayden threw his head back and this time he let out an unrestrained laugh.

"Your Honor—" Barber began to plead.

"Mr. Ash, I will not remind you again about your unacceptable behavior in this courtroom. Mr. Wilson, please counsel your client. I will not tolerate this type of conduct. Mr. Barber, please proceed with your questioning of this witness," Calder ordered.

"Mr. Murray, how did Amanda get involved in attending The Church of True Believers School?" quizzed Barber.

"Well, she met some little friends who told her about the church and the school. Margaret and I had been unhappy for some time with the local school district, but we couldn't afford to send her to a private school. And when we were told that she wouldn't have to pay no tuition—well, we thought it was the answer," John responded.

Ayden smiled as he wrote a note on the table in front of him. He passed it to his attorney. *The dumb sonofabitch just put two negatives in one sentence!*

"Were you pleased with her academic progress in the church school?" Barber probed.

"At first, we were. She seemed to be doing good work. She brought home good grades. But then we started to worry," John replied.

"Worried about what, Mr. Murray?"

"We couldn't figure it out. She was just different. She would start to argue with us for no reason. We couldn't ask her any questions about the school. She would get real mad and say we were getting on her back and stuff like that. I chalked that up to normal teenage rebellion, if you know what I mean."

"Did Amanda ever indicate that anything out of the usual was taking place at the school?"

"Objection," both Berman and Wilson stated.

"Overruled," the judge replied.

"Did she ever give any indications that anything sexual was taking place in the school?" Barber steadfastly asked.

"Hell, no! If she would've, we would have taken her out of that hellhole right away."

Wilson then began his cross-examination.

"Mr. Murray, you are not married to Margaret Hoffman, are you?"

"Objection, Your Honor. Mrs. Hoffman's marital status is irrelevant," Barber emphatically stated.

"Your Honor, I'm trying to examine the home environment in which Amanda lived. I feel this is vital to my client's case," Wilson pleaded.

"Overruled. Continue, Mr. Wilson."

"Mr. Murray, are you married to Margaret Hoffman?" Wilson asked once more.

"No," John emphatically replied.

"How long have you lived with her and Amanda?"

John began to look uncomfortable as he shifted in his seat. "Bout three years—maybe a little longer. But we can't get married 'cause she's not divorced, and we cannot find her husband."

"Do you perform the duties of a father?"

"Sure. I earn the money to put food on the table and pay all the bills. I take good care of both Margaret and Amanda." John said sternly."

"Good care? Does that mean you take care of Amanda when she has health problems?" Wilson inquired.

"Sure. When she gets sick, we take her to the doctor. Our family physician can vouch for that. That's a dumb question if you ask me."

"How about the time Amanda got a rash? Was it you who put salve on her?" Wilson said as he moved closer to the angry man.

"I don't like your tone, mister. What the hell do you mean?" John said defensively.

"Wasn't it you who put the lotion on Amanda's legs—on the area between her crotch?" Wilson asked sharply.

"Wait a minute. I won't—" John bellowed.

An exasperated judge said, "Mr. Wilson, this line of questioning is not appropriate."

"Your Honor, my client is accused of a criminal act. I am trying to establish that Amanda has had previous sexual experiences and—"

"You bastard, how much is that fucking child molester paying you. I did not touch Amanda in any sexual way," said John, who was now standing up and waving his fists at the attorney.

"I have no more questions for this witness," Wilson said as he backed away from the witness stand.

"Mr. Berman." Calder said.

"I have no questions for this witness, Your Honor," Berman stated.

"The hour is getting late, ladies and gentlemen. We shall recess for lunch. Court will resume at 2 p.m.," Judge Calder directed.

John had a difficult time regaining his composure. But, when he did, he walked up to Ayden and stood directly in front of him.

"What do you want, black boy?" Ayden whispered.

For a moment, John remained perfectly still. Then, he took a deep breath and spit in Ayden's face. Confusion ran rampant throughout the courtroom as those who were aware of what had happened began clapping. While the deputies were trying to regain order, one man slipped out, ran to the elevator, and disappeared into the crowd on the sidewalk. Twenty minutes later the same man, now wearing a delivery man's cap and carrying two bags, walked up the front steps of the courthouse and entered the elevator. After pushing the button for the fourth floor, he held his bags even tighter. When the doors opened automatically, he peered into the courtroom and was pleased to see that everyone was gone. He then hurried down the hall, pulled the old rusty chain that dangled from above, and climbed up into the dirty attic. Before he closed the opening, he hid the chain from view by pulling it up and laying it on the floor beside his feet. *All is ready. All I must do is wait until they bring him back across the street.*

The man held his breath while he tugged on the sooty window and was delighted when it opened easily. He was able to see the wide concrete portico that jutted out of the building from the fourth floor. Some of the railings looked badly chipped and the walkway was covered in pigeon dirt, but nothing hindered his view of the jail across the street. He checked his watch. The deputies would be bringing Ayden and Sarah back to the courtroom in about a half-hour. He opened the bags and placed their contents on the floor. Then, he carefully loaded his .357 pistol. His hands were shaking—he needed to get himself under control. He took the wrapper off a Hershey candy bar and quickly devoured the delicious chocolate. Suddenly, he heard the loud beating of a drum. Off in the distance, he could see a crowd of people carrying placards. As they neared the courthouse, they began to chant "*Guilty... guilty...guilty*" and marched in time to the beat of a big bass drum as they formed a circle from one side of the street to the other, stopping traffic in both directions.

"Sonofabitch," he said. "Not now. I'm ready for him." He knelt down and placed his .357 on the splintery windowsill. "*Ready or not, I'll take him out today.*"

As soon as the protestors sat down on the cement pavement, he practiced aiming his pistol at the spot where he expected to see Ayden.

He spotted the deputies first. They stood in the open doorway of the jail and waited for the police to move the protestors away. He knew that he would have only one chance to hit his target. Then, suddenly, he saw him. As bile rose up in his throat and, with his eyes focused on Ayden's bald head, his finger caressed the trigger of the pistol. Then, with a gleam in his eye, he pulled it.

CHAPTER 4

(Two months before Ayden was arrested)

All was ready for the séance. Colorful satin pillows had been tossed haphazardly on the floor in Ayden's private library. Several dozen candles had been placed around the perimeter of the room. When the candles were lit, eerie, kaleidoscopic patterns danced on the walls and ceiling. Heavy drapes on the windows prevented anyone from the apartments across the street from seeing what was going to happen on the second floor of The Church of True Believers.

Ayden had selected his guests carefully. This was to be a very special evening—Ayden was going to try to contact his dead brother James. For months, Ayden had been immersing himself in books about the occult. In addition, he also had attended several séances conducted by others and was certain that he had mastered the secret of crossing into the world of the dead. Besides, he had also prepared a spectacular incident that was certain to endear him to those in attendance just in case his powers to reach the dead failed him. His guests loved excitement, and Ayden was about to give them something that they had not seen before.

For days, Ayden had been removing bricks from the side wall. It was easier than he had thought it would be. The building was old and the wall had been renovated several times when his father owned it. The mortar was loose, and with a minimal amount of chipping, it had fallen to the floor in little pieces. He had carefully calculated the spot where the hole had to be so that it would remain unseen from the outside. When he had broken through the outer wall, he had seen the reverse side of the sign which proudly heralded the words *The Church of True Believers* and he knew that the climbing ivy would provide the camouflage needed.

Ayden needed a place to hide the small piece of marble that he had chipped off his brother's crumbling tombstone. He had planned to fire this morsel over the heads of his guests at just the right time so that it would appear to have come right through the outer brick wall. To make certain that the wall board looked as if this really happened, Ayden had cut the opening in an uneven fashion. Ayden had taken great precautions when adjusting the spring; he needed just the right tension in order to get the momentum required to hurl the chunk into the air.

He had moved the altar from the sanctuary and had placed it against the wall in the library where he had created the opening. It was an unusual piece that had, at one time, served a local congregation for many years. The front of the two-foot square wooden altar had been devotedly carved by craftsmen in the early twenties. A small ledge on the top provided a resting place for Bibles or other religious books. The altar would play a major role in his performance. The base would provide the ideal space to cloak the pedal which would put the whole works into motion. After a few trial runs, Ayden was confident that the crude mechanism would function properly. It had to look real. He had to make certain that the catch and the spring remained out of sight after the piece of marble had been flung into the air. Only for a fleeting moment had Ayden thought about the safety of his guests. While he didn't intend to hurt anyone, his need to elevate his power had far outweighed any other concerns.

Now, his hands began to sweat and his body was filled with excitement and anticipation as he discreetly lifted the picture, which covered the opening, to check that nothing had been disturbed. Tonight he would demonstrate his power in its purest and most compelling form.

Power. That's what the world is really all about. There are only a few ways one can obtain it: money, position, sex, or mind control. And, from the time that he was young, Ayden had been determined to get power one way or another. He stayed hidden while the guests arrived. He needed to keep his mind clear, and he didn't want to get caught up in meaningless conversations.

Eddie, his newest convert, was filling the incense dishes, making sure that they were placed at just the right spots so that the aroma would not be too overpowering. The total atmosphere had to be perfect. Ayden had always maintained that most institutionalized religions failed to use all the senses, concentrating mainly on hearing and seeing while the senses of smell and touch, which stir much emotion, were completely overlooked. Tonight, his guests would be free to explore their innermost desires once again. *They would be unchained from tradition and allowed to soar to new heights. He would give them encouragement to lose their inhibitions and, in turn, they would give him the power he so richly deserved. Few people have a thirst for inner substance and vision. As a result, they would never experience the glory of losing self-limitations and discover the secrets that are lying there deep within, just waiting to be detected.*

From his hiding place, Ayden concentrated on Eddie, who was moving around the room so gracefully, making certain that everything would be appealing to the guests. While Eddie was small in stature, he had amazingly strong shoulders and arms. His wavy, long blonde hair and his brilliant blue eyes complimented his alabaster skin. He smiled readily, for he truly loved people. He was a gentle person, fond of all God's creatures, but he especially adored Ayden.

The two had met several months ago when they had accidentally bumped into one another as they were searching the stacks in the basement of the State Library. It had been a very funny sight, each so intent on browsing the old, dusty shelves, that neither had been aware of the other's presence. There they were, apologizing profusely and trying to retrieve the books that they had dropped when they collided. Their friendship had grown rapidly since they had a common passion—books and the marvels that they held—a passion that soon drew them into a physical love for one another.

Eddie was a unique individual. He would disappear from time to time, riding off on his motorcycle, seldom offering an explanation of where he was going. Ayden had demanded no explanation of his whereabouts and, each time Eddie came back, they would resume their relationship as if there had been no interruption. They made no demands on each other and no recriminations were ever hurled. A loyalty developed between them—a loyalty that Ayden had not been able to give to anyone else.

Tonight, no children were present. They had been sent home or to various babysitters. Ayden had arranged to have Jake Mnbonu attend a conference on biblical interpretation so he would be away for a few days. This was no place for anyone who was not ready to free the sexual soul. Jake was not prepared for any of this. As Ayden parted the heavy drapes slightly, he saw that Dr. Jenson had arrived, wearing a stupid wig—a sign that the pompous ass was still unsure of his right to do with his body what he wanted.

The voices of the guests were high-pitched with excitement as they hurried into the building and up the stairway. Rebekah and Melody escorted each couple into the room and encouraged them to select a spot and make themselves comfortable on the pillows. Sarah moved quietly among the crowd, offering glasses of a special punch that Ayden had prepared for this occasion. He saw that Eddie was paying particular attention to a couple who were sitting in the most dimly-lit corner of the room. The woman was a red-haired beauty who seemed a bit nervous as she hung on to a young man's arm.

The ambiance was perfect. The air was heavy with incense. The darkness was softened by the glow of the candles. Only last week, Ayden had finally found a record of Stephen Halpern's new age music in a vintage clothing store. Halpern's music would provide the perfect background to enhance his guests' consciousness, peace and self-realization.

Ayden's research indicated that séances originated in the mid-1800s with spiritualists, who wanted to communicate with the dead. He needed to help his guests to be open-minded—to rid themselves of mental blocks. Nothing must occur to prevent them from being active participants in the séance. His guests, except for the new couple in the back, had already proven their willingness to let go of conventional mores by participating in several sex parties that Ayden had hosted in the past. Ayden waited until his guests had finished their punch before he began his ceremony. He wanted them loose, very loose.

Sarah had made Ayden a long, flowing robe of maroon velvet. She edged the bottom of the robe, as well as the sleeves, with sparkling gold braid. Under his direction, she had also sewn two large pockets on the inside of his new vestment. As soon as he stepped into the room, a hush came over the small crowd. As the wide sleeves of his vestment moved back and forth, the candlelight picked up the glimmer of the gold braid—an impressive, exotic sight. The guests gasped.

"James, my brother, come forward. Give me a sign—anything that will let me know that you are willing to communicate with me," Ayden said, in a low chanting voice. Ayden kept calling his brother's name over and over.

Some of the guests willingly joined in calling, "James, James."

Ayden raised both arms into the air. "Hush, my friends, you may frighten him away. James, I need to know that you approve of what I am doing. James, a sign, any sign, is all I need to guide my flock."

Ayden kept repeating his brother's name and chanting for several more minutes. Finally, he pushed on the hidden pedal.

Suddenly, there was a loud crash as the small piece of granite hit the edge of a metal lamp shade and fell to the floor, just inches from Eddie's head. Eddie quickly picked up the object. At first he thought it was just a stone, but on closer examination, he found that it was a piece of a tombstone. "Master, you did it…you did it! You contacted your brother."

A small contingent examined the stone carefully, and they all agreed with Eddie that it was indeed a piece of tombstone. The stone was small but the letters "*Jam*" were clearly visible. Ayden was being congratulated and given accolades on his ability to reach across the sea to the dead. Several guests stretched their necks up to look at the opening in the wall, marveling at the wonderful feat that had just occurred before their eyes. Ayden made certain that during the confusion he picked up all the pieces of the wall board and hid them under his flowing robe. He moved slowly among his guests, enjoying their exuberance.

After the crowd settled down, Ayden said, "My friends, you have helped me to fulfill my dream. I was able to connect with my dear brother, and I thank you for your participation. My ladies are here, and they are more than willing to help you fulfill your sexual needs. Feel free to choose among them or, if you wish, exchange partners with anyone in the room. This is my reward to you for your faithfulness."

In no time at all, the guests started removing their clothing and the couplings began taking place—moaning and groaning filling the air. However, Ayden noticed that the red-haired beauty, who had started to undress just moments earlier, was putting her clothes back on. She looked frantic as she grabbed her sandals. Pulling a necklace off her neck, she threw it angrily at the young man and headed for the stairway. Her young, naked companion made a ridiculous sight as he ran after her with his clothing dragging all over the floor. Ayden made a mental note to warn Eddie not to invite the ungrateful couple to one of the sessions again.

CHAPTER 5

(The Trial: Day 2- Afternoon Session)

Pete Forster was holding his reporter's notebook in his right hand when the shot rang out, and he instinctively fell to the ground. The protestors, who only moments earlier had been chanting, began screaming. As they tried to flee the scene, people starting pushing and shoving one another. As a result, some were trampled. Deputies were attending to Ayden as he lay sprawled on the bottom concrete step of the jail. Someone yelled, "He's dead. The rotten bastard is dead!"

As Pete managed to squeeze his way through the clamoring crowd, he was shocked to see that Ayden was sitting up—he certainly was not dead. While there was a small trickle of blood streaming down his face, it appeared that the shooter's bullet had only grazed Ayden's head.

No one noticed that the small window above the portico of the courthouse was being closed very slowly. The man inside the attic sank to the floor and cried when he realized that Ayden's wound was only superficial. He unloaded his pistol and placed it back into the bag. He would probably have to wait until dark before he dared to leave his hiding place. A new plan must be made—one that would have no chance of failing.

Pete managed to snap a picture before a burly policeman pulled him away and ordered the crowd to disburse. The deputies hurriedly ushered Ayden and Sarah back into the jail and six officers, standing shoulder to shoulder, prevented anyone else from entering the building.

Pete turned around and began examining the crowd. He was positive that the shot had come from the courthouse, but, with so many people scampering here and there, he couldn't be certain. After taking a few photos of the crowd, as well as the police guard at the doorway to the jail, Pete hurried to his office to make the deadline for the evening edition.

When the announcement was made that the trial was not going to resume for the afternoon session, Pete went back to the courthouse to look around. His first thought was that perhaps the shooter had been among the protestors. But he kept looking up at the portico—maybe that's where the shot had come from. Going into the courthouse through a side door, Pete proceeded to the fourth floor by using the stairway. He was surprised at how much he was huffing and puffing when he reached his destination. Most of the offices on this floor looked deserted. He walked toward the front of the building, looking for a doorway to the portico. When he heard muffled voices ahead, he abruptly stopped. As he tugged at a soiled, dark red drape that was hiding a French door, he spied three detectives who appeared to be examining the shabby-looking portico. Pete knew better than to barge in on them so he hung back in the corner.

"Nothing here," one of the detectives said. "There's no evidence that anyone has been out here for a long time."

"I still think the shooter was in the crowd. I think we should concentrate on those people. After all, they wanted him dead."

"Frank, watch that banister there, it looks wobbly. Christ, this place is strictly from hunger. I thought the Commissioners were going to build a new courthouse. I think it's overdue. Wow, all this pigeon shit is really getting to me. Let's get out of here."

As the three men barged back in through the doorway, they failed to see Pete as he huddled in the dark corner. He listened to their footsteps as they hurried down the linoleum-covered steps. Pete waited a few more minutes before doing the same thing. He casually walked to the front of the building, scrutinizing the area as he went along. By now, the sun was setting over the courthouse and, when Pete looked at the top of the building, he did not notice the small attic window.

Feeling pangs of hunger, he decided to have dinner at the Italian Courtyard, just across the bridge. Choosing a small table in the tiny café, Pete began paging aimlessly through the notes he had taken at the trial. He still could not believe it. For the past two years he had been friendly with both Ayden and Sarah and had supported their efforts on behalf of their church school. Pete had met Ayden at a lecture, given by the curator of New Valley's museum. Afterwards, the two had gotten into a conversation about several of the most famous historical buildings in the area. Ayden had invited Pete to attend an open house at his little religious school, and out of courtesy and a reporter's curiosity, Pete had attended. Pete had been surprised when he received a signed copy of one of Ayden's historical books in the mail. The book looked very professional, and Pete had given it a favorable review in one of his columns. While Pete had no particular religious loyalty, he respected the rights of others to participate in whatever cloister they chose. But if Amanda was not lying, if Ayden had violated her, then his friendship with Ayden was over.

"Hey, Pete, you sure this is enough?" asked the handsome young waiter as he placed a small salad in front of the brawny reporter.

"Sure, Tony. I don't have much of an appetite. Just bring me a few slices of that good garlic bread. This will be plenty."

Pete was lost in thoughts. Could Amanda have been lying? What about the wild stories she had told the school's counselor? And, he was not sure that John Murray had told the truth, either. Could he have been the one who defiled Amanda? Suppose Ayden was innocent? But, on the other hand, what if Ayden really was the bastard that Amanda claimed? He could not picture Sarah being involved in something like this. She simply was too sweet. However, he had always been uncomfortable with Ayden's passion with the occult. It seemed as though everything Ayden had done was in some way wrapped in secrecy, always mysterious in nature. Supernatural agencies and their effects on everyday life had been just a few of Ayden's obsessions. Ayden had told him that he would spend days working on horoscopes for his friends, and the few that Pete had seen had struck him as strange and a little foreboding.

Pete liked to concentrate on facts—just facts. He did not want his emotions to spill into his coverage of the news. His colleagues had long classified him as aloof, a disseminator of information. But Pete thought of himself as a political interpreter, and he had always taken great pride in not interjecting his own personal opinions in his articles—except in his book reviews. He loved New Valley and its people and was at his best when he wrote about what he loved. His late wife, Estelle, used to kid him that he wrote like a telegraph machine, direct and rapid. One time Ayden had labeled him as a private man in a public profession. That probably suited Pete to a tee.

Perhaps he should have turned over the coverage of this trial to one of the other reporters. Pete wasn't certain that he could remain distant from the defendants. Maybe his unaccountable, mild friendship with Ayden—admittedly a strange one—might prevent him from being unbiased. It might even cloud his normal frame of reference and force him to abandon his usual methodical style. But exactly what he thought about Ayden, at this time, was still incredibly cloudy.

The perplexed reporter began to underline certain parts of his notes about the trial. He didn't fully trust Amanda. He knew that if the girl on the witness stand had been his little Cindy, he would have been as angry as John had been in the courtroom. And, if what Amanda had testified to was true, he was ready to excuse what John did to Ayden.

"Mind if I join you? It looks as if all the other seats are taken."

Pete looked up. He was genuinely surprise to see Jeanette Logan, a fellow reporter whom he had met last year at a press conference in Philadelphia. "Oh, hi Jeanette, are you here covering the Ash trial?"

"Do chickens have lips?" teased the slender, black-haired woman as she sat down next to Pete. "No wonder you look so good," she said, pointing to the small salad. "Is that all you are going to eat?"

"Not hungry," grunted Pete as he munched on a fork full of lettuce."

"Well, I'm starved. Don't worry, Pete, old boy, I'll pay for my own food. The *Philadelphia Daily* pays me well. Besides, I'm from the enlightened generation," Jeanette replied as she moved her chair closer to Pete.

"Don't you people in Philadelphia have enough crime to report on? How come you have this assignment?" Pete asked.

"Well, I do have a bit of personal interest in the case," Jeanette responded.

"Personal? In what way?"

"Oh, no, you don't, you slick country-bumpkin reporter. I like you, Pete, but I'm not going to give away something that I may have on

Ayden that you may not know. I'm not sure that it would have any bearing on this case, but, for the time being, I'll keep this information to myself," Jeanette said in a teasing manner.

"What do you really think?" Pete mumbled, motioning toward his notes.

"Guilty. He even looks like a creep. Did you get a load of those eyes? There's decadence behind those beady peepers."

"Maybe Amanda was lying."

"Sure, and maybe the Pope's not Catholic. I admit that Amanda may have had just as much sex with her boyfriends as she has had with Prince Charming, but that's different, Pete. How about the ring he gave her?" Jeanette challenged.

"A trinket—perhaps?"

"Bullshit," Jeanette said as she watched the muscular waiter walk away. "Look at that back view. That's enough to get a girl to leave the big city!"

"Look, before you jump to any conclusions about Ayden, you better wait until he testifies. Remember, there are two sides to every coin."

"I'm telling you, Pete, he's guilty."

Pete sat back in his seat and observed his dinner companion. Her makeup had been applied perfectly, just enough to bring out her especially fine features—a stunningly striking woman. She had been a reporter for only the past two years but had already achieved an almost incomparable feat of obtaining the respect of her colleagues. But he was certain that most of them would love to spend one night with this vision.

"You're good for me, you know that?' Pete said, his expression softening.

"I'm here in your fair city until the end of this circus," Jeanette said, placing her hand on top of his.

Pete felt the warmth of her touch and it felt good. He was about to say something when the waiter returned with Jeanette's order.

"Thanks, sweetie-pie," Jeanette said, dismissing the young man with a sexy wink of her eye.

Pete laughed. "You amaze me. Do you flirt with everyone?"

"Not quite. What do you say we share our night? It's awfully lonely in this one-horse town."

Pete looked at the lovely woman sitting next to him. He wanted to take her up on her offer, but his heartstrings wouldn't let him do it. The memories of his wife, lying in that hospital bed months on-end, dying a slow death due to cancer—were still too vivid in his mind. He had no idea how long he would have to go through this. It was hard for him to accept that she had been gone for over a year now. Why couldn't it have been him instead of her? He had no answer to that question.

"How about dinner tomorrow evening? A new restaurant just opened on the other side of town and I heard that the food is great," Pete said, surprising himself by offering the invitation.

"Well, I've made some progress with you. And I warn you, Pete, I'll be packing my toothbrush!"

CHAPTER 6

(One year earlier)

It had rained continuously for nine days. The storm had moved from the Gulf of Mexico and hit New Valley during an extremely mild June. Abigail was her name and she was a Category 1 hurricane. While the local television station had been warning listeners that the hurricane would hit, very few people had taken it seriously. But, inevitably, the disastrous flood had caused the Valley River to overflow, turning little streams into wild torrents. As much as seven feet of water had covered some of the intersections in the downtown area. Quaint little houses that sat near the banks of the river had been engulfed with muddy water. Most of the back yards of the narrow row houses near the courthouse were turned into pools since the water had come down faster than the obsolete sewer system could handle.

In the mountains that surrounded the city, the rain had created hundreds of little currents. Roads had been inundated, making access to many of the smaller communities impossible. A helicopter had been put into service to rescue several hundred people, including a troop of girl scouts who had been camping in the mountains. Small streams were swollen and many had overflowed their banks. New Valley's water supply had been classified as in danger of contamination and, for the first time in over one hundred years, local newspapers suspended publication.

Most city residents had lost their electrical power. Curfews were put into effect and National Guardsmen had patrolled the streets to prevent looting. And even more astonishing, the State offices of New

Valley had been closed for three days, providing an unexpected holiday for both Sarah and Melody.

Extensive damage had been caused by the run off of grease and oil from the New Valley steel plant. And, when the water had finally receded, oil slicks covered the streets, making travel extremely difficult, especially for the emergency vehicles engaged in rescue missions. Businesses and offices had also suffered extreme water damage and valuable papers and goods had been rendered useless.

Ayden's bookstore had not escaped misfortune. Many items stored in the basement were soaked and had to be discarded. However, all the important books and pictures had been moved to the upper floors of the school by Sarah and Melody. Since the students had been unable to leave the school to return to their homes for two days, they also helped. The children had made a game out of moving items by using the old wooden dumbwaiter to transport small loads of books from the basement to Ayden's private library on the second floor. They had pretended that they were pirates as they pulled on the old ropes which raised and lowered the anachronous dumbwaiter.

Ayden had taken full advantage of the children's long stay in his home to further his control over them. He had ordered the children to sit on pillows on the floor in his library with the drapes wide open.

"See…see what fury the Lord can bestow upon us? We must all follow his teachings. I can lead you, but you must not question my authority. See how hard the rain pellets are hitting the window? That is power, children, that is power. The Lord has passed that power on to me."

Sarah, fearful that the window pane would break and hurt the children, had tried to get them to move back farther into the recesses of the darkened room. "No," Ayden shouted, "they must become aware of what power means and respect such authority!"

Having the students there for several days had made Sarah very edgy. She had a difficult time handling her jealousy, especially when Ayden had given so much attention to Amanda. The most difficult times were those when he had taken Amanda by the hand and led her away with orders that no one else was to leave the room. And, when

Sarah learned that Ayden had taken Amanda as his bride, and had even given her a ring, her hatred for the young girl grew even stronger.

After the children were finally able to go home safely, Sarah had taken on much of the clean-up activities. Wearing old black boots, she had waded through a foot of murky water that still filled the church basement. For the past two hours, she had been carrying water-soaked trash up the rickety wooden steps and placing it on the back porch so Ayden could move it to the curb. Her legs were weary and her back ached. But she knew better than to complain. Exhausted, she sat down on one of the steps and began to massage her aching muscles. The basement had an unpleasant odor and she wished that her task was completed. Melody had been given the easy assignment of working in the photography studio, and Rebekah had been charged with making revisions in the English curriculum. Only Sarah had been sent down to the smelly catacombs. She began to muse over her plight. *Why do I do this? Why didn't I rebel and demand that the others help me? You know perfectly well why you didn't—you're afraid that if you don't do what he tells you that you'll lose him.*

Sarah began pushing her feet back and forth in the dark water, trying to send the ripples over to the far wall. *That's it, Sarah, push those evil thoughts away. You know that Ayden speaks of the true meaning of life and the way the Lord wants all of us to live. He is your reason for being. Without him you have nothing. He is your Master. He is your husband and none of the others can say that.*

As Ayden carried some of the water-soaked rubbish to the curb to be hauled away by the city's trash crew, he spotted a group of sightseers who were driving past, snapping pictures. These morbid thrill seekers had been causing incredible traffic jams throughout the city and impeding recovery efforts. As one of the cars came to a stop, the driver emerged, adjusted his very expensive camera and snapped several pictures of the devastation near the church.

"Hey, bud," Ayden yelled. "Wouldn't you like to go down to the morgue and get some shots of the dead people? What about some fantastic pictures of the thousands who were injured? That would sure get it up for you, you fucking bastard," Ayden added as he gave the finger to the astonished man. The photographer quickly jumped back into his car, but not before returning the gesture.

As he went back inside his property, Ayden was muttering to himself as he approached the top of the cellar steps. Sarah looked up and asked, "What happened?"

"Some damn sightseers. They really piss me off. They probably live in Country Club Estates and like to come over here to have a good time at our expense," Ayden said, his irritation quite evident.

Ayden was grateful that his printing press had been located on the second floor. If he had allowed it to remain in the basement, where it had been previously, and where Jake had wanted him to keep it, it probably would have been damaged beyond repair. Fortunately, his newest publication had just been completed before the storm had arrived. He was extremely proud of his latest creation, *Sylvia: From Child to Woman.* Melody and he had worked long hours in preparing this manuscript for publication; he had written the text and Melody had created the startling pen and ink drawings that aficionados of pornography loved. Since his book would undoubtedly be castigated by many of the local residents, he used a pseudonym so that he would not jeopardize the lucrative contracts he had been receiving from the State.

"Let's knock this off and take care of the cartons up here," Ayden said as he motioned for Sarah to come up the stairs. He lovingly stroked the cover of his new book. Once more, he flipped through the pages. Melody's drawings demonstrated her talent—her ability to capture the activities, just as he had imagined them, was nothing short of mystical. He and Melody formed a perfect team—one destined to go on to greatness.

Sarah removed her dirty boots and began packing copies of Ayden's book into several small boxes, designated to be shipped to certain dealers on the East coast. The more she packed, the more she became annoyed. Ayden had spent endless hours with Melody as they were writing the text and designing the accompanying pictures. She knew that she would not be able to tell Ayden that she found the book repugnant. The drawings were disgusting. She hated the way they depicted the deflowering of the child. But she would remain silent; she did not want to lose him.

"Well, that does it," Sarah said as she taped the last box shut.

"This book is going to do better than the last one," Ayden said very confidently as he patted the cover of his newest brainchild. "If only enough people would read it, they would begin to understand so much. You know, Sarah, the morals brought to this country by the Protestants and the Catholics and other oppressive religious sects are unnatural. They are intolerant," Ayden preached. "This state, this very state in which we live, was founded based on religious freedom. But look around you—what do you see? People with narrow minds, that's what. We live in a country which demands that its men and women live a lie. We have not progressed at all in all these years—not a bit."

Sarah merely nodded. She wanted to cry out that it was he who needed to question what he was doing. But she could not. She was not nearly as intelligent as Ayden, so how could she challenge his statements. He had warned her just last week that her questioning was no longer tolerable. He had even grabbed a suitcase one night and offered to help her pack if she wanted to leave. And then, he had abruptly reached for her and had tenderly held her in his arms. For awhile, for those few precious moments, nothing else had mattered. She hadn't cared that he had only wanted her for such a short period of time. Nothing had mattered at all except the feel of his body and the heat of his desire. He had dug his fingers into her flesh and then covered her face and neck with kisses. She had needed him so much. Then, just as suddenly, he had released her and walked away.

While Ayden never hit her, he had been physically abusive to the children now and then, especially when they resisted his demands to undress. She rationalized in her mind that such punishment was necessary in order to bring the children to the Lord. But the mental pain was almost too much to handle.

"Did all the children get home safely?" Sarah asked, hoping to keep him in her sights for a bit longer. "I guess they were glad to get home," she said, trying to sound casual.

Ayden gave her an angry look. He studied her for several seconds before he responded, "Look, don't start. If you can't handle any of this, you know what you've got to do. Don't go Puritanical on me."

Sarah turned her back and began walking away. She could not bear to undergo another verbal attack.

"Now, that's intelligent. Just walk away. You know the children could not have made it past the bridge without drowning. The streets were flooded. What did you want me to do? Let them go home and take a chance that they would be swept away?" Ayden said as he sneered at her. "Besides, it wasn't like anything that happened while they were here didn't happen before, you included."

"No, of course I didn't want anything to happen to them. It's just that sometimes I feel, well, I just feel that I'm not your wife anymore," Sarah said almost in a whisper.

"That's crap and you know it. Look, here's my wedding ring. What more do you want from me?" Ayden asked haughtily as he pointed to the simple band of gold.

"Sometimes I'm not sure that we should—"

"Should what?"

"Well, you know." Sarah began to weep.

"If you doubt my teachings, then you have the problem, not me. I'm living the true meaning of The Word just as God has instructed. If you can't do that, Sarah, then you know what your alternatives are. I'm tired of babying you. You did not object the other night when you watched me with Amanda, now did you? Now you have second thoughts? You have something here that most people would love to have. If you cannot handle the freedom that I have given you, then leave. The door only swings one way—if you leave, you will never be allowed to return. However, Alice stays with me. I don't want her living with a mother who has rejected the true way of life. You will be living in the darkness. You will no longer be in the inner circle of my bright orb. So, if you are unhappy, just go—I will not stop you. "

"I don't want to leave you. I love you," Sarah pleaded.

"Love—are you sure you know what that means? Love is giving; it is all inclusive. It's not restrictive. Love is creating oneness with God—something which, apparently, you have not been able to achieve. You have had your share of our joy in uniting with others and don't say that you haven't," Ayden taunted. "Jealousy is a sin before God. It is not an enviable characteristic. Remember: *Bright is the spirit of loving. Dark is the soul that is filled with envy.*"

"But, I...well..."

"You don't know what you mean, Sarah. You stand around like a little girl exuding false innocence. I've made you come alive. I've helped you remove the chains that would have kept you fastened to outdated morals, which restrict your spiritual intellect. I have given you freedom," Ayden said dramatically, emphasizing the '*I*' each time. "And now you bring shame, not glory, to the Lord."

Ayden began to stomp around the shop, busying himself with cleaning up the debris. "You know, Sarah, you should have been concerned only about whether the children were safe—whether they were being loved. While they were here, they were cared for better than they ever were at their homes. I'm getting tired of your inane jealousy. It doesn't belong here in this place—not in our little group."

"But—"

"No, no *buts*. If you are stupid about a subject, you should not offer an opinion. Every time you do that, you make a fool of yourself. Ignorance is not a quality to exhibit before the Lord. It's time you rise above such common thinking."

"I'm sorry, Ayden. You are right. I have much to learn. I promise I'll try harder. Please don't be angry with me. I love you."

Ayden stormed out of the room and up the stairs. He went directly to the dark room where he knew Melody was working on some projects. He pushed the door open and said, "Guess who?"

Melody smiled. "I guess it's time to place fire on the altar one more time. Come on in."

CHAPTER 7

(The Trial: Day 3)

Pete had managed to get out of bed in time to take a bike ride before going to the courthouse. He had pedaled alongside the river on the macadam bike path for almost an hour when he decided to get off the bike and sit on one of the wooden benches facing the Valley River—he had some thinking to do. Pete stretched his long legs across the wooden slats, which were sorely in need of a new paint job, and opened his notebook. But he could not keep his mind on the trial. As he watched the water flowing along at a leisurely pace, he allowed himself to think about Jeanette. *"It's been a long time,"* Pete said to himself, *"a long, long time."*

Visions of Estelle drifted into his mind. *Can I ever let her go?* Suddenly, he became aware of the passage of time. Checking his watch, he knew that he had to hurry if he wanted to get to the courthouse before the gavel was rapped.

As he entered the courtroom, he saw Jeanette but decided it would be better if he stayed his distance during the proceedings, if not for any other reason than to maintain his ability to concentrate on the testimony. Most of the seats had already been taken, but he managed to find an unoccupied metal folding chair which looked terribly uncomfortable. He winced as he sat down on the hard seat in anticipation of the extreme pain that he would probably be experiencing after spending any length of time sitting on a chair without any measurable back support—a condition that could be credited to his college football days.

Pete was taken aback when he spotted Ayden entering the courtroom with his forehead wrapped in a white bandage. While reports of the shooting indicated that the sniper's bullet had barely grazed his head yesterday, apparently, Ayden wanted to get as much sympathy from the jurors as possible. Every once in awhile, Ayden would raise his hand and gently touch the bandage—a movie-star performance.

"The State calls Margaret Hoffman to the stand."

After Margaret managed to squeeze her large body into the chair in the witness box, Barber asked, "Mrs. Hoffman, can you tell the Court how your daughter came to be enrolled in The Church of True Believers School?"

"Like John said, Amanda found out about the school from friends and she wanted to go with them. Me and John, we talked it over and, well, we didn't like the school she was going to anyway, so we let her go."

"Were you charged any tuition for her schooling?" Barber asked as he turned dramatically and looked at Ayden.

"Nah, it was free. We sure didn't have the dough to send her to a private school," Margaret stated.

"How were the Ashes able to permit children to attend the school without charging tuition?" Barber asked.

"Objection, calls for an opinion," Berman stated.

"Sustained," Judge Calder answered.

"Mrs. Hoffman, did you investigate the school in any way before you permitted Amanda to attend classes there?"

"Sure, I went down there and talked to …him…," Margaret said as she pointed to Ayden. "He gave me a big line and talked about the horrible conditions at the school that she was attending and how he wouldn't want any of his kids to go there. Then, he showed me a list… what do you call it…like the subjects the kids would be getting, and it had stuff like history, math, and English. He showed me the certificates of the teachers and an official state education seal so I thought he was legit," Margaret emphasized.

Taking his time, Barber asked, "When did you start to become concerned about what was happening at the school?"

"Well, me and John, we talked about it a couple times with my daughter but we couldn't get much out of her; Amanda's real closed-mouth. Finally, one night, Amanda came to me and she was crying. Here that little rotten sonofabitch had been bopping her right over there in the school. Can you imagine? Right in the school," Margaret almost shouted.

"What did you do next?"

"Called the cops, that's what I done. Amanda got real mad at me and didn't talk to me for days, but I wanted to see him punished," Margaret responded sternly.

Margaret then went on and, in graphic detail, described several sexual encounters that Amanda claimed had happened at the school. The jurors seemed to be in a trance as the rotund woman went on. The defense attorneys objected several times but were overruled.

Slowly, very slowly, Barber was able to get all the seamy details out in the open. Margaret began weeping as she spoke about what her daughter had revealed. She turned to Calder, "Judge, this is hard for me. Children should not know about stuff like this—sex between adults and kids. My daughter shouldn't know about fellatio and cunnilingus." Margaret was now weeping uncontrollably and her large, ungainly frame shook rapidly as the sobbing grew more intense. She raised her head and yelled, "You goddamned SOB!"

Calder leaned toward Margaret and said, "Mrs. Hoffman, I realize how difficult this must be, but please try to remain as calm as possible. I cannot condone name calling and outbursts regardless of the circumstances."

Margaret sniffed backed her tears and lowered her head. Her corpulent body strained at the seams of her flowered cotton dress as she tried to get her breath. Her feet were jammed into shoes that appeared to be much too small. Little rolls of fat covered the wide leather straps which held the shoddy shoes in place at the bottom of her heavy legs. She kept trying to smooth her dress in a vain attempt to make the wrinkles seem a little less noticeable.

"Your Honor, I submit Doctor Nesbit's report on his examination of Amanda as Exhibit A," Barber said as he handed an envelope to the bailiff. "I have no further questions for this witness."

Claude Wilson stood up, tugged on the cuffs of his shirt, and said, "Mrs. Hoffman, it is still Mrs. Hoffman, is it not?"

"Objection," shouted Barber. Mr. Wilson seems to be implying—"

"I see no implications at all in the question, overruled," Judge Calder ruled.

"Mrs. Hoffman, you are not married to John Murray, are you?" Wilson asked the distraught witness.

"Are you deaf or something? John told you we wasn't married," Margaret replied, as she wiped her nose with a torn facial tissue.

"Oh, I see," Wilson responded as he faced the jury. "In other words, you two are just living together, is that correct?"

Barber jumped up and said, "Your Honor, I think—"

"The jury is instructed to disregard that last question. Mr. Wilson, I see no point in belaboring the fact that Mrs. Hoffman and Mr. Murray are not married, and I feel that it has no relevance to this trial. Now get on with it," Calder ordered.

"Mrs. Hoffman, after Amada came to you with her story about Mr. Ash, isn't it true that you did not call the police immediately? Isn't it also true that you called Mr. Ash first and demanded that he give you five thousand dollars?"

"I called him first, but I didn't ask for money. That ain't true. I told him that I was gonna put his ass in a sling. What kind of woman do you think I am?

"I'm sure the jury already knows that," Wilson said, smirking as he watched the obese woman fidget in her seat.

"Mr. Wilson," Calder almost shouted. "You are an experienced attorney. I should not have to remind you that your personal opinions have no place in the courtroom, at least not in mine. Now, please proceed and step carefully. Consider this a warning."

"Mrs. Hoffman, let's change the subject. How would you describe the relationship between you and your daughter?"

"She's like most young girls—she keeps secrets. That don't mean she's doing bad things. At times, she's confused. It's hard growing up in a world like this. But I believed her then, and I believe her now about what that bastard did to her. Look, I know I'm not much, but I love my daughter."

"I have no more questions for this witness," Wilson stated.

"Cross-examine, Mr. Berman?" Calder asked.

"I have no questions for this witness," Berman stated.

"Mr. Barber, you may call your next witness," Judge Calder said.

Much to the surprise of many in the courtroom, Barber said, "The State rests, Your Honor."

"Ladies and gentlemen, since the hour is late, court will reconvene Monday morning at 9 a.m.," and with a loud rap of the gavel, Judge Calder ended the proceedings for the day.

Pete stood up, rubbed his aching back and moved toward the rear corner of the courtroom. There, he pressed his back against the wall and started to flex his muscles—an old trick a buddy had taught him that helped to relieve the pain he experienced from time to time. He watched the people begin to file out the large doorway—a curious mix.

To his relief, neither Ayden nor Sarah seemed to have been aware of his presence in the courtroom this afternoon. He had been trying to listen to the proceedings with his reporter ears and not his heart. Pete wondered whether he was simply feeling a bit guilty about avoiding Ayden since he had been the only one allowed to interview Ayden right after his arrest. At that time, Pete had been inclined to believe Ayden when he had professed his innocence—he no longer felt that way. Thinking back on that interview, he now realized how good Ayden was at manipulating people. He surprised himself by not recognizing a long time ago that Ayden was truly an evil person.

Lost in his own thoughts, he was startled when he heard Jeanette say, "What time?"

"Oh, Jeanette, sorry I didn't see you. I'll pick you up at seven in front of the New Valley Inn. Will that be okay for you?"

She simply smiled a smile that made him weak in the knees. "Baby, I will be there with bells on." And, as quickly as she had appeared, she turned and was lost in the crowd.

Pete stood for awhile, just looking around the courtroom when he heard a sound coming from the balcony. There, in the upper corner, he saw a disheveled man holding his head in his hands. Pete could hear his sobs. Hurriedly, Pete climbed the staircase and approached the man from behind. Something drew him to this pathetic creature. As he sat down on the bench beside the man, he placed his hand on the stranger's shoulder.

Little by little, the man raised his head, and with tears streaming down his pock-marked face, he said, "It's my fault; don't you see…it's my fault."

Pete was at a loss for words. He tried to think of something to say to console this man in shabby clothes. All he could get out was, "Now…now…"

As if he had been insulted, the man stood up, pulled back as far away from Pete as he could get, and said through clenched teeth, "She's mine…mine…and I failed her."

With that, the man headed for the doorway and ran down the steps. Suddenly he stopped, turned around and looked at Pete who was still on the top step and, after clenching his fist and waving it in the air, he said, "I promise you this. I will get that bastard, wait and see. That's the least I can do for her."

CHAPTER 8

(Day 3 of The Trial – Later that evening)

Getting ready for a date was something Pete had not done in a long time. He felt a bit giddy even thinking about Jeanette. He was taking an inordinate amount of time in dressing for what was supposed to be a casual dinner date. The dark blue pin-striped suit had been taken out of the cleaner's bag, the new shirt that his sister had given him for his birthday had finally been removed from the gift box, and a striped tie was lying on top of the pile.

A strange feeling was developing in the pit of his stomach. The very thought of Jeanette's provocative behavior was weighing heavily on his mind. Erotic mental images of her loveliness kept flashing in and out of his thoughts. He hadn't felt this horny since his days in high school. He tried to remind himself, *dinner—that's all it will be—just dinner.* He had to stop thinking about anything else.

Mrs. Morton had just left a few minutes ago with his daughter Cindy in tow. She would be spending the weekend with her favorite babysitter. He owed a lot to this woman. She had been a blessing. The day that Estelle had died, Mrs. Morton had knocked on his door, extended her condolences, and offered to take care of his daughter until after the funeral. And, by that time, Cindy and the woman had developed a special bond for one another, a feeling that had grown more intense with the passing of time.

Cindy had just turned nine and was a carbon copy of her mother—warm and tender, sweet and adorable, but with a strength of purpose that sometimes overwhelmed Pete. However, Cindy had a mind of her own, unlike Estelle who lived only to please others. Pete had been grateful that his daughter had been so strong, for he felt that he had let her down during his mourning period. Oh, Cindy had cried. He had often found her weeping into her pillow long after he thought she would have been asleep. But she had adapted. Maybe she had not fully accepted the fact that her mother was gone, but she had accepted the reality of the situation much better than her father.

He had enjoyed watching his daughter grow. Friends had advised him to let her go to Miami and live with his mother, and he had almost acquiesced. But he was glad that he had decided against their well-intended suggestions. Each day, he had found something new about her, something that he had not noticed before. He was always thrilled to observe the subtle changes in her physical and mental make-up. She would come home from school and hold the most delightful conversations with him. And, oh, the questions! More than once he had to run to others for advice on how to handle the delicate probing of a little girl, wanting to know what would happen to her as she became a woman—one who would naturally leave her father's home some day and start a family of her own.

Pete had long ago given all the credit to Estelle for how his daughter handled herself. It was she who had laid the groundwork with the child. It was she who had explained her illness and her imminent death to Cindy. He remembered looking in on the two of them one time. Mother and daughter had been sitting on the bed, side by side, with their arms wrapped tightly around one another. He did not know exactly what Estelle had told the child, but he knew a bond had been established between the two of them that was precious. Cindy could talk about her mother now without crying. She would talk about the good times they had had together, but not once did she mention those private times—those times when the two of them had wrestled with having to leave one another—an inevitable fate, one not of their choosing. But somehow Estelle, as sick as she had been, had found the inner strength needed to help her daughter face reality. She had given Cindy the strength to go on without her—the greatest gift that she could have given her at that time.

Now it was time for the husband to move forward, too. Time to venture forth like Cindy and not be afraid of what the future would hold—nor fear the memories of the past.

As he drove to center city to pick up Jeanette, his nervousness grew stronger. *How does one go about reentering the dating game*? It all seemed a little foreign to the handsome reporter as he stole one last look at himself in the rear view mirror.

She was standing on the corner, waving to him as soon as she spotted his car pulling up to the curb. *A vision of loveliness; no, pure unadulterated sex*, Pete thought. She was wearing a blue, two-piece silk suit. Even from inside the car, Pete could see that the top buttons of the jacket were opened, exposing her soft breasts. A single, silver chain lay around her neck and large, silver earrings sparkled as they nestled in her dark hair.

Pete hurried from the car, ran around to the other side, opened the door and said, "Allow me, madam."

"Madam? That makes me sound old," Jeanette teased.

Pete could not help but notice her legs as she moved into the passenger's seat. Three-inch heels helped to accent those long, lean, and lovely limbs.

"You look great," Pete said as he inched the car forward.

"Is this where I'm supposed to say that you don't look too bad yourself?" Jeanette kidded.

"Might be nice to hear."

"Well, you do. There's something about a man in a suit, shirt, and tie that gets to me. Where are we headed, handsome creature?" Jeanette asked as she crossed her legs, exposing a great expanse of a well-proportioned thigh.

"I thought we'd really do it up right. I made a reservation at a little French restaurant, Chez Paris. Would you believe that name?" Pete asked, not quite covering his nervous state of mind.

"Sounds marvelous, I'm starved," Jeanette said as she adjusted her skirt. "By the way, did you happen to see the news on Channel 6? God, I swore I would not watch that station, but I wanted to hear their take on the trial."

"No, did something explode?"

"Not really. One of the local yokels was interviewing some of Ayden's neighbors. Of course, they all claimed that they knew something weird was going on. But none of them could really add anything to what we have already heard. Do you think that there's the remotest possibility that the Ashes could be innocent?"

"God, Jeanette, I don't know. I used to think Ayden was innocent, but I've changed my mind. I think he is evil incarnate," Pete responded. "When I look back on my contacts with him, I now realize that he snookered me. At first, I didn't want to accept the possibility that he could have molested Amanda. After all, she had to be about twelve when the molestation began—damn, that's tough to even think about," Pete rationalized. "But, when it comes to Sarah, I am vacillating. She just looks so pure."

"Pete, of all people, you should know better than to let your emotions get in the way of a story—you just can't do that," Jeanette reminded Pete.

"But sometimes, Jeanette, that's how good stories can be developed. Just suppose—now wait a minute before you say anything, just suppose she's not guilty."

"I can't see how the molestation could have happened without Sarah's knowledge. Then, there is Amanda. While she is definitely a child in one sense, her body is maturing faster than her mental understanding of what is happening to her. And, quite possibly, she may still think that she's in love with Ayden and that he loves her, too."

As Pete mulled over this possibility, he could feel the warmth coming from Jeanette's presence and became aware of the intoxicating aroma of her perfume. "I love the perfume you're wearing."

"Glad you appreciate something that's twenty dollars an ounce. It's supposed to drive men into a wild frenzy. It better work tonight, or I'll go back to Macy's and demand a refund," Jeanette said as she placed her hand on Pete's arm.

Pete chuckled. It felt good to feel so alive once again. To be with a lovely woman and to be aware of her every move made Pete realize that perhaps his life, as he once knew it, was not gone, but was reawakening. "Now don't distract the driver," Pete cautioned.

"You really want me to stop touching you?" Jeanette asked as she leaned forward to look into his face.

"To be honest, I don't want you to stop; but, unfortunately, we've arrived at our destination."

Jeanette removed her hand and said, "To be continued later."

The meal was only a bit above average but Pete didn't care. He hadn't laughed this much in several years. Jeanette was a marvelous dinner companion and was as charming as she was lovely.

Pete refilled their wine glasses and said, "I want to propose a toast—to a lovely woman who has made a tired man feel young again."

"Young again? My God, Pete, you make yourself sound like an ancient pelican. You're only five years older than I and you look terrific. Didn't you see that woman over there give you the eye as we walked by her? Wake up, Pete—smell the roses. Don't let the parade pass you by," Jeanette said as their wine glasses met.

"How did you get through everything, you know..."

"Well, it wasn't easy. When my husband was murdered, I thought my life was over. Death isn't easy to accept, let alone when you lose someone so violently. You're certainly no stranger to that, Pete. But whether someone you loved, loved very dearly, died a slow, painful death like Estelle did, or whether they were in the wrong place at the wrong time, like Frank was, it must be faced. I went through all the stages. First was the disbelief that Frank had been in his office at the bank one day, alive and well and, through one person's unforgivable act, dead in a moment. It's still hard to handle," Jeanette said softly. She put both her hands on his and said, "I was angry with him for dying—like he had an option—how dare he die and leave me alone. Imagine, I was blaming everyone for his death—even him. I blamed him for standing in the line of fire."

"Sounds familiar. I used to go around the house slamming doors and drawers and blaming Jeanette for getting cancer. But, I had Cindy to think of, and I truly believe that, if it had not been for her, I would not have gotten through all of it."

"It's okay to let go, Pete," Jeanette said as she took Pete's hands in hers. "Now I deal with it by trying to be the same individual that Frank fell in love with. I loved him deeply. But I know that that phase of my life is over. There will always be times when my thoughts will be with him, just as yours will be with Estelle. There are things that I wished I would have told him—things he should have known. But the time for crying, the time for mourning, has ended. I'll always be grateful for what I had. Pete, no one can ever take Estelle from you. But, don't make a martyr out of yourself. We can't change the hands that we were dealt. We both got raw deals. What we must do now is go on living and make them proud."

"I would have given my life for her," Pete said.

"Don't you think she knew that? You had a good marriage and you have Cindy. Count your blessings. Enough of this morbid conversation—let's dance."

Holding hands, they walked to the tiny dance floor. Pete placed his arm around Jeanette and pulled her toward his chest. They moved in perfect unison to the rhythm of the music. She turned her head slightly and kissed his cheek. At that moment, Pete felt the thrill of desire filling his body. They finished their dance without saying a word to each other. Slowly, they walked back to their table and stood there for a few seconds just looking at one another. Pete helped Jeanette with her jacket, placed money on the table to cover the check, as well as an ample tip, and guided his lovely companion to the door.

The conversation on the way back to Jeanette's hotel was light. They discussed things like the weather, sports, and movies—afraid to say what was really on their minds.

"My hotel has a great piano bar. Let's stop by for a nightcap. I'll treat," Jeanette said as Pete neared the parking lot.

"Good idea. Who said female reporters can't think?" Pete teased.

As Pete pulled into a parking spot, Jeanette said. "Pete, I have something for you. Give me your hand." She gently placed her room key in his warm hand.

Pete let his fingers curl around the metal key. He looked at her once more and knew for certain that his time to love again had arrived. "Let's forget that drink," he said. Pete moved like a zombie through the dimly-lit, hotel hallway, still clutching the key in his hand. As he pushed the door open, Jeanette stepped in and turned on the lights.

They clung together tightly, each afraid of letting go, but more afraid to go ahead. Finally, Jeanette said, "Let me make a few adjustments. This is too good not to do it right."

She moved to the window and opened the drapes. When she turned the dresser light off, the room was bathed in a soft amber color from the lights on the North Bridge. "Isn't that better?" she asked Pete as she slipped by him.

Pete found himself alone, standing there like an awkward young man waiting for his first sexual experience. He could hear Jeanette moving about in the bathroom.

"Put some music on, darling," she called from behind the closed door.

When he heard '*darling*' he almost fell apart. Pete found his favorite radio station and sauntered back to the window. He watched the cars moving across the bridge and was immediately awed by the beauty before him—New Valley never looked so good to him.

He suddenly became aware that she was standing behind him. She put her arms around him and began to investigate his body. He stood immobilized, hoping that this feeling would not end.

"Turn around," is all she said.

"My God, you're lovely," Pete replied softly.

Later, much later, Pete awoke to the sound of running water in the bathroom. His body was totally relaxed. The world could stop at this moment, and he would have no regrets. He curled up on his side and firmly hugged his pillow.

Jeanette crawled back into bed beside him, deftly placed her hand on his hip and rolled him over on his back. "Now, my darling, just relax and let me take over."

CHAPTER 9

(The Trial: Day 4)

Ayden settled back into his chair and assumed a confident manner. He was certain that both John and Margaret had come across to the jury like a couple of buffoons. How could they believe those uncouth people? Ayden felt that even the uneducated people, who were sitting in judgment of him, had to be able to understand how superior he was to the average person. Anyone with any sense at all should be able to tell *quality*. And, John and Margaret certainly did not represent good character.

He replayed Margaret's phone call over in his mind. She had been screaming at him that he had been a disgraceful pig and that she was going to be sure he was punished for his crime. Margaret had, indeed, offered her silence for money—how commonplace she had been. Of course, he had refused her offer. In fact, he had been grossly insulted by her proposition. He recalled telling Margaret that she would have a difficult time proving Amanda's charges.

Claude Wilson and Wally Berman began the fourth day of the trial by calling a parade of character witnesses for their clients. Most were testifying on Sarah's behalf. Only Dr. Jenson, from the Department of Education, had reluctantly agreed to testify in reference to Ayden.

Dr. Jenson was a short man with a distinctive, full head of gray hair and a well-groomed, short beard. He was immaculately dressed in a blue serge suit, white shirt and a bright red tie. He wore short black boots with elevated heels. His total appearance shouted "ladies man." But Jenson had a quick mind and had been one of the few visionaries at the state level. He hadn't wanted to testify, but when he was subpoenaed, he knew that he had lost the fight. The uneasiness that he had been feeling for the past few weeks had not disappeared. In fact, it had intensified. He had been fearful that his testimony would taint his educational reputation, which he guarded jealously. Only after Claude Wilson had assured him that the prosecuting attorney would not question him about his personal life had he begun to cooperate.

"Dr. Jenson, how do you know the defendants, Ayden and Sarah Ash?" Wilson asked.

"Sarah works at the State Library, and I really don't know much about her. But Mr. Ash and I have had dealings involving the production of films for school districts," Jenson said as he nervously stroked his short white beard.

"What types of films did Mr. Ash produce for you?"

Jenson hesitated for a few moments. "The last job we gave him called for a series of short films, focusing on the problems experienced by children who run away from home. The contract also required Mr. Ash to produce teacher study guides to accompany the films," Jenson explained. "You see, when the Department needs films, which are not available from commercial vendors, we contract out for them. This was just such an incident."

"I see. Was the work done to your satisfaction?" Wilson inquired.

"Yes. While they were certainly not up to commercial, professional standards, we found the films to be quite suitable for the students."

"Did they meet all the requirements of the contract?" Wilson asked.

"Yes," he said.

"While Mr. Ash was working for you, were you entirely satisfied with Mr. Ash's behavior and demeanor?"

"Yes. He was always professional in his dealings with me."

"Thank you, Dr. Jenson. Your witness," Wilson said as he looked at Barber.

"Mr. Jenson, excuse me, I mean Dr. Jenson, were all of your dealings with Mr. Ash held in your office?" Barber asked in a skeptical tone.

Jenson stiffened. "Yes. I had no reason to meet with him anywhere else."

"So, you did not have any occasions to visit the school or talk with any of his students. Is that correct Dr. Jenson?"

"That's correct."

"That means that you cannot testify about his moral character?" Barber asked with a slight smile on his face.

Jenson tensed his body and sat upright.

"Objection," Wilson said. "Dr. Jenson was very specific, regarding his level of knowledge about the defendants."

"Sustained," Calder responded.

"Dr. Jenson, did you ever have an occasion to visit the school building in the evening hours? Let's say for a party or a get-together?" Barber asked with the confidence of a man who knew something.

Ayden shook his head. He didn't know how people like Jenson got their positions in the Department of Education. Should he stand up and tell this moronic jury that the good doctor had not even looked at the films? Melody had told Ayden that Jenson, despite being the person responsible for the production of the contracted educational films, had merely turned them over to staff for distribution to the field without checking on their quality and appropriateness for middle school students. But, as soon as Ayden had been arrested, Jenson had called in all copies of the films. Then, and only then, had Jenson taken the time to review the films. Much to his relief, the end products had fulfilled all the requirements of the contract. But because of all the publicity, the films had never been released again, which angered Ayden.

Ayden really wanted to tell the jurors about Jenson's attendance at the best sex orgy that he had ever held. *That's it, Jenson, pretend that you're clean. It's all in my favor anyway.* He had told Wilson about Jenson and the orgy, but his attorney had advised him that it could prejudice the jury against him, so they would not bring this to light.

Jenson had played a major role in implementing the affirmative action plan for the Department of Education—a fact that greatly irritated Ayden. In Ayden's mind, choosing employees not according to merit, but according to class, was ludicrous. In fact, he could not understand how women could be considered a minority when they made up the majority of the population—another example of the stupidity of today's society.

"No. We transacted all of our business in my office." Jenson said as he tugged on his lapels with both of his hands in a Napoleonic gesture for which he was noted.

Barber paced back and forth in front of the nervous witness. He had no evidence to link the good doctor with the Ashes socially. But he had a hunch. His intuition told him that this cocky, little banty rooster had been more involved in this whole mess than he had admitted so far.

Jenson was looking more apprehensive every minute. His body was becoming very warm. The heat started creeping up his neck and began to show as a bright red flush on his face. As he tried to regain his composure, he started to bite nervously on his bottom lip.

When Barber realized that his fishing expedition had not been successful with Jenson, he reluctantly said, "I have no more questions for this witness, Your Honor."

As one witness after the other testified to Sarah's pure behavior, Ayden was getting aggravated. You would think that they were talking about some virgin—annoying as hell. Ayden glanced around the crowded courtroom. He was irritated when he spotted Pete. Wilson had approached Pete and asked him to testify as a character witness for his client. The snooty reporter had refused and provided some lame excuse why he couldn't. Ayden glared at his old friend—someone who apparently did not know the tenets of a true friendship. It certainly wouldn't have hurt his case if Pete had gotten up in front of the jury to testify on his behalf. Ayden vowed to remember this snub.

Wilson said, "I call Ayden Ash to the stand."

The courtroom became hushed. The click of Ayden's heels produced full resonant tones as he strutted across the hardwood floor. He took his place slowly, his eyes scanning the faces of the jurors. Faces he swore that he would not forget—ever.

"Mr. Ash, you are the Director of The Church of True Believers, located at the corner of Jackson and Commerce? Is that not correct?"

"I am the Primate of the church, sir," Ayden gently responded.

Wilson was his usual confident self. He was used to winning cases and he wanted this one badly. The publicity alone would be invaluable as he sought to further his political ambition. Ayden was paying through the nose for his services, but that was not the driving reason that he had agreed to represent him. There would be lots of photos, lots of press coverage, and Wilson thrived on that. He realized that Ayden held some strange beliefs, but then so did many people. While his client was definitely kooky, that didn't mean that he was guilty. No one had been killed. And if the rape had happened, although he was still not certain that Ayden ever had sex with any of the children, they would soon forget what happened and it would all be water under the bridge.

"As the Primate, what are your responsibilities?" Wilson asked.

"I AM the church, you might say." Ayden responded in an authoritative voice. "I not only attend to the spiritual needs of my little flock, I handle all of the financial transactions and tend to their personal needs. Without me, my members would not survive."

"And what are your duties as far as the school is concerned?"

"The church—the school—they are one. When you speak of The Church of True Believers, you speak of me. It's just that simple," Ayden responded, sounding very much like an evangelist.

"You also established the curriculum for the students, hired the teachers, and administered the program?"

"Of course, but when you say 'hire the teachers', I must explain that our teachers did not get salaries. They volunteered their time. Some of them lived at the school, others did not. But no one, including myself, received a salary as such. All expenses were paid for by the school," Ayden recounted in an official tone of voice.

"I see. Where did the funds come from that you used to pay these expenses?"

"Quite frankly, most of them came from private endowments and contributions made to our little church. And, of course, some financial help came from the contracts that I was granted by the Department of Education. In addition, I authored several books and produced some films. The women, Sarah and Melody, contributed their paychecks," Ayden explained. "You see, what belongs to one member of the church, belongs to all."

"Mr. Ash, you have heard allegations made about you from this witness stand, regarding sexual activities occurring in your school," Wilson said, taking time to look more intently at the faces of the jurors. "Are you guilty of these crimes?"

Ayden caught the spirit of the moment. Sensing that the jurors were currently sympathetic toward him, he looked directly into their faces and said, "No, I am not. I love my students, but not in a sexual manner. You see, man is endowed with a divine soul, distinguishing him from the creatures below, who need no self-realization. However, we humans have souls, so we find self-realization through our love for one another. And much to my dismay," Ayden said as he lowered his eyes, "this love that I have for them, this pure adoration, has somehow been misconstrued into something malefic."

"Did you give Amanda a ring?"

"Yes. I presented rings to several girls to symbolize their holy connection to the church. They were tokens of my love for them," Ayden said as he chuckled. "We all know how impressionable young girls are. They have a tendency to fall in and out of love several times a day. I thought they understood that the rings were just little gifts to represent my affection. I guess some of our teachings might be a little too complex for their tender souls to comprehend. You see, God put all in the hands of Aaron and for a short period of time, the time that I walk on this earth, I represent Aaron to the true believer. You cannot lead anyone, help anyone, or guide anyone in the true direction if you do not love everyone."

"If you were not sexually involved with Amanda, why do you believe she made these charges?"

"First, you must realize that Amanda is a product of her upbringing. She loves to make up stories—stories that are very difficult to believe. She reads trash magazines and those ridiculous love stories, and then she begins to confuse what she has read with the real world. I tried my best with her, but I can only do so much for children who have been reared in revolting circumstances."

"Objection," Barber said, "calls for an opinion."

"Sustained."

"Mr. Ash, can you think of any other reason that may explain why Amanda accused you of violating her?"

"I feel that in an innocent way, I may have had some influence on her. You see, one day she entered my bedroom while Sarah and I were making love. It startled me so much that I raised my voice to her. After this incident, Amanda began pursuing me. She wanted me to do with her what I had been doing with my wife. I tried to explain to her that my love for her was different than my love for my Sarah. But she persisted. And after each rejection, she became more and more agitated with me. I honestly believe that you will find her mother at the heart of these charges. You see, she needs money and—"

"Objection," Barber stated empathetically.

"Mr. Ash, just answer the questions directly. Do not add your personal opinions," Calder said.

"That will be hard for one who leads a church, Your Honor," Ayden said as he smiled at the judge.

The spectators, as well as the jurors, broke into laughter.

"Mr. Ash, I must ask you a very difficult question. To your knowledge, have any sexual activities involving children occurred in your school?" asked Wilson.

The jurors riveted their attention on Ayden and the spectators were unusually quiet. Ayden, taking full advantage of the stillness, turned toward the jury and said convincingly, "Not to my knowledge. You do not know what kids will do, but as far as I know, there were no such incidents, at least between adults and children. But I wouldn't be surprised at anything that Amanda would do since she—"

"Objection, Your Honor. Mr. Ash is making allegations which he cannot prove," shouted Barber.

`Surprisingly, Ayden stood up in the witness box, shook his fist at Barber and said, "How about the allegations she made about me?"

"Mr. Ash," Calder said loudly. "Sit down. Counselor, please counsel your client that one more such disturbance, and I will restrict him from the courtroom."

Wilson walked over to Ayden, placed his hand on the angry man's shoulder, and said something so quietly that no one else could hear.

"Mr. Ash, did you receive a phone call from Mrs. Hoffman on the night she pressed charges against you?" Wilson asked, trying his best to bring the jury back to a level of compassion.

"You bet I did. She told me that, unless I paid her cash money, she was going to go to the police with her trumped-up story. She was yelling at me, calling me names, so I hung up on her. I thought she was just getting back at me."

Wilson pulled his eyebrows together and asked, "Getting back at you for what?"

"One day, when Sarah had the children on a field trip to the State museum, she walked into the school. She had been quite blunt about what she wanted." Looking at the jurors, he then said, "Excuse me for this, but I must tell you what she wanted me to do—she wanted me to… well—take her to bed. She told me that she was tired of seeing black skin on her."

Margaret jumped up, knocking her large purse on the floor. "Liar, you fucking liar!"

Judge Calder pounded his gavel loudly, but it took almost a minute before the courtroom calmed down enough for him to be heard. "Mrs. Hoffman, one more outburst like that and I will have you removed from the courtroom."

Begrudgingly, Margaret sat down, muttering to herself. John tried to say something to her, but she turned her head and wouldn't listen to him. She gathered up the items which spilled when her purse fell on the floor, closing the clasp with such force that the plastic handle broke. She crossed her arms over her large stomach, all the while gritting her teeth and taking deep breaths.

Wilson was delighted. "Mr. Ash, at the time when Mrs. Hoffman asked for money, how did you respond?"

"I said *no* very emphatically. She promised to get even with me. Why, she had even begun to remove her clothes—what a repulsive sight that was," Ayden said as he let out a little chuckle.

It was obvious that Margaret was seething. She tightened her jaws and pressed her lips together, while little tears began to roll down her chubby face.

"Did Mrs. Hoffman ever contact you again about the charges?"

"Only by phone—she had been letting me know that she was still interested in having sex with me. One day I received a package in the mail, and it was filled with adult sex toys. I know she sent—"

"Objection, calls for a conclusion," Barber stated.

"Did John Murray ever express any concerns about what was happening in your little church school?"

"No, he never came to the school. But he's not too smart so..."

"Objection, Your Honor, these degrading remarks need to be stricken," urged Barber.

"Sustained. Mr. Wilson, this cannot continue. I have previously warned your client and he continues to cause havoc in my courtroom. I will have him removed," Judge Calder ordered.

"Let's cut to the chase, Mr. Ash. Did you ever violate Amanda?"

"Absolutely not!" Ayden stated firmly.

It was now time for Ray Barber to cross-examine Ayden. He was pleased that his time had finally come. He had waited a long time for this opportunity. He wanted to get this man so much he could taste it. Of all the criminals that he had prosecuted over the years, he hated child molesters the most. The memories of the times that his uncle had forced him to do those things when he was small were as vivid as if they had happened yesterday. His family had refused to have his uncle arrested—they argued that, after all, it was family and family must be protected. But Ayden was here—here in this courtroom—Barber was determined that he was going to even the score.

"Mr. Ash, you claim that you are the Primate of the Church of True Believers. Is that correct?"

"I don't claim to be, Mr. Barber, I *am* the Primate," Ayden said proudly.

"How did you become Primate? Did you earn a degree of any kind?" Barber asked in a sarcastic tone.

"The Church of True Believers does not require its leaders to attend any college," Ayden answered. "You see, I was anointed."

"How does one get anointed, Mr. Ash? I am sure that the jury is curious about that," taunted Barber.

Ayden smiled weakly and said, "Several bishops from Philadelphia participated in a ceremony at the church, and then they presented me with a certificate which qualifies me to serve as the Primate."

"Certificate? What does that mean? Did you complete any formal schooling or training to become the...what did you call it? Primate?" Barber scoffed.

Ayden drew himself up in the witness chair and responded haughtily, "One does not necessarily have to attend formal schooling to become educated. One needs only to study humanity to learn the truth."

Barber smiled broadly. "So, you did not have to attend classes in order to earn your *certificat*e. Did you have to pay for it?"

"Yes, I paid five dollars—" Ayden said, as the courtroom burst out in laughter.

Barber took full advantage of the levity by strutting back and forth in front of the witness and shaking his head while chuckling loudly.

"Oh, now I understand. For a mere sum of five dollars, and for participating in some mumbo jumbo, you became a Primate. Is this correct?"

Ayden was showing signs of losing control. "It may be mumbo jumbo to you, but to us it is a sacred ceremony. Don't knock what you do not understand," Ayden stated emphatically.

"If I give you ten dollars, Mr. Ash, can I become Primate of two churches?" Barber asked as he faced the spectators and shrugged his shoulders. Margaret laughed the loudest of all.

"Your Honor, the Prosecutor is belittling my client," Wilson exclaimed.

"The jury will disregard Mr. Barber's last remark" Judge Calder said as he looked at the smiling Prosecutor.

Barber was pleased with himself. He was enjoying every moment of Ayden's discomfort. He couldn't wait until he had this sanctimonious, phony charlatan hung out to dry.

Letting Ayden squirm for a few seconds, Barber took his time before he asked his next question, "Who owns the church building, Mr. Ash?"

"I do. I inherited it. I own it free and clear," Ayden stated in a rapid fire manner. "It is mine—all mine."

"None of your students paid tuition?" Barber asked.

"That is correct. All my little ones attended the school at no cost to their parents. Just because people are poor should not be a reason for their children to be denied a good education. My flock and I supported the school," Ayden answered proudly.

"And children at your school got a good education—a proper education?"

"I'll match my curriculum against any in the state."

"Does the curriculum include sex education?"

"Objection," shouted Wilson.

"Your Honor, I have asked a legitimate question. Most curricula across our state now include courses in sex education. I am merely trying to determine if Mr. Ash's school includes such studies."

"Overruled, the witness may answer," the judge ruled.

"No, it does not. Our staff decided that such teaching should come from the parents. We covered the core courses as well as the humanities. Our children always progressed very well. But, before we could administer state tests, well…"

"The State closed your school. Is that what you were going to say, Mr. Ash?"

"Yes, but the move was unfair. We should not have been closed because nothing had been proven and nothing can be proven," Ayden firmly said.

"I beg to differ with that conclusion. Now let's move on. Mr. Ash, how many wives do you have?"

"One, of course; Sarah."

"Isn't it true, Mr. Ash, you have also made Melody Baker and Rebekah Montgomery your wives in secret ceremonies conducted in your church?" Barber asked, leaning in toward the witness so close that they were almost eye-to-eye.

"First of all, there were no secret ceremonies. My flock is always in attendance whenever we have religious activities. Secondly, in this state, sir, in case you do not know it, one is permitted to have only one wife," Ayden snickered.

"Oh, I know that, sir. However, I was not certain that you knew that. Did you conduct ceremonies at which time you took Melody and Rebekah as your wives?"

"No. I think of them as my wives but only in the biblical sense. It is part of our faith. But all of this had nothing to do with Amanda and her ridiculous charges," Ayden responded.

"Biblical sense—does that include having sexual relations with your wives?"

"I can see that you still do not understand. Melody and Rebekah are my responsibility. They look to me for guidance. They depend on me for their spiritual needs. Is that plain enough for you to understand?" Ayden said.

"And their sexual needs? Do you take care of those, too?" Barber asked.

"Human needs cannot be classified in neat little boxes. They cannot be controlled by man-made laws. People react to one another on different levels. And, what happens between consenting adults should be no one's business but theirs," Ayden responded.

"So, you have a church full of people with loose morals, and you are asking us to believe that Amanda made up her story? That the child is a liar even though the medical report states otherwise. Is this what you are asking this intelligent jury to believe?"

And before Ayden could answer the barrage of questions, Barber threw his hands up in the air and announced, "I have no more questions for this witness, Your Honor."

As soon as Calder dismissed court for the day, spectators filed out the door, and the rush was on to get on the elevator. Outside, on the cement steps, several reporters formed a small group and began to discuss the happenings of the day.

"Imagine, five bucks…that's how he became head of a church… totally unbelievable," said the youngest. "Hell, even I could afford that."

"Since when did you have five bucks?" asked another.

"Hey, listen to this," one of them said. "There was this blonde who was in a bar and…" The little group closed rank and they leaned in so that others could not hear what was going on. After the punch line, the group broke up into wild laughter.

One of them spotted Pete and called to him. "Over here, Pete!"

Pete breathed a short sigh and headed toward the small gathering. He would have preferred to spend time with Jeanette, but she had disappeared somewhere in the crowd. Every time her name crossed his mind, he smiled. And, he had been smiling a great deal since the other night. The world was completely different now: colors were more intense, songs were more melodious, people were kinder, and his disposition had been remarkably brighter than it had been in a long time.

With the gait of a much younger man, Pete approached his peers. "What's up, gang? Is this some kind of union meeting?" Pete asked as the group parted to admit him into their inner sanctum.

"Pete, what's the real scoop? Is that cock-eyed bastard sane? Are there more kooks like him in this town?"

"You know as much as I do," Pete answered as he shrugged his shoulders. As he leaned backwards to glance around to see if he could spot Jeanette, he said, "We still haven't heard from his wife, yet. Perhaps she'll shed some light on the whole mess."

"Well," said a pimply-faced young man, "I'd like to take that bastard and cut his damned cock off. He'd never touch another kid again."

Suddenly, one of them said, "Oh, my God, will you look at that!"

Jeanette was coming down the courthouse steps, the slit on her black skirt just opening wide enough to expose a bit of her thigh.

"What I wouldn't give to have a tumble in the hay with her," he said, as he banged his forehead with his hand.

"Dan, she'd kill you. A skinny little runt like you couldn't handle a woman like her. What she needs is a man…a man like me, and I'm more than willing to sacrifice myself and volunteer!" said one of Dan's friends.

The hair on the back of Pete's neck stood up. He wanted to hit the acne-plagued youngster. Instead, he just smiled, looked at Jeanette and said, "Hi."

Jeanette walked toward the small clan. Pale pink lipstick and a white silk blouse perfectly accented her dark hair. She was wearing the same earrings that she had worn when Pete had taken her to dinner—earrings that Pete would not forget. He could still see them glistening on the night stand, where she had placed them, before she had undressed. Pete swallowed hard and tried to remain calm as his new lover approached.

"Hello, darling," Jeanette said as she placed a small kiss on his cheek.

The reporters became very quiet, with their mouths hanging open to the gentle fall breeze. Pete could feel the warmth of a blush creeping up his neck and into his face.

"Well, gentlemen, have you come to any conclusions yet about our creepy defendant?" Jeanette asked the astonished group.

"The hell with that—what's this '*darling*' business?" the scrawny young man asked.

"You're a reporter—what does it look like to you?" Jeanette asked as she took Pete's hand.

Ordinarily, Pete would not have relished such a public display of affection, but somehow, this was different. He liked the feel of her. He liked the smell of her. And, to his surprise, he was enjoying being the envy of his counterparts. Pete could only guess what was running through their minds and gave them all a smile that let them know just how close he had been with this gorgeous woman.

"Sorry, boys, I'm stealing him away. We have a date." Jeanette said as she guided him away from the group.

After they had turned the corner, Pete said, "I didn't know we had a date."

"Sweetie, you have a lot to learn."

CHAPTER 10

(The Trial: Day 5)

On the fifth day of the trial, the sky was extremely overcast and it appeared that a thunder storm might be imminent. Dark clouds were rolling in and the air was heavy with moisture. Even the birds had stopped their usual chatter. The atmosphere had manifested itself in the behavior of the spectators, who were far more restless than they had been on previous days. The noise level in the courtroom had reached an almost ear-drum-breaking level as the rush for seats began once again. Ayden made no attempt to hide his displeasure—his concentration was being interrupted and his space was being violated by the discord.

Ayden was irritated that Wally Berman had hustled Sarah into an anteroom for a consultation just minutes after they had arrived at the courtroom this morning. He was angry that he was not given an opportunity to provide his wife the guidance she needed before she testified—he was afraid that Berman might be planting ideas in her head—ideas that would be counter-productive to Ayden's defense. Several minutes later, Ayden was relieved when he saw that Sarah was being led to the defense table by her attorney. After taking a good look at his wife, his concern returned. She sat perfectly still, looking straight ahead, and did not even acknowledge his presence. He felt that, if anything unusual happened this morning, he might be doomed—without his advice, she could be a detriment to their entire case.

Both Berman and Barber had completed questioning Rebekah Montgomery, producing much the same results. Rebekah adamantly corroborated Ayden's testimony and vehemently denied that any of the children had been molested. She came across as a cold woman who judged things either black or white with no in-between. But she steadfastly gave credit to Ayden, her Primate, for leading her to the Lord.

Melody Baker, however, was a different matter all together. As she testified on behalf of the defendants, her arrogance and self-assuredness came across loud and clear. The well-directed questions presented by the defense attorneys produced a long and meritorious list of the generous and giving nature of the accused. According to Melody, all the children were treated with kindness by a loving church school staff.

Now, at last, it was Barber's turn to cross examine Melody. "Miss Baker, you have testified that you are a member of The Church of True Believers and that you contributed your salary to the operation of the church and the school. Did you at any time serve as a teacher?"

"No, I gave my secretarial skills. Sometimes I filled in for Jake Mnbonu, but I'm also an amateur photographer as well as an accomplished artist. I helped in those ways," Melody responded in an arrogant tone.

Barber was annoyed that law enforcement had failed to locate Jake Mnbonu, who had acted as the school's principal. The African man, who spoke almost perfect English, had disappeared the day that the Ashes had been arrested. As far as Barber could determine, the man had not been involved in any of the acts with the children, but he felt that Jake could have cleared up many of the concerns that still bothered him about Ayden.

Now he was facing Melody Baker for whom he had a distinct aversion. Perhaps it was her smirk that irritated him so much, or maybe it was the way she held her head to one side. He just could not put his finger on why this obnoxious woman aggravated him. Barber was certain that Melody was as evil as Ayden, but he didn't have any evidence to support his belief. She looked like one of the hookers that he had to drag through the court system day after day. Hookers he could understand—they sold their services. Children, however, had no voice in their molestation—they were helpless victims.

Barber approached Melody slowly, almost hesitantly. He had to try to question her without letting his hatred show. He wanted to demonstrate disgust but did not want to reveal his real emotions. "Miss Baker, do you consider yourself to be married to Ayden Ash?" he casually asked.

"Only in the eyes of the church," Melody answered.

Barber strutted back and forth in front of the witness. A sense of expectation seemed to fill the air. "Miss Baker," Barber said in a loud voice, "are you pregnant?"

Sarah finally lifted her head. She let out a little whimper, covered her face with her hands, and lowered her head.

"Objection, Your Honor. Miss Baker's physical condition has no bearing on this case," Berman argued.

"Your Honor, it is my contention that the environment in The Church of True Believers had a great deal to do with the abuse of children and I—"

"Your Honor, no abuse has been proven," Berman pleaded.

"I'm going to overrule your objection, Mr. Berman. Mr. Ash has already testified that he considers himself married to this woman. I instruct the witness to answer the question," Calder ruled.

"Miss Baker, are you pregnant?" Barber asked.

Melody looked at Ayden and then at Sarah who still had not raised her head. Holding her head high, Melody responded, "Yes. I'm pleased that I will be bearing a child for the Lord sometime in April." Then, she raised her hand and said very proudly, "And, Ayden, my beloved Primate, is the father of my child—our very special love child."

Claude Wilson looked as if he had seen a ghost.

Ayden straightened himself up and threw his shoulders back, letting out a loud cheer. While he had been intimate with Melody when he was out on bail, he hadn't known! She had not told him! He gave Melody a big smile and her eyes glowed as she returned his gaze. He allowed himself to enjoy the news as he pondered what he had just learned. *It will be a son. I can tell just by looking at her. She does not disappoint me. She will bring forth a son. Now I will have a son—a son who will some day take my place, walk in my footsteps---and keep my faith alive. A son will keep my name alive. Now, you bastards, no matter what you do to me, I will endure!*

Different thoughts, however, were going through Sarah's mind and filling her body with spasms. She could feel a migraine headache beginning to advance behind her eyes. *I will lose him. Now I will lose him. My God, what have I done to deserve such punishment?*

Barber continued his cross-examination of Melody. But Ayden's thoughts were not with the trial any more. His excitement escalated to a height that he had not experienced lately. Thoughts of a son ran in and out of his mind so rapidly that he hardly had time to grasp the meaning of all of them. *My son, such beautiful words—my son—words that he had been waiting to hear for so long. His name shall be Adam. He will bring forth a new birth of faith. He will be my rock.*

Suddenly, Ayden was brought back to the immediacy of the trial when he heard Berman say, "The defense calls Sarah Ash to the stand."

Sarah walked lethargically to the witness stand, keeping her head bowed, without glancing right or left. Just as she was about to take her seat, lightning illuminated the entire courtroom, followed by a loud crash of thunder, making her cry out. Sarah grabbed the arms of the chair and, at long last, lifted her head. As her eyes moved upward toward the ceiling, she appeared to be praying. For the first time during the trial, Ayden was frightened. He quickly forgot about Adam and turned his attention to his wife. He leaned toward his attorney and said, "She could be my nemesis. She is afraid of thunderstorms."

"Mrs. Ash, are you all right, my dear?" a concerned Berman asked.

Sarah looked like a frightened child as she tried to respond to her attorney's question. "I…I guess so."

"Sarah, you have heard the testimony in this case. Charges have been made against you and your husband, regarding sexual misconduct involving a minor child in your church school. Did you at any time have any type of inappropriate contact with any of the children?"

Sarah sat perfectly still. The thunder storm was growing more intense. A bolt of lightning hit the generator just outside the building, creating an arc of light across the courtroom, sending sparks in all directions. Bright white and yellow beams of light zigzagged down the rear wall. Clamorous rolls of thunder followed several amazingly brilliant streaks of lightning. Rain began pounding on the large, arched windows with such tremendous force that several of the jurors covered their faces and many of the spectators cringed in their seats. The thunder was almost deafening as the storm seemed to concentrate directly on the old, stately courthouse. When the lights flickered off and on several times, the atmosphere became extremely frightening.

After pausing for a few minutes, waiting for the worst of the storm to pass, Judge Calder asked, "Mrs. Ash, are you able to proceed?"

"I'll be fine now," Sarah said with an angelic smile on her face. In a reassured voice, she said, "I know now what I must do."

"Shut up, you stupid bitch!" Ayden screamed.

"Mr. Wilson, please restrain your client. Mrs. Ash, are you certain that you want to go ahead with your testimony?"

Very quietly, almost inaudibly, and with a smile now replacing the fear she demonstrated just minutes ago, Sarah responded, "Yes, I am certain."

Berman stopped dead in his tracks. He desperately wanted to get Sarah off the stand, and he almost lost his usual courtroom composure. Ayden's eyes were fixed on his wife's face. The spectators became extremely noisy, pushing one another, and voicing their opinions to one another.

Judge Calder had to rap his gavel several times before he could bring the courtroom back to order.

Jeanette leaned over to Pete and said, "Look, would you believe it… as soon as she answered, the storm dissipated. Is that creepy or what? She's smiling ear to ear. I can't believe any of this."

"Your Honor, this comes as a complete surprise to me. I would like to request a recess so that I may confer with my client," Berman pleaded.

"No," Sarah said loudly. "The Lord has spoken. I must obey him. I want to confess my sins now. There were others, at least five that I know of. There were other little girls."

"Mrs. Ash, for your own benefit, I will recess now and reconvene tomorrow morning so that you have time to meet with your lawyer and make an informed decision about your testimony," Calder ordered.

Sarah stood up slowly, raised her eyes to the ceiling once again and said with certainty, "I have heard you. I have seen your signs and I will obey your commandment. I will lay my offering upon the altar and burn it as a sacrifice—an offering made by fire is a sweet savor unto the Lord!"

CHAPTER 11

(The Trial: Sentencing Day)

Judge Calder looked down at the two convicted people standing before him. Only a few days before, both husband and wife had been found guilty of child molestation and were now awaiting their sentencing. The morning newspaper had devoted several columns on the front page, focusing on this very unusual trial. Sarah had broken the case wide open when she had admitted that several children had been molested. However, she claimed that while she observed the molestation, she did not participate in any sexual acts.

Sarah stood with her head hanging down, not looking at the judge or her husband. Ayden, with his shoulders erect and his head held high, faced Calder as if he were getting an award. He exuded a confidence that indicated that he simply did not care what Judge Calder was going to order. Last evening, he had written a letter to Melody to explain his inner most feelings. After tossing out several drafts, he had finally written, *'My precious Melody, I know that I have not done anything wrong. The court has no right to interfere with sexual matters. It is not it's jurisdiction. They may put me away, but I will not be kept behind bars too long. I'm much too smart for that. My flock will not desert me. Eddie will be in charge until I can, once again, take over. I am an ingenious person. Our son, Adam, will need me. Take care, my beloved; I will be with you soon.*

Judge Calder took a deep breath, looked down at the guilty couple, and began, "As a judge, I have been exposed to all types of crimes, and I have had to sentence many people. But the crimes for which you have been found guilty are among the worst. You must be censured for hiding your sexual gratification and appetites behind a mask of religion and education. You knowingly secured a license to operate your school from the Department of Education. This was a calculated act. Your crimes involved a child. Our society has long accepted the responsibility of protecting our children from harm. You have violated this sacred trust. The child involved in this case was led to believe that you were special… that somehow you were ordained by a Superior Being to lead her, to show her the proper way to behave. All of this was done to cloak your insatiable need for sex.

Your crimes are heinous, and decent people everywhere despise them. I think they deserve an equal response from me on behalf of the entire community.

Ayden Ash, I sentence you to twenty years in the state penitentiary on charges of statutory rape." As Calder paused, both Rebekah and Melody shrieked. Rebekah started weeping, while Melody shook her fists at Calder. Margaret, however, crossed her arms and smiled broadly.

"Furthermore," Calder went on, "I also order you to pay all court costs. You have been found guilty on charges of indecent assault and corrupting the morals of a minor." Calder's expression did not change—his look of utter disgust and abhorrence was evident.

"Sarah Ash, I am sentencing you to two years in prison and placing you on five years probation. Your crimes, while not on the level with those committed by your husband, are as egregious. You watched many of the acts being committed and did nothing to prevent them from happening, nor did you attempt to shield the victim from being used in such a manner."

Heaving a big sigh, Calder continued, "Both of you profess to believe in Almighty God and claim that you committed these vile acts in the name of your religion. I cannot comprehend that you could have derived such a meaning from the Holy Scriptures as you have claimed."

Several reporters were huddled together in the balcony of the courtroom. They were approaching the end of the trial with mixed emotions. On the one hand, they had enjoyed the time they had spent together; on the other hand, they were delighted that the defendants were judged to be guilty. Jeanette and Pete were taking notes as rapidly as they could. No one in the balcony, except Pete, took notice of the shabby man who got up and quickly headed for the stairway. He recognized the man as the one whom he had found sobbing last week.

"I hope that parents in this community will take a bitter lesson from all of this," Calder said. "Placing children in the hands of others cannot be done lightly. In fact, it must be done with great care. I also hope that the Department of Education will review it's standards for granting licenses to people to operate schools and that out of such a review, will come a tightening that will prevent such an incident from ever occurring in our state again," Calder said forcefully. "Perhaps time will heal you. Perhaps some day you will become aware of what you have done. When I reflect on the damage that you have done to an innocent child, I am filled with loathing," Calder said.

"Religion may yet help both of you. I only hope that something, or someone, can intercede with you, and that you may never commit such despicable crimes again."

Margaret sat like a peacock—proud and pleased with the verdict. She clapped her hands together in a joyful celebration.

As the bailiff approached to lead the two convicted criminals away, Ayden turned and looked up at the balcony where Pete was sitting, Lifting his right arm in the air, he glared at Pete and he shouted, "I will get my revenge against those of you who turned your backs on me—casting friendship aside. Even if I die, I will reach across the wide divide and strike you when you least expect it. The fire of truth shall ever be burning on the altar—the flames will never go out!"

Over the noise in the courtroom, Margaret yelled back, "Well, you pervert, your fire is out for awhile now. You fucking bastard!"

Rebekah Montgomery, who was crying hysterically, was being helped out of the courtroom by Melody and Eddie. A flash bulb went off in their faces, and Melody took off after the photographer who had just snapped their picture. She chased him down the cement courthouse steps, but she was unable to catch him.

The man who had left the balcony earlier had hurried down the staircase and out the front door. He was livid with rage. He could not understand why Sarah had gotten off so easy. Ayden needed to be executed. Several policemen were stationed around the paddy wagon that would soon be transporting Ayden and Sarah to state prison. The man looked at the five-foot-high pedestal that was the resting place for the giant cement lion and, with remarkable agility, he scaled it quite easily. He waited. He clung to the lion, trying to gain his balance, so he could aim his pistol. Leaning to one side, he raised the .357 and pulled the trigger. His shot went over Ayden's head and lodged in the door of the paddy wagon. He slowly lowered his hand and took aim once again, but before he could squeeze the trigger, a policeman's bullet hit him in the chest. With his left hand clutching his heart, he fell forward, still holding his pistol, and landed with a thump on the cracked sidewalk.

"Who is he? Does anyone know him?" a policeman asked as he turned the body over.

Margaret Hoffman's eyes opened wide and she screamed—she had finally found her long-lost husband.

PART TWO

ON THE RUN

If you have sinned, what do you accomplish against him? And, if your transgressions are multiplied, what do you do to him?
Job 35:6

CHAPTER 12

(1974, ten months after the trial)

It was Pete's first vacation in many years. He stretched his long legs out across the chaise lounge, placed his hands behind his head, and watched Jeanette as she came out of the ocean. What a gorgeous sight! They had been on the island for only two days, and she had already managed to get a golden tan. The white bikini that she was wearing left little to the imagination—the rest Pete knew by heart.

She came running toward him, shaking the water out of her hair. "Why you lazy bum," she teased. "I thought that you were coming in the water with me. You're going to get fatter and lazier than you are already—just lying there, sipping God-knows-what from that tall glass."

"But sweetheart, this is my vacation. On a vacation, one is supposed to be lazy and sip strange drinks," Pete said as he slapped her playfully on her behind.

"Whoa...that's war," Jeanette challenged.

"Choose your weapon, woman," Pete responded as he picked up the little plastic sword that had recently held a maraschino cherry.

"I'm a lover, not a fighter," she reminded him.

"Oh, don't I know it," he agreed.

Jeanette wiped herself dry with a huge, yellow beach towel. Just then, a young beach waiter stopped directly in front of her and asked, "Mrs. Forster, may I get you a drink?"

Bestowing a smile upon the smitten boy, Jeanette said, "No thanks, Jeffrey, but how sweet of you to ask."

As the young man walked away, Pete said, "He can't get enough of you, my dear."

"Oh, he's just a kid," she giggled, "a kid who likes to look at women in bikinis."

"I'm not a kid, but I like to look at women in bikinis, too," Pete said as he pulled his sunglasses down to take a peek at an attractive girl who was passing by.

"Behave yourself, you monster. Here," Jeanette said as she handed Pete a plastic bottle, "put some lotion on my back, please. That might keep your mind occupied so that you stop ogling other women."

"Oh my, man's work is never done," Pete said as he began to moisten Jeanette's back with the warm, oily substance. He rubbed the liquid into her skin in gentle circular motions. "You know, I kind of liked it when Jeff called you *Mrs. Forster.* Did you catch that?"

"Yeah, I caught that," Jeanette said as she tried making herself comfortable on the slatted, beach lounge chair.

"Well?"

"Pete…now come on…let's not start this again," Jeanette responded as she sat up. "Roll over, I better put some of this on your back or you might turn into a red lobster."

Pete was completely relaxed. There was simply nothing else that he could possibly want. Not only was he vacationing on this gorgeous island, but he was with the woman he loved. He had hoped to find the right time to propose to her but so far she had been avoiding discussions regarding marriage. Pete was determined to remain patient—she was well-worth waiting for.

Out of the corner of her eye, Jeanette took a long appreciative look at her lover. She loved how his body looked—all glistening with the oily substance she had just applied to his firm skin. *If only I would have met you sooner, before all those others. How can I tell you? Will you hate me if I do? I will try to make you happy, my darling, but I can't tell you yet. Maybe in a few weeks. I need more courage.*

After baking in the sun for another hour, Jeanette said, "I think it's time we head back to our room. How about it?"

Reluctantly, Pete opened his eyes and said, "Hey, are you trying to lure me into a compromising situation?"

"Think I could?"

"Well," Pete said, "I'm very hard to get, but I have an extremely long list of satisfied clients that will testify that the fight will be well worth it."

Jeanette laughed and said, "Come on, help me gather this junk, and then I'll see whether or not I will be able to seduce you."

From the hallway, they could hear the phone ringing. Pete said, "Hark, what is that I hear? It's probably some woman begging me to meet her."

"Don't answer. It may be that ugly chick in the yellow bikini."

"If it is, I will try not to break her heart," Pete said as he hurried to stop the clanging noise.

"Hello," Pete said. "Are you the girl in the yellow bikini?" At that, Jeanette tossed a bed pillow at his head.

"What the hell are you talking about?" a gruff voice responded.

"No, my dear, I cannot meet you. I don't care if you cannot live without me," Pete continued.

"Pete…Pete.. goddamn it, cut it out. This damn call is costing me an arm and leg. Do you hear me?"

"Yeah, Walt, I hear you. This better be important. I asked you not to bother me for four whole days. What's this all about?"

Walter Worthington was not only Pete's editor, he was also one of Pete's closest friends. In fact, it was Walt who had taken turns with Pete sitting with Estelle when she lay dying from cancer.

"You're not gonna like this," Walt warned.

"What?"

"He's out."

"Who's out?"

"Ash, damn it," Walt shouted.

"What the hell do you mean, Walt? He's been in jail for less than a year," Pete replied while holding his head in astonishment.

"He escaped."

"You're kidding…escaped…that rotten bastard."

"He flew the coop…took off…skipped town…"

"When?" Pete asked.

"This morning. Pete, you won't believe this story. You better sit down. Better yet, have a drink…a stiff one. He used a ladder. Can you imagine anything so stupid? A goddamned ladder, climbed up over a roof…jumped to the ground, and sped off on a waiting motorcycle. Just like a James Bond movie…"

Pete scratched his head and said, "How the hell did he get a ladder?"

"Beats the crap out of me—maybe he ordered one through a damned mail order catalog. The latest report indicates that someone was waiting for him on a motorcycle and the two of them rode away without one goddamned shot being fired by the guards—sounds fishy as hell to me!" Walt explained.

"On the motorcycle—man or woman?" Pete inquired.

"No report on that yet, but it had to be someone from his cult."

"I agree. Find the women and we'll find him!"

"None of them are around. The cops checked and they're all gone. What the hell does that little creep have? Christ, I can't get one babe to give me the time of day, and he has several chasing him all the time. Oh, by the way, what or who, is *Kabbalah*?"

"*Kabbalah* is the Hebrew word for *tradition*. Why?"

"It was written on the wall in Ayden's cell with some kind of screwy drawing or diagram," Walt replied.

"Like circles and triangles?"

"Christ, I don't know. Why?" Walt's gruff voice asked.

"If the drawing looks like a union of triangles and circles, it could represent the Tree of Life in Jewish mysticism," Pete replied.

"Say what? Ayden's not Jewish. You know that," Walt said cantankerously.

"I know…I know. But some of this is starting to make sense. The *Kabbalah* is based on the Old Testament revelation. Those who practice *Kabbalah* believe that knowing God is achieved through illumination, not direct encounter. I remember that Ayden had told me that his religion was based only on the Old Testament. But I never knew that he was into mysticism."

"You're doing it again, Pete," Walt said.

"What?"

"You know damned well...you talk all this hoity-toity crap and you lose me. I don't care what the bastard believes. I want you on this story and quickly," Walt emphasized.

"Get all the background stuff you can, and I'll get on it as soon as we return," Pete said as he began to pull his swim trunks off. "Meanwhile, give Jimmy a try at this...see what he can do until I get back."

"Jimmy will need lots of help—he's a cub! But, if anything else breaks, Pete, I'll call you. Now don't do anything that I wouldn't," Walt said as he hung up the phone with a loud guffaw.

"What happened? Ash escaped? How?" questioned Jeanette.

"The bastard used a ladder and got away on a motorcycle. A lousy motorcycle—sounds so juvenile that I can't believe it. Christ, it was only three weeks ago that the plot to get him out of the prison yard with a helicopter blew up in their faces...now this. What the hell were they thinking...where were the extra guards? I bet all that I have that Melody was the one on the motorcycle...I just know it," Pete said as he paced back and forth, not aware of his nakedness.

"How'd he get a ladder?" Jeanette asked, shrugging her shoulders.

"Who knows? That guy's so clever that it doesn't surprise me. He probably had help from the inside. Can you beat that?" Pete said disgustedly as he continued pacing. "They found *Kabbalah* and a drawing on the wall of his cell. I never knew—"

Jeanette began laughing. "Darling, do you realize what you look like...pacing the floor stark naked?"

Pete stopped pacing, looked down at himself and began to feel embarrassed. Jeanette came toward him slowly, still wearing her small white bikini. "No sense in only one of us being naked, now, is there?"

Jeanette turned her back to him. Pete reached for the tiny string that held her top and gave it a gentle tug. It fell to the floor.

"We can't do anything about Ash right now, but I was challenged earlier to seduce you. On a scale of one to ten, how am I doing?" Jeanette asked as she wrapped her arms around him.

"A fifteen!"

After they had made love, Jeanette curled up in Pete's arms and fell asleep. Pete loved looking at her when she didn't know he was watching. As he stroked her hair, he began to mull over Walt's call. *Where could*

Ash have gone? Did he leave the country? Were all his women with him? What about money? How were they going to survive? What's the key...there's got to be a key. He had to have help on the inside to get a ladder. Could Ash have possibly convinced someone, perhaps a woman, on the inside to get that stupid ladder?

While the two slept side by side, that special world of slumber that only lovers can visit, the patio door opened slowly. A man, wearing a muscle shirt and jeans, slipped quietly into the room and walked toward the bed. He smiled when he looked at Jeanette. He spotted her purse on the night stand, and just as he was putting something inside the straw bag, Jeanette opened her eyes. She saw him and began screaming.

A startled Pete sat up, trying to bring himself back to the land of the living, in time to catch a brief glance of a man jumping over the small porch railing. Pete grabbed his robe. Flinging the patio door open, Pete began chasing the intruder. "Stop him...stop him...," Pete yelled. The man darted into the heavy foliage surrounding the back of the pool. Pete was running as fast as he could, trying desperately to find the man. But it was all in vain—the man was nowhere to be seen.

"Mr. Forster, what happened?" said the young lifeguard who had caught up with Pete.

"The bastard was in our room," Pete managed to get out in between breaths.

"Who?"

"How the hell would I know, kid. We woke up and there he was. Sonofabitch. I wish that I would have caught him," Pete muttered disgustedly.

"You get a look at him?" the lifeguard asked.

"Only a glance—he was about six feet tall, dark hair, about thirty-five or so and he was wearing jeans and a muscle shirt, blue, I think. I have no idea who he was. Oh, my God...Jeanette...," Pete shouted as he started running back toward his hotel room.

Nearing the pool once again, Pete was relieved to see that Jeanette was standing on the patio, wrapped in a white terry cloth towel. He scampered across the lawn, leaped over the small patio railing once again, and took her into his arms. "Thank God you're safe."

Neither one said a word for several seconds. They hung on to one another tightly. Some of the sunbathers were stretching their necks to see what was going on, but Pete was oblivious to anything but the fact the Jeanette was secure in his embrace.

"Did he get away?" Jeanette asked hesitantly as she guided Pete back into their room.

"Yeah…sorry—I lost him in the bushes. Did you get a good look at the sonofabitch?"

Without looking directly at Pete, Jeanette said very softly, "No."

Pete dressed hurriedly. "Wait right here for me. I'm gonna talk to the manager. Meanwhile, keep the patio door locked."

As the door closed behind Pete, Jeanette walked over to the sliding glass door. She bolted it with a sharp pull of the handle. She put on a pair of pink shorts and topped it with a white tee shirt emblazoned with little pink elephants. After brushing her hair slowly, all the while staring at herself in the mirror, she formed a pony tail and tied it with a matching pink grosgrain ribbon. She looked directly into her own eyes until the guilt became too overwhelming. Suddenly, she noticed that her straw bag was lying on its side, exactly where he had been standing. With shaking hands, she dumped the contents out on the glass-covered bureau top. When she heard the clanking of metal and saw the leather chain, she knew that it was her old peace necklace. She picked it up and held it up to the light. It looked as new as the day he had given it to her. Leaning against the plate glass door, she began crying. *Why now? I haven't seen him since the orgy. Why now? Why here? Oh God, why now?*

CHAPTER 13

(1976, two years after the escape)

The hills of Ohio were ablaze with color. The oranges, golds, and reds were a dazzling sight to behold. Ayden was basking in the warmth of the early fall sun, taking in the glory displayed before his eyes. The world was good. And, he was making progress in his efforts to become one with God.

Ayden had succeeded in leaving the dismal atmosphere of prison behind him and, once again, had proven that he was smarter than all of the others combined. While the first prison break attempt did not come off as anticipated, the second one—the simplest plot of all—had manifested itself into his freedom. Ayden knew that his luminescence had come about from his ability to disassociate himself from the world, detaching his ego from his body—a gift that others in this world would never be able to achieve.

It was too bad that the first prison break failed, but that was all Sarah's fault. It would have been so very dramatic. Sarah was supposed to commandeer a helicopter, force the pilot to fly into the prison grounds, and carry Ayden away—like a bird soaring into the heavens. But, as usual, Sarah, weak-willed as she was, had not been able to carry the plan to fruition. So, he would never count on her again, no way, regardless of the situation. He would punish her in a variety of ways until she learned her proper place.

After being in prison for only a few weeks, his keen observation powers had allowed him to pick his targets early on—Mary and Martin Culver. Mary was a prison nurse and Martin was a guard. Ayden had moved slowly. He had approached Martin as a colleague and frequently engaged him in conversations. Ayden had sympathized with Martin's problems and focused his attention on the man's obvious inferiority complex. Martin had been passed over twice for a promotion and that had severely destroyed his self-image. Ayden had taken advantage of the situation by employing his technique of *'it's you and me against the world'*. It had worked well with Martin. In fact, Martin had often revealed small prison secrets and gossip to Ayden, who had used these tidbits, some true, some false, to his advantage in order to gain favors from the superintendent.

Ayden had used one excuse after another to get into the infirmary, where Mary had been the head nurse. He had known instinctively that she was a needy soul. And, when the topic had turned to religion one day, Mary revealed that she had been searching for spiritual guidance. That's all Ayden needed to hear. After almost a year, it had become obvious to Ayden that Mary would be willing to do anything that he asked of her. It had taken some time, but now Ayden had Mary and Martin under his control. Freedom would not be far away.

Martin had informed Ayden ahead of time that work was going to be done on the prison air ducts in his cell block. Martin had offered to leave the door to the workroom unlocked on the day that he was on turret duty at the far corner of the prison yard. The plan had been that Ayden would slip into the work room, where he would find a ladder that he could use to navigate over the top of the yard.

On the assigned date, Ayden had followed Martin's instructions to the letter. He had easily climbed through the open air duct, pulling the ladder up with him. Once on the roof top, he had crawled to the far edge of the building, slid the ladder across the open yard space, leaning it on the top of the razor-wire fence, and crawled across. Before he had scampered to the ground, Ayden even had had the audacity to stop and wave good-by to Martin, who, with rifle in hand, stood guard duty in the only turret that had a full view of the escape route. As he hit the ground, Eddie had been there with his motorcycle to carry him to freedom. No one had realized that Ayden had escaped until one of the guards noticed a ladder that looked out of place.

Ayden had moved his little band to this modest farm house within days of his escape. Using one of his pen names, Ayden had purchased the property several years prior as a possible site for a permanent residence for his flock. He had never dreamed that he would need this haven quite so soon. The wooden frame house was in dire need of a new paint job. But the fall flowers, which almost surrounded the entire building, and the stunning panorama of the hills, softened the atmosphere and gave the house a look of unconventionality. Three very wide steps led up to a rickety porch lined with several old wicker chairs and rockers. A small toy box, filled to overflowing with childhood delights, was stashed in the corner under the large living room window. White curtains had been hung with precise care in every room on the first floor.

Rebekah, Melody and Sarah were in the kitchen preparing fruits and vegetables for the winter. Ayden could hear their voices through the open doorway. He was watching his newest wife, Mary, as she worked in the garden. Ayden was proud of his newest conquest. While Mary was plain in looks, and a little on the heavy side, she was rapidly becoming one of his most faithful followers. He had been so certain of Mary, and her attachment to him, that he had told her ahead of time about his planned prison escape, and exactly where she could find him. However, he had given her strict instructions not to tell Martin anything about his whereabouts. He had known that once he was on the outside he would no longer need Martin. He had been right about Mary. She had kept the secret and had even emptied out her husband's bank account before she had fled to their little sanctuary. Mary had stayed in her position at the prison for six weeks after Ayden's escape, feigning surprise that he was gone. Martin, on the other hand, had claimed that he had had a diabetic attack and had fainted only moments before the escape. The Culvers had managed to stay out of the line of suspicion.

Alice, his daughter by Sarah, and little Adam, his son by Melody, were having a good time playing in the yard. And soon there would be two more since both Rebekah and Mary were pregnant. Adam was indeed his favorite. He was the bright one.

Ayden had judged him a born leader—one to be groomed to take his place.

Ayden believed that in order to be able to understand God, to climb the Tree of Life to become one with the Omnipotent, he had to prove that he could live in the world and handle the problems it presented. He also believed that, by yoking himself to God, he was developing a power of love so great that he was bringing the godly influx into this imperfect world. He would produce many children—children who would obey him and create other children just like themselves. It could be done. The human race could be controlled—he was convinced of that. He would teach them early that their bodies were instruments of his divine rights. And, before too long, they would all emulate his behavior.

Mary came trudging up the dirt path with her arms filled with chrysanthemums. Her large stomach, filled with Ayden's child, served as a resting place for the huge bouquet. She smiled as she said, "I know what we will call our child if it's a girl—Beth. Isn't that lovely? Beth means wisdom…that's what you have given me, Ayden…wisdom to see the truth, the light."

"Beth is perfect," Ayden said as he got up to help her into an old wicker porch rocker.

Mary chuckled as she said, "If it's a boy, may we call him Abulafia? You said he was one of the great masters, the Martin Luther of Judaism. Would it be too presumptuous?"

"We may call our child anything we like…and if you like Abulafia, then that's who he will be."

"I wasn't sure that I was good enough to use his name for my child. I don't know if I will ever understand the way you do," Mary said as she leaned toward him and lovingly took his hand. "It took me so long to face the truth—so long to come to the Lord."

"Mary, my sweet Mary, all creatures were created because of the good inherent in them. If this were not true, they would not have been created. You must study the works I have given you. But, most importantly, you must follow my commandments. You must also meditate. Remember, Abulafia developed a system—a method to meditate. You see, Mary, he felt that the soul had knots and seals so that it could function in our finite world. For, if these did not exist, the flood of the divine would overwhelm it and blind it. I was hand-picked by God to lead this little flock. Mortal fools cannot understand him, and I am honored that he chose me. I have a divine mission and I must work to that end. God has given me the intellect, the leadership qualities, and the superiority a strong, vibrant leader must have in order to accomplish his mission. Remember, Mary, God speaks directly to me. He gives me the strength I need to carry out his mission. Therefore, all of us," he said, gesturing toward the house, "must learn how to untie the knots, open the seals, and let the divine flow slowly. When we remove the prosaic and throw off the chains which shackle us to man-made laws, we will enter a state of consciousness—an intimate clinging to God."

Mary gazed at Ayden. "I will...I promise I will. I've never been as happy as I am now. I used to be afraid of so many things. I was afraid of my own sexuality...afraid of dying...afraid of living...I was so confused. You took that all away. My life was empty with Martin. He was so shallow. He could not understand my fears, my dreams, the real me. But you, Ayden, you instinctively knew what I needed. For that, I thank you."

"Do not fret about Martin. He will survive. He could not possibly have lived with us. He's still chained to the ridiculous beliefs that society has forced upon him. It is difficult to explain to others how an infinite God, a transcendent God, can communicate with a world that is only capable of grasping the finite. You owe nothing to Martin. He never would have been able to grasp our teachings. But you, Mary, have been all that I could have expected. The women also love you. Our flock has come a long way...we have found our paradise," Ayden said as he gestured toward the paragon of nature that surrounded them.

"The money, Ayden...do we have enough to survive?" Mary inquired. "Remember, I have a few worldly trinkets that I can still sell. I have an unusual pearl necklace and a few more coins that I can sell."

Ayden reached for Mary's hand, patted it gently and replied, "Thanks to you and Eddie, we'll be fine...for awhile at least...but don't give money another thought. I will provide for you and all the rest... now tell me, how is that baby behaving?" Ayden said as he placed the palm of his hand on the woman's swollen stomach.

"It must be a boy," she giggled. "It kicks all the time."

"You look wonderful," Ayden said quietly. "This place, our way of life, certainly agrees with you."

"Did I tell you that Eddie's gonna make a cradle for the baby? Isn't that nice? That's what's so wonderful. Here, we are all one. We all work together, live together, and love together," Mary said as she began rocking gently. "Eddie has so much common sense for one so young. Don't you think?"

"Eddie's a faithful follower of The Word. I am very proud of him."

"He never talks of home," Mary said.

"Mary, *this* is his home," Ayden reminded her.

"Of course. I'm sorry. You see, I've so much to let go of. Please be patient with me," Mary begged.

"Eddie has found a place where he can be accepted for what he is. He doesn't have to try to live up to someone else's expectations. His family, that is, his former family, placed too many demands on him. The only thing I expect of him is to follow The Word and obey my commandments, which are really from God."

Just then Melody came out the front door. "Children, time for a nap. Come along," she called. "Remember," she said as she glanced toward Ayden, "we need to go over those application papers for our state certification renewal. The process is a bit more complicated now that we have over ten children enrolled."

Ayden stood up and followed the children through the doorway and went directly to his study on the third floor. He opened the window wide and leaned out to once more gaze at the countryside. The back of the house was built directly against a hill and one could almost touch the bushes that grew there.

He closed his eyes and started to meditate. Just a few weeks ago he had achieved a miracle. He had entered a space…a space where there was a Tree of Life whose branches were made up of ten different colors. According to *Kabbalah*, that meant that he was truly ready to climb the Tree and make his ascent to God. Ayden, while not Jewish, embraced Jewish mysticism. Of course, there would be those who would argue with him that his interpretation was wrong. They were fools! He was certain that he represented the new Aaron, the one to lead others to the glory of God. God had chosen him, a non-Jew, to accomplish this deed.

He was ready to expand their little school. He knew that he needed a steady flow of income, and a school, one filled with many children, would provide a constant stream of money.

As Ayden and Melody worked on completing the necessary paperwork for the state, they were not aware that they were being watched. If they had looked out the window, they would have seen the bush on the side of the hill moving ever so slightly. A few twigs cracked sharply as branches parted to make way for the intruder to get closer and closer to the open window. But the occupants of the house didn't take notice of any of this nor did they hear the words uttered softly by the lone figure perched so closely to them, "I have found you at last, you bastard!"

CHAPTER 14

(October, 1976)

Pete leafed aimlessly through the mound of papers that had accumulated on his desk. He was having a difficult time concentrating on any one story. His mind kept going back to Ayden Ash. He was particularly disturbed that he hadn't found the key yet—the key to Ayden's escape.

News was breaking all around The Hill. Charges were being thrown at one senator that he had given a sweetheart deal to a relative to supply concrete for an addition to the state capital building without going through the proper channels of putting it out for bids. Rumors were circulating about a possible sex scandal involving members of an important House committee. And, as if that wasn't enough to get any reporter's blood flowing, an upstanding citizen was caught with his hand in the cookie jar of his local church.

Last week Pete had finished an expose on a city councilman involved in a job-selling scheme for positions in some of the school districts. Even though Pete had received accolades for his coverage of the story, he had found the experience very tiring and depressing. Maybe it was time for him to get out of this racket and move on to something else.

"Hey, Pete, do you have the file on Senator Mitchell?" Jimmy Moyer inquired from across the room.

"It's here somewhere." Glad for the interruption, Pete pointed to the conglomeration which surrounded him but made no effort to find the file.

Jimmy, looking more like a teen-ager than a reporter with four years of experience under his belt, leaned back in his swivel chair and said, "Christ, Pete, how the hell do you find anything in that mess?"

"Never mind, I know where the important stuff is," Pete responded as he finally started to flip through the stack of files which were on the floor. "I told you…here it is…you see, there *is* some organization in this disorganization."

Jimmy's long legs enabled the junior reporter to get to Pete's side in only a few strides. "Do you know what I think about our infamous Senator Mitchell? Well, I think he's as guilty as sin. Awarding all those contracts to his brother-in-law is probably just the tip of the iceberg," Jimmy said as he rummaged through the sheets of paper which made up the senator's file. "Wow, I didn't know that his wife was such a looker… do you really think he plays around with that at home?" Jimmy asked as he held up Mrs. Mitchell's photograph for Pete to view.

"That's the scuttlebutt," Pete said as he took a sip of coffee from an old chipped mug and propped his feet up on his desk.

"I could comfort her on those nights when hubby's not home," Jimmy said as he rolled his eyes and smiled knowingly.

"You must have more sex hormones than the rest of us put together. Women...that's all you talk about," Pete chided.

"Well, you should talk, my fine friend…you've got Jeanette," Jimmy said as he outlined a woman's figure in the air with his hand. "Why, even Walt's got a woman now. I must be the only one here without female company."

"Maybe you should advertise in the want ad section…they're running a special rate all this month," teased Pete.

Jimmy looked at the top file on Pete's desk and asked, "Are you still working on that Ash thing?"

"Sort of…"

"Look, there's been no sign of the guy and his broads for a couple of years. Personally, I think he's left the country. Besides, there are bigger fish to fry," Jimmy said as he waved the senator's file in the air.

Pete watched the young reporter walk back to his desk without responding. Perhaps Jimmy was right. Maybe he should let the damned thing go. But somehow, every now and then, Pete would review the records of the trial and escape, trying to find a sign to indicate where Ayden could be now. He would need an out-of-the way place—a place where his flock would be able to remain unnoticed.

Jimmy was right about things heating up on Capital Hill. Almost every other day charges were being made that unscrupulous dealings were becoming a way of life in state government. Actions like this hadn't taken place in New Valley for several years. Pete should have been inspired, but instead, his obsession with a real scumbag—a child molester hiding his sexual appetite behind a mask of religion—had been consuming him.

Walt had been more than generous with the time that he had allowed Pete to pursue his own investigation into Ayden's whereabouts. But all of his leads, even those he had gotten from prior cult members, hadn't panned out. All of them had led to dead ends.

"Pete, I just thought about that time when you were in the islands... remember when that guy came into your room...you ever find out anything about why he was there?" Jimmy inquired as he held the picture of Mrs. Mitchell up for closer examination.

"Nah, I guess he was just a beach bum looking for cash and stuff he could sell easily. Never heard a thing from the police, but I can tell you, he scared the crap out of me," Pete said, making an attempt to get back to work.

"This Mitchell story is gonna pop soon. I feel it in my bones. I never liked the guy. My sister says its because the senator's so good-looking. You think he's good-looking?"

"The women do. But that's only because they just don't appreciate real handsome men like you and me, kid."

"I don't know. There's something about that guy that gets to me. I think he's creepy. You know what I mean? Like, when I look at him, I get negative vibes," Jimmy said, as he examined the clippings of the senator which helped to make up his voluminous file.

"Negative vibes?" Pete chuckled.

"Yeah, he's in deep, I just know it. What's his kid like?" Jimmy questioned.

"I've never met him personally. Never heard...hey, wait a minute..." Pete shouted as he suddenly sat upright in his chair.

"What...what?" Jimmy asked eagerly.

"I just remembered something about Mitchell's kid," Pete said with a tone of excitement in his voice.

"Well?"

"Maybe its too farfetched, but I remember that at one time he was supposed to be tied up with Ayden and his flock."

"Your Ayden?"

"How the hell did he become '*my Ayden*'?" Pete asked, obviously annoyed at the connection.

"It's you who keeps bringing up the Ash mess. It's you who went traipsing around the country trying to find him. It's you who pours over his records again and again; furthermore, I—"

"Okay, okay, kid, I get the point," Pete responded rather meekly.

"What's the connection with the school?" Jimmy asked.

"Not the school...with Ash when he was doing some research on his books," Pete said, getting more caught up with the idea.

"The smutty ones?"

"Nah, it was the one he did on the history of the county. I have it right here somewhere," Pete said as he pulled out a cardboard box he had stashed under his desk. "I put some stuff in here during the trial and I think that...Christ, here it is."

Jimmy jumped out of his chair and rushed over to Pete's desk. Pete was busy flipping through the pages of the cheaply-bound book "I think he mentioned him somewhere...let's see...I know he didn't give the kid any credit for the research, but I believe...yeah, look here...see what he wrote, '*My thanks to Edward Mitchell for his kind assistance.*' When I asked Ayden about this one time, he told me that the kid had dug out maps and charts from the library for use in the book."

"That sure doesn't get me turned on," Jimmy said disappointedly.

"Look, kid, you have to go beyond what you first see. Don't underestimate Ayden's power of influence and manipulation. He's a master at drawing people into his web. I know that the Mitchell kid was involved with Ash. He was never investigated when Ash flew the coop. But maybe, just maybe, there's a stronger connection," Pete said not knowing whether he was trying to convince himself or Jimmy.

"He wasn't involved in the trial," Jimmy said. "His name wasn't mentioned anywhere."

"I know, I know...but," Pete said as he shook his finger in the air, "but something clicked just now. I remember that he was there, in the courtroom, with Rebekah and Melody, on the day that Ash was sentenced. Perhaps...just perhaps he might have been more involved than we thought. Bingo! Jimmy. The damned motorcycle. That's it, kid. The damned motorcycle."

"What motorcycle?" Jimmy asked innocently.

"The one Ash used to get away from the damned prison. That's the motorcycle," Pete responded as he shook his head in disbelief. "I was concentrating on Sarah and Melody...but the Mitchell kid, Christ, he rides all the time."

"Sounds like you're reaching, Pete."

"Maybe, kid, maybe," Pete said as he pulled the legislative phone book from the shelf and began paging through it vigorously. He bypassed the senator's office number and concentrated on his home phone. Nervously, he dialed the number and waited patiently. After the fourth ring, his waiting was over.

"Hello," a lovely voice said.

"Hello. Is Edward there?" Pete asked.

"No, I'm sorry, he's not," the voice responded.

"Ah, do you know when he'll be home?" Pete asked hesitantly.

"Oh, I'm not sure of that. You see, he's been touring the country on his motorcycle. I have no idea when he'll return. Maybe I can help you? I'm his mother."

"This is Pete Forster. I just wanted to talk to Edward about a motorcycle I'm considering buying, and I was looking for some advice. I thought perhaps he could help me," Pete said, trying to sound casual.

"I haven't heard a thing from him for a few weeks. But the last time he called me, he said he was in Ohio. I'm sorry that I can't be of more help," Mrs. Mitchell said sympathetically.

"If you hear from him, will you please ask him to give me a call at the *New Valley Press*?"

"Yes, I will."

"I appreciate your help, Mrs. Mitchell. Thank you very much."

Pete put the phone back in its cradle and sat for a long time staring straight ahead. The Mitchell kid's in Ohio…took his motorcycle…and Ayden escaped on one. Pete's heart began beating a little faster as he started to imagine what might have happened.

"Ever been to Ohio?" Pete asked Jimmy.

"No way. I'm a big city guy," Jimmy replied.

"Then, what the hell are you doing in this town?" Pete teased.

"Waiting for my big break—this is only my first step in a long career. Walter Cronkite…move over…here comes Jimmy."

"Hey, Cronkite Junior, what do you know about Ohio?" Pete persisted.

"Sort of like our state, why?" Jimmy asked as he put down the senator's folder and gave Pete his full attention.

"I think that's where Ash is," Pete said with a gleam in his eye.

"Lots of places to hide in Ohio, by God," Jimmy said. "You know, there are some isolated areas where the Amish live. Could he have gone there?"

"They wouldn't have anything to do with a creep like Ash."

"He's fooled a lot of people, you know."

"I know. I know. But where would a guy like Ash go? He's certainly not Joe Average."

"You're the expert. Don't ask me," Jimmy said, getting up and putting his jacket on. "I'm headed for the Senate building in case the governor needs me."

"Yeah, yeah, I'll forward all messages. Get the hell out of here," Pete said laughingly.

Pete got up and rushed into Walt's office. "Hey, boss, I think I just got a lead on Ash," Pete said, hardly able to contain his excitement.

"Oh, no, not *that* again," Walt responded.

"I think he's in Ohio...and I think…I think he's probably operating a school. Is your friend still with the Department of Education in Ohio?" Pete asked hopefully.

"Yeah, but not so fast, Pete. How'd you get this?"

"Jimmy and I were talking about Senator Mitchell when I remembered his kid had been mixed up with Ash some time ago."

"What's the association?" Walt asked Pete, who by now was frantically pacing back and forth like a caged animal.

"He helped Ash with one of his books and I think that—"

"Hold on now, Pete. Are you getting carried away again with this story? Just because the senator's hitting the newspaper doesn't make his kid guilty of anything," Walt reminded his best reporter.

"No," Pete said as he stopped in front of his boss's desk, pointing his finger at the man. "But the kid's got a motorcycle."

Shrugging his shoulders, Walt replied, "So do thousands of other kids."

"Remember, Ash escaped on a motorcycle," Pete said excitedly. "The kid's been touring the country on his cycle and, according to his mother, the last time she heard from him he was in Ohio. I bet that's where Ash and his followers are," Pete explained, once more resuming his pacing.

"And, the Department of Education—how does it fit in?"

"It'll know who has applied for licenses to operate private schools. He's probably right back in his old business. That bastard will never change," Pete responded.

"You really think he would be that foolish? I can't believe he would do that," Walt stated.

"Of course, he would. He needs money to take care of his followers. Hell, his ego's as big as a house. Not to mention his sex drive. Walt, please call your friend and see if he can trace anything for us," Pete urged.

Just then Walt's phone rang. "Hang on, Pete, let me get this. Yeah... what—Ohio? You have to be joking! Hold it..." Walt put his hand over the receiver and said, "Okay, Pete, what's the deal...are you pulling my leg or something? I'm too busy to be farting around with practical jokes!" Walt removed his hand from the receiver and said, "Marcie, are you part of this? Are you sure this is legit? Wait, I'll put you on the squawk box...okay...go ahead...Pete's with me now...go ahead."

"Guys, we just got a call from Detective Nonnenmocher from the New Valley Police Department, claiming that Ayden Ash has been picked up in Center County, Ohio. They're certain that it's Ash," Walt's secretary related. "Nonnenmocher wanted Pete to know immediately."

"Marcie, did he say how they found him?" Pete questioned.

"An anonymous telephone tip…that's all I know," she said.

Pete leaned forward to get closer to the telephone. "Did he say anything about Ash operating a school?"

"No. Are you going to Ohio, Pete?" Marcie asked.

"You're damned right I am," Pete said, as he hurriedly left Walt's office.

"Pete…Pete…" Walt called. "Wait a damned minute. Call me as soon as you have something to report." Walt doubted that Pete had heard him. He had never seen Pete move so quickly. Too bad…the guy was finally on the right track when someone else had beaten him to the punch. "Talk about timing," Walt said to no one in particular. "Timing is everything."

CHAPTER 15

(October, 1976)

The Center County police moved quickly when they received the telephone tip, regarding a prison escapee who had been convicted of child molestation. In cooperation with the Ohio State Police, they raided Ash's commune and arrested him on an outstanding warrant. At first, the man had argued that he was not Ash, but they ignored him and placed him in handcuffs. The police had their hands full as Mary and Melody maintained that Ayden was not the man they were seeking. Rebekah and Sarah managed to get out the back door, and they were hiding in the woods, where they clung together weeping.

Ayden could not believe that he had been located. He had been so very careful and had stuck to his plans and was confused now that his world had caved in on him once again. "Sir, my name is Thomas Gable," Ayden said in this most elitist voice. "I've done nothing wrong. I'm the Primate of our little church. You have made a grave mistake. You will rue this day, I warn you."

"Oh, that's a good one—you warning me," Steve Huddock, the Center County sheriff replied. "We'll see who you really are very shortly, I warn you!"

Huddock was a big man, standing almost six feet, six inches tall with a strong muscular frame. He had been the sheriff for almost eight years and was considered one of the best in Ohio even though the county he represented was the smallest in the state. While a little rough around the edges, and not the most articulate of people, he was thorough and knew his business extremely well. When he received the call from the tipster, he wasn't sure at first that it was a legitimate claim. He quickly made several calls and, before he had even arrived at the commune, he knew that he was about to arrest an escapee.

As they escorted him off the porch, Ayden drew himself up, threw his shoulders back, and said, "My friends will be hiring an attorney to represent me. And I want to speak to him as soon as possible. That is, if you hillbillies are civilized enough to know that I have certain rights which are—"

"Yeah…sure you have rights, fellow. I understand that you're a child molester. How about that, Harry," the sheriff said to his deputy. "Imagine. He likes to have sex with kids—nice man isn't he?"

"Gentlemen, let's stick to police business," one of the state troopers said.

After the officers shook hands, and the local police thanked the troopers for their assistance, they loaded Ayden into a rather battered police car. The officer in the back seat with Ayden said, "Let's see how you react when the cell door closes behind you. You won't break out of our little jail—you can bet your life on that."

The deputy led Ayden down a small hallway to the holding area which contained two compartments approximately ten by fourteen. Each cell had a bunk bed attached to one wall with long, rusty chains. A toilet stood in the corner, a yawning obscene vessel that looked as unpleasant as it smelled. And a small unpainted table, accompanied by an old wooden chair, completed the furnishing of what was to be Ayden's newest domicile.

"How long am I to remain here?" Ayden questioned.

The deputy leaned against the bars, propped his hand on his hip, and said, "What's the matter, fellow? This ain't good enough for the likes of you?" The deputy was obviously enjoying Ayden's displeasure. "Perhaps you'd rather stay at the Holiday Inn. I'll call and see if I can get you a reservation," the deputy replied facetiously.

"There's no privacy here, sir. It looks like that cell is occupied," Ayden said pointing to the next cell. "Why, I can hardly believe that there is no wall between, just open bars. Really, I can't—"

"Ah, ain't that too bad now. You afraid that Willie's gonna see you when you have to shit?" the deputy sneered. "From what I hear, little man—and indeed you are a little man—walls don't bother you anyhow. But let me tell you something. You ain't gonna get out of here with no ladder. You can bet your sweet ass on that."

"There's no reason to become vulgar, sir. I'm at a distinct disadvantage here, but I do resent not having my privacy," Ayden said as he tried to reason with the man.

"Oh, it ain't you who should worry," the deputy replied. "It's Willie. He'll be back soon from work release. I guess I better warn him about you. But, of course, he ain't no kid, so maybe you'll let him alone."

After the deputy slammed the door behind him, Ayden sat down on his bunk and began to reflect on his fate. He knew that he had to get out of this dump, and it had to be quickly. He stretched out across the paper-thin mattress and propped his head up with his arms, hesitating for a moment as he looked disdainfully at the well-worn bed linens. This was certainly no place for him. But, more importantly, he had to get out before extradition papers could be served.

Ayden got up and walked over to the bars that separated the two cells. A colorful afghan, neatly folded and placed over the bottom of the bunk, looked oddly out of place in a sea of grey-cement blocks. An old wooden chair was the resting place for a large maroon-colored cardigan sweater. A small pile of books, with an old, dirty shoelace tied around them, was sitting in the center of a splintery desk.

"Company's here," Ayden heard the deputy say as the hall door opened once again. "Willie, we got you a nice fellow here. This here's Ayden…Ayden Ash. He's a real important person. You better watch him, though, Willie—he likes to fool around with little kids. But you ain't no kid any more, are you, Willie" The deputy laughed loudly and locked Willie in his cell.

"Sir, has my lawyer arrived?" Ayden asked.

The deputy stopped, moved his head slightly, and replied, "Well, no Mr.-Ash-child-molester, he ain't here yet. Oh, by the way, Holiday Inn is full up…they can't take your reservation. So, I guess you're forced to stay with us," he chuckled. Ayden could hear the deputy's raspy laughter long after the door had been slammed shut.

Willie was a very large man. His six-foot-four frame carried about two hundred and fifty pounds of raw muscle. Wiry, red hair and a full beard made him look like a mountain man. But when he spoke, he had a gentle voice. "Hello," he said nervously. "Don't mind the deputy—he's always like that. He don't mean nothing by it," Willie said.

Ayden reached his hand through the bars and shook his neighbor's hand which was rough and full of calluses. "You work outside?"

"Yep. I work over at the saw mill. But I must come back here each night," Willie said as he put his head down. "Some bad people call me *retard*, but Mama says that I'm just slow. Do you hurt kids?"

"No, Willie, I do not. You see, I am God's emissary."

Willie wrinkled up his face and said, "Emmi what?"

"I am here on a mission from God," Ayden responded.

Willie's eyes opened wide. "You mean the God that's up in the sky?"

"Yes, Willie, that's the one," Ayden replied softly.

"Then, why are they being mean to you? People mustn't be mean to each other. They must be kind. That's what Mama tells me all the time," Willie said rather proudly.

"She's right about that, Willie. I can tell that you are a good person who is never mean to anyone."

Willie's shoulders rose and he appeared to be pleased with what he had just heard. "I am. I work real hard." He hung his head and quietly said, "You see, I did a bad thing. I took a radio and some stuff that wasn't mine. I wanted it, so I took it. God wouldn't like that, would he?"

Ayden's spirits began to rise and he felt a surge of hope. "No, Willie, he wouldn't. But he knows how good you really are, and I'm sure that he's not angry with you any longer. You see, God wants us all to be friends and help one another," Ayden said compassionately.

"Like I do when I carry packages for Mama and stuff like that?" Willie asked.

"Oh, yes. And when any of your friends are treated badly by others, you must help them and that makes God smile."

"Will you be my friend?" Willie asked hopefully.

Now it was Ayden's turn to smile. "Sure, Willie. From now on we're best friends."

"Will you read me stories? Stories like what's in these books?" Willie asked as he carefully untied the old shoelace and held up some Little Golden Books for Ayden to see.

"Why, of course I will. And when I need help, Willie—real help—will you do what I ask?" Ayden asked cautiously.

"Whatever my best friend asks me to do, I will do. I never, ever had a best friend. But I can't read stories to you. I can't read. But I'm strong. See..." Willie said as he rolled up the sleeves of his checkered shirt and proudly displayed his muscular arms for Ayden to admire.

"Oh, I wish I were that strong, Willie."

Willie rolled his sleeves back down and said, "After supper...after we eat...read this one to me." Willie handed Ayden one of his battered books, and Ayden knew that he would be out of this jail before the weekend had arrived.

CHAPTER 16

(Two days later)

Willie was walking back to the jail with a leisurely gait. He kept feeling his jacket pocket to make sure that the gun Melody had given to him was still there. He hoped that it wouldn't fire and kill him dead. This was just like the movie that he had seen on the television before he was sent to jail—now he was around a good-looking woman, a gun, and lots of excitement. Melody had told him that she loved him and that she wanted him to be her boyfriend. And Melody had taught him some tricks—tricks she said that people in love play with each other.

The first time he had seen Melody was when she had visited Ayden on the night he was arrested. He loved her right away. She was pretty and she had smiled at Willie all the time, especially after Ayden had whispered something in her ear. Now he and Melody had been sweethearts for two whole days.

He wasn't going to have to serve six more weeks in jail—Melody had promised that they were going to run away and get married. The very thought of her was doing funny things to his body. He had often played with himself in the dark of night, but Melody did it to him in the daylight, while he stood beside a big tree. It had never felt *that* good before. The more he thought about Melody, the more excited he was becoming. He felt himself getting hard again. He crept deeper into some thick bushes and sat down. He did it to himself, closing his eyes tightly and picturing how Melody had looked when she had opened her blouse. Before he crawled back out of the bushes, he looked around. But he was a man--Melody had told him that—and he could do anything he wanted with his body.

Mama wouldn't agree with Melody, and she would be mad at him if she knew what he had done with his new girlfriend. Mama just didn't understand what it meant to be a man—Melody did. Oh, she was as pretty as the girls in magazines. Daddy used to tell him that he would never find a girl because girls didn't like retarded men. Willie didn't know what that meant. He knew that he was not smart enough for a lot of things, but there were plenty of things that he could do. He was strong. He could move things that other men couldn't even budge. And, he was a good worker at the saw mill.

Soon he would be with Melody all the time. *When we get married then we can play those tricks all the time.* He dug his hand deeper into his pocket, slowly letting his fingers run over the hardness of the gun. In the movies, all the heroes had guns. Now he has one, too. Now he could be a hero for Melody.

Sheriff Huddock was sitting at his desk and was busy with a mound of paperwork—a task he hated. Without lifting his head, he said, "Willie, you're a little late. We were getting worried about you."

Willie, looking very sheepish, said, "I wasn't doing nothing bad."

The sheriff lifted his head and said, "I didn't say that you did, Willie. Hey, boy, your fly is open." Huddock said laughingly. "Willie... Willie...Willie...were you playing with yourself again?"

Willie put his head down and refused to look at the sheriff. Deputy Smith piped up and said, "Never mind, Willie. It won't hurt you and it won't fall off. Come on now. Back in the cage you go."

Ayden heard them coming down the hallway. His heart began beating at a rapid pace. A lot had to go the right way today—his freedom depended on everything working out as he had planned. Eddie must be able to secure a gun. And since Ayden planned on taking Willie along, Eddie also had to steal a car. Melody had to make sure that Willie would be willing to smuggle the gun into the jail. In addition, she would be making a call to lure Sheriff Huddock away from the jail. He was certain that Melody would do her part, but he wasn't sure that Eddie could get his assignments done so quickly. Willie was another matter. Ayden wasn't sure that Willie, in his excitement, wouldn't tell someone about Melody and the gun.

Deputy Smith opened Willie's jail cell and nonchalantly let the big man enter the little space. Willie waved his hand at Ayden and winked his eye. He had seen James Bond do that in the movies, and Willie was beginning to feel just like a spy.

Ayden couldn't wait until the door closed behind the deputy. Willie took off his jacket and hung it over the old wooden chair and sat down on his bed.

Ayden whispered, "Did you get it?"

Willie jumped up and said, "I almost forgot. Sure I did. Here it is, my friend."

Willie passed the gun through the bars, and Ayden quickly put it under his mattress and placed his pillow on top. Now all Ayden had to do was to wait until suppertime and this place would be history.

"Ayden," Willie said very quietly, "Is Melody your girl?"

Ayden smiled broadly. Melody must have done a real number on this kid. "No. Why do you ask?"

"I'm glad she's not—she's in love with me. She told me, but I didn't want to tell you 'cause I thought she was your girl."

Melody had done her assignment to perfection. She always did. "Nah, Willie, don't worry, she's all yours."

Willie untied the shoelace that held the stack of story books and was about to hand one to Ayden to read to him. Suddenly, he stopped, put the book back in the pile, and re-tied the shoelace. He didn't need these anymore. He had Melody now.

Eddie wasn't in a hurry. He was enjoying the time alone and the feel of the wind on his face as he rode his motorcycle through the back roads leading toward the commune. The plan was ready. Everyone, except Melody and him, had already left and were making their way to their next safe haven. All was in place. Ayden, the Master, would be free in only a few hours.

As he approached his favorite spot, he decided to stop and enjoy the view for probably the last time. He brought his cycle to a halt, propped it against an old oak tree, and trudged the short distance to the top of the mountain. He stood with his hands in his pockets, surveying the wonders that Ohio offered its citizens. Soon the trees would be bare, but not for long. God, in his infinite wisdom, would permit the trees to bud once again and the leaves to return to protect the floor of the woods for the little creatures living there. Perhaps by spring God might permit him to also return to this beautiful spot.

Eddie had had no problems in securing a gun. He had gone to one of the local sports shops and had told the clerk that he was going to be traveling across the country on his bike and needed one for protection. He had prayed that Ayden would not need to fire the weapon. Stealing the car had been a bit more risky. He had parked his motorcycle in the woods behind a shopping center so that he could watch people as they parked their cars. When the back row was filled with vehicles, he wandered down the embankment and strolled around the parking lot. Suddenly, he spied it—car keys dangling down from the ignition. Within five minutes, he had taken the car. He drove it to a deserted barn just a few hundred feet from the jail.

By now, Melody should have passed the gun to Willie. Tonight, she would be calling Sheriff Huddock, pleading for protection from her fictional, abusive husband—that was certain to get the sheriff out of the building, leaving only the bumbling Deputy Smith on duty. The night shift replacements were not due to report until midnight, giving Ayden plenty of time to get far away.

Tonight, after he dropped Melody off near the escape car, Eddie would be on his way. All he had to do was throw his duffel bag on the back of his Harley and find his way to Kentucky. He found an old tree stump and sat down. He pulled his right boot off and removed a dirty, wrinkled envelope. Slowly, he counted the money that his mother had sent him several weeks ago. He hadn't told Ayden about the money. Even though Eddie admired and appreciated what Ayden had done for him, he didn't feel comfortable without having a sum of money that was all his. *If I become a wanted fugitive for what I did for my Master, then so be it.*

Ayden was having a difficult time keeping his eyes off the mattress of his bunk bed. He felt as if the gun was going to surface at any moment and jump into his hands. While he hated guns, it was going to be his ticket to get out of this hell hole.

Ayden began pacing. Back and forth…back and forth…all the time Willie was watching him. If this clever plan of his was to come to fruition, Melody and Eddie had to execute their next duties perfectly—Willie had come through with flying colors. He glanced at Willie. Perhaps Ayden had underrated this huge man who had the mind of a child. While Willie was slow and had limited intellectual ability, Ayden sensed that there was a great deal more to this man than one could judge at first glance. Ayden winked at Willie and Willie winked back with a smile on his face. Thank God for Melody. That girl was his treasure. Poor Willie didn't have a chance. Melody probably had been Willie's first experience with a woman.

Ayden put his finger in front of his lips—a signal for Willie to be quiet. It was time for meditation. As he put his head down into his hands, he cast a side glance at Willie who was doing the same thing. *How simple it all is. How very simple. People struggle their entire lives looking for answers to life and death. Why can't they see? I must help others to understand, to realize that once the sexual bonds are removed—once men and women begin to unite their bodies without putting any conditions on the act itself—they will be free.*

Ayden was unable to take himself into the depths of true meditation. He was not able to lose himself and enter the space that releases all worldly ties. There were more pressing issues to be addressed. He needed to be free. His imprisonment was unjust. He looked over at Willie—another jewel in Ayden's crown—perhaps the short time that he would be spending in this honky-tonk jail would be well worth all his inconveniences.

He glanced at his watch—it was seven o'clock. Any second now Sheriff Huddock should be leaving the building in response to Melody's call for protection. Ayden knew that Huddock's ego would not allow him to send his deputy to answer the call for help. Now it was five after seven and Ayden's heart was beating very rapidly. *What's taking so long?* Then, he heard the sound of a car door slamming. That's it. Ayden jumped up on his bunk and strained hard to get a look out the small, barred window, but all he saw was the top of the police car moving out toward the dirt road. He nodded to Willie and motioned for him to lie down.

Ayden stretched out across the cement floor. "Sheriff...Sheriff," called Ayden. Help...Sheriff."

He heard the door unlock and just as Ayden had predicted, Deputy Smith walked in.

"What's the problem, lover boy?" he smirked as he looked at Ayden who was doubled up and rolling around the floor.

"Ever since supper...I feel terrible. Pain...I have excruciating pain... please help me," Ayden replied as he rolled around on the cold floor.

Deputy Smith looked at his prisoner with hatred in his eyes. He would really like to go into that cell and beat the living shit out of the creep. But Huddock would never put up with that.

"Ash, you got a little tummy ache?" Smith mocked.

Ayden's moans grew louder. He rocked back and forth as if he were in excruciating pain. Carefully, he cradled the gun in his arms. Suddenly Willie stood up and said, "He's hurt. His face is turning blue. You better help him or he may die."

Deputy Smith hesitated for a moment. *Suppose this is some kind of trap? Oh hell, the jerk is only half as big as me. I can take him in a minute.* He opened the cell door and knelt down to roll Ayden over on his back. Suddenly, Ayden's knees came up with a force that belied his small stature and landed in the deputy's groin. As Ayden pointed the gun at Smith's head, the deputy drew himself into a fetal position. Ayden grabbed the deputy's keys, jumped up, and slammed the cell door shut with a loud bang.

As Smith was gasping for breath, he shouted, "You bastard...you fucking, no good sonofabitch. You won't get away with this."

"Go ahead, Smith. Yell to your heart's content. No one's going to hear you way out here in the boonies," Ayden said as he unlocked Willie's cell door. "Come on, boy, we're on our way."

As the two fugitives ran out the front door, Melody was pulling up in the stolen Chevy. Willie's face lit up like a Christmas tree when he saw her.

"Get in, baby, get in," she shouted.

Willie assumed that she was talking to him and leapt into the front seat. Ayden, smiling broadly, obligingly took the rear.

CHAPTER 17

(Three weeks later)

Pete was getting dressed to go out on the town to celebrate Cindy's twelfth birthday. He had figured that it might be the last time that she would want to party with her dad. Cindy had been showing all the signs of developing into an independent teen-ager, and her father would probably be the last one that she would want to spend time with on her next birthday.

Cindy was tall for her age. At times, she was like a young willow, swaying in the breeze, needing no one to shield or protect her. And then there were those times when she was very much a little girl, wanting to be hugged, and held, and cuddled. She had what Pete referred to as a *Florence Nightingale* complex. She wanted to heal all the wounded creatures that she found in the woods and to befriend all of the friendless kids that she met in school. Cindy sincerely believed that she could change sows' ears into silk purses. When she took others under her wing, they had found a friend for life. She gave her lunch money to kids at school when she had found out that they had none. Many a night Pete had found her, hunched over her typewriter, finishing a school paper for one of her lost souls. One day she wanted to become a teacher; the next a veterinarian. One day she could be as happy as a bug in a rug and the next she was a modern day image of Camille. Pete was amazed at how frequently her behavior changed. She was an enigma—a lovely, unpredictable puzzle.

Pete planned to take Cindy and Jeanette out for dinner and then stop by Cindy's favorite arcade. Cindy then would be able to challenge

Pete at a pinball game once again. The brightly-lit games had always fascinated his daughter, and she had quickly developed skills that surprised and delighted him. Pete had not been able to rack up the number of points that his daughter could amass in a short period of time. As she jostled the machine, she would dance gleefully each time that she had beaten the odds. Cindy had seemed oblivious to the young teen-age boys that had come out of the woodwork whenever she played the pinball machines. Pete only hoped that he could keep them away from his daughter for a long time. Cindy had won every prize that the arcade had to offer. In fact, she had earned so many free games that the owner of the arcade constantly encouraged her to try her luck at someone else's establishment.

With the exception of his disappointment about not having found Ayden, Pete's life was back in order. Jeanette had done that. But Cindy—she had been his lifeline, the link to the past, but more importantly, his hope for the future. Much to his pleasure, Cindy and Jeanette really liked one another. What more could he want? Ayden, that's what.

As soon as he had heard of Ayden's escape from the Center County jail, he had gone to Ohio where he had spent two days trying to uncover a clue that would lead to Ayden's current location. The only help that he had received came from Eddie's mother who had provided Pete with the post office box address where she had mailed her son several thousand dollars. Strangely, though, the post office had been almost fifty miles west of the commune where the cult had been located. But the trip to that little town had led Pete to a shop where Eddie had been identified as a purchaser of a small hand gun, a revolver that *could* have been used in Ayden's escape. And although residents had seen Eddie many times, riding the back roads on his motorcycle, no one could place Eddie directly at the commune at any time. While, admittedly, the events involving Eddie were only circumstantial in relation to Ayden and the cult, Pete felt certain that the fair-haired young man was traveling with Ayden and his entourage. But, where they were now was still a mystery. Even though Eddie's name had not been mentioned in the paper, the rumor mill—much more efficient than any other means of communication—had the young man connected at the hip to Ayden.

Senator Mitchell had become extremely irate when Pete had questioned him about his son Eddie and his relationship to the cult. The senator had accused Pete of trying to smear his political future by linking his son's behavior to the investigation regarding the concrete used in the new state office building. The angry man had threatened to initiate a law suit against Pete since there had been no evidence that Eddie had done anything wrong. Mitchell had also reminded Pete that, as a state senator, he had friends in high places that could end Pete's newspaper career.

When Pete had returned home, he had spent hours tracking down people who might know any of the cult members, hoping that someone could provide a lead that would help his investigation. One person, who still bothered the hell out of him, was Mark Jenson from the Department of Education. Pete had an instinct that this Beau Brummel knew more than he had, so far, been willing to share. What he had found out, however, was that Jenson had been a full-time skirt chaser—but that didn't prove that he had been involved with Ash, other than on a formal level. But, birds of a feather often fly together. Pete was certain that here was another association that he had been unable to untangle.

Ayden's banking records had been scrutinized by the DA's office in an effort to determine if the crafty escapee had purchased any other properties that could possibly serve as a new hiding place for the cult. But no such transactions had been found. Pete had received an unsigned letter, indicating that the group had fled the country and hinted that the writer had been involved with the cult at one time. Ironically, the letter had been mailed from New Valley, but to Pete's knowledge none of Ayden's cult members had been left behind.

Pete had spent considerable time looking into Sarah's and Melody's backgrounds. Those who worked with the women had become extremely paranoid and had avoided the press like the plague, refusing to discuss the case at all. Even family members of the two women couldn't, or wouldn't, provide any clues as to the whereabouts of the cult. One of Melody's relatives had moved out of the area, claiming that she was too embarrassed and ashamed of the vile acts that her cousin had committed.

Margaret Hoffman had been on the phone constantly with Pete. She had cried, pleaded and begged Pete to get Ayden behind bars once again. Her greatest fear now was that Ayden might come back and take out his revenge on Amanda. Pete had tried to convince her that Ayden would not be that foolish, but he totally understood the woman's concern.

As he sat on the edge of his bed, he picked up the letter he had received this morning. The letter was written in perfect penmanship with each character formed correctly, all loops were closed, all *t's* were crossed exactly the same way, and each *I* was dotted with similar pressure. The writer had used a fountain pen with dark ink—no cheap ball-point pen for the writer of this letter.

Pete read the letter out loud. *Dear Sir, I understand that you are eager to locate Ayden Ash for reasons which are obvious. You are not the only one who would like to see this fornicator punished. But the Lord will eventually be triumphant. I found him once, I will find him again. Look for the answer in Matthew 13: 44-46.*

Pete had immediately looked up the passage in the Bible and wrote it down beneath the brief letter. In fact, he had almost committed the words to memory: *The kingdom of heaven is like treasure hidden in a field; then in his joy he goes and sells all that he has and buys that field. Again, the kingdom of heaven is like a merchant in search of fine pearls; on finding one pearl of great value, he went and sold all that he had and bought it.*

He had spent significant time this afternoon wrestling with these words. Were they meant as a clue that Ayden had purchased another property? The reference to pearls and treasure seemed to be jumping off the page—what connection does this passage have to Ayden? Or could someone be playing mind games with him?

Pete had not shared this letter with Jeanette. He had felt a little guilty about not doing so; so much, in fact, that he had avoided talking to her this afternoon about the case. Lately, she had appeared to be dealing with issues of her own, but Pete couldn't get her to open up. Perhaps Jeanette was only playing the same game as he. Maybe she, too, had some information that she was not sharing with him. *That* he could live with. What he couldn't accept, even dreaded, was the possibility that she was getting tired of him. He couldn't bear to think of this world without her.

Damn. Maybe I'll share this letter with her later on tonight.

—∞—

Yesterday, Jeanette had submitted her resignation to *The Philadelphia Daily*. She knew that if her relationship with Pete was going to lead to the next step, she needed to cut her ties to Philadelphia. She had extended her lease with the owner of the small condo in which she had been living for the past two months. And, ever since Ayden had escaped once more, she wanted to give Pete all the room he needed to be the one to help crack the case. How Ayden had been able to captivate his members and convince them that he was their Master was still hard for Jeanette to understand.

Last week, at the request of FBI agents, unlawful flight charges had been filed against Ayden, and he had been classified as "armed and dangerous." Ever since the escape from the Ohio jail, Pete was once again obsessed with the case. This worried Jeanette. While Pete had stopped discussing the case with her, she knew that he was still searching for something—anything that might lead him to Ayden's whereabouts. It had all been so simple at first—the guy was convicted and sent to jail. Jeanette had been convinced that she would never have to tell Pete her secret. Then Ayden got out—not once—but twice.

Pete had never questioned her about her past. He had given her his love. She was afraid that if he knew all about her that their relationship would end—something she couldn't bear to think about. She hadn't even planned on going to that damned séance. She did it out of anger at her husband. Walking in on him like that was one of her most painful memories. His secretary was kneeling on the floor, bare-assed naked, while Frank was right behind her with his pants on the floor. The image was burned into her mind like an indelible etching.

In the beginning, she had thought that she and Frank would be together forever. People had often referred to them as the ideal couple. But it had all just been a fantasy—one that was shattered in an instant. She hadn't told anyone what she had seen in Frank's office—not even

Frank. She had carried her devastation around with her like a heavy bundle. It had created a constant aching in her stomach, a feeling that she would not ever be whole again—an agony that had disappeared only after she had met Pete. She couldn't lose him; she just couldn't.

She regretted all those sordid things that she had done. One time, after a particularly sweet love-making session, she had almost confessed to Pete. Damn that Greg. Why the hell had she gone to the séance with him? At that point in time, she had never heard of Ayden Ash and his church. As soon as they had arrived at the church, she had had a gnawing feeling that she should not be there. But her mind was dead. It had been as if she were sleep walking—not even aware of her own heartbeat. Her only thought had been to block out what she had seen in Frank's office—block it out so the hurt would stop. But there was no doubt that she had been at the séance, had taken her clothes off, and almost participated in the orgy.

She had allowed herself to become immersed in self-pity and hate for a man she had once loved with all her heart. When she had left him, Frank claimed that he had no idea why. He had called—written many letters—but to no avail. All she had done was to concentrate on her own misery and that terrible empty feeling in her body.

Then, the realization had come over her that she had become her husband. The séance was the trigger. Men had found her attractive, so she did not have any difficulty finding lovers, regardless of their marital status. Once in an elevator. Once in the back seat of a taxi cab. She shuddered when these memories came flooding back. She even had a brief affair with Frank's brother, making sure that Frank knew all about their relationship.

None of these actions had eased her pain. In fact, it had grown sharper—more intense, more excruciating. She had walked in a daze most of the time—zombie-like. Then, Frank had been killed, and ironically, her anger grew stronger. *How dare he die? How dare he leave her alone to face the hurt, the humiliation?* For a long time she had put all the blame on him. Perhaps his death had been a form of punishment—another burden that covered her like a heavy cloak, providing a shield of armor that had prevented any feelings from entering or exiting her body. She had deserved this castigation. She had never faced him, never told him what she had observed, nor had she given him an opportunity to confess, to repent, or to ask for forgiveness. Then, Frank was shot down by a crazed lunatic intent on seeking revenge on a bank that had foreclosed on his business. Frank was gone. And she was left alone in her self-constructed prison.

As a young girl, Jeanette had been extremely shy and introverted. Tall and lanky, with not much of a figure, she had classified herself as one of the ugliest girls in junior high school. Her only solace was her diary. She would hide under her blankets and write about her most private thoughts, her innermost fears and dreams. Her thoughts were sprawled across the paper in an almost incomprehensible handwriting. But the periods and commas were neatly recorded and the exclamation marks were like little works of art.

As a teenager, Jeanette had enmeshed herself in layers of guilt. When her parents divorced, she had been certain that it was all her fault. When her dog had gotten hit by a passing car, she had taken the blame for that, too. When anything happened to her friends, she had always assumed a burden of guilt for either saying something or not saying anything—it was always her fault.

After Frank had died, for a short period of time, she had tried therapy. She had spent hours spilling her guts out to a fat, bald-headed man who had charged her fifty dollars a session. But it was Pete who had made her well. Pete, with his gentle loving ways, had managed what no one else had done—he had taken the pain away.

This should be a time of rejoicing. But now it was her own past behaviors that haunted her. She had been there—in that damned church. No man could accept that. Not even one as terrific as Pete.

CHAPTER 18

(1978)

The cult was together once again, safe and secure. The small, rural home in Kentucky, while not providing some of the amenities that they had had in Ohio, would suit their needs, at least until Ayden could find better accommodations. And that would come from an unexpected source, Dr. Jenson—Ayden's old friend from the Department of Education.

Ayden was sitting by himself in the small country kitchen, sipping from a mug of hot chocolate. *We have to be careful, very careful. Jenson must be contacted and the transaction completed without tipping our hand to the authorities.* Thank God for the pictures he had taken at the séance. As he spread the photos across the linoleum-covered table, Ayden smiled broadly. There was no doubt about the man's identity—it was Jenson, naked as a jaybird, leaning on the back of the church altar. And, along side the educator, two very lovely naked women.

The damp night air was beginning to make Ayden uncomfortable. He didn't want to make a fire in the old upright stove. It was just too much work. He was agitated that he had not been able to discover how they had been located. While he had been grateful for the two years that they had had in Ohio, he really was not happy in this new location. It just did not suit him—in fact, it was beneath one of his importance. Ayden realized that he needed a new plan, one that would bring in a large sum of money immediately—money was the key to his future happiness.

Ayden had to remind himself that all problems in the world are only temporary. He had to shake off this inexplicable feeling of sadness. *Inward*—he had to go *inward*—into his very soul, where he could regain the strength that he had possessed before his recent incarceration. There, in the space beyond, the place where so few could reach, he began to feel the quiet, the peace, he so desperately needed. He believed that every little seed, every snow flake, every grain of sand, was different in some manner—just like he was different from most men. *I must not let the actions of uneducated men draw me into the abyss of ignorance. I must stand tall. I must concentrate on a new plan.*

Somewhere there was a Garden of Eden—a place where he and his flock would be able to live undisturbed. The stillness in the room deepened as Ayden focused his attention on bringing the higher and lower together, hoping to break through the barriers that still separated him from the True Light that he knew was out there. Here, in his sadness, in his humiliation, he had to seek out the joy. He believed that no matter what was in a man's soul that makes itself evident, there was a possibility of the beginning of deliverance.

Ayden was now the proud father of several more children. He and Rebekah had a lovely baby girl just three months ago and Mary delivered Abulafia, his second son, last year. Sabrina and her sister Emma, young twins who joined the cult only ten months ago, both delivered girls. In addition, Mary was getting close to her time to deliver his second child with her. Mary was so certain that she was carrying a girl she had made a pink quilt with the name *Beth* embroidered in the center. On the other hand, Sarah had not been able to conceive—making her difficult to live with. Ayden needed to discipline her before her jealousy would eat away at the harmony he had tried so hard to maintain among his cult.

Eddie entered the room so quietly that it was several minutes before Ayden realized that Eddie had joined him at the table. He gazed into the young man's blue eyes with a steady stare—beauty—undeniable beauty—that was his Eddie. He reached across the table and took the young man's hands in his.

"Guess where Willie is?" Eddie asked playfully.

Ayden smiled. "I don't have to guess. I know. Melody finally met her match. The two of them never wear out."

"You don't mind?"

Ayden shook his head slowly. "Willie deserves some fun. While he cannot understand our ways like you do, my precious one, he certainly deserves to be rewarded for helping me to get out of that stinking jail. Mark my words, Willie will always be there for us—thanks to Melody."

Eddie cast a glance at the pictures Ayden had secretly taken at the séance. "You're not going to give him all the negatives, are you?"

"You bet your sweet ass I'm not. Just these two," Ayden said as he pushed the photographs toward Eddie. "Tell him that's all we have. But, if he doesn't come up with the money, these little gems will be sent to the Governor's office. Hell, he doesn't want that to happen. He'd be finished in education if the press got wind of this."

"It's too bad that so few people understand your philosophy. Why can't they find the wonders and the signs which we can see? If only they would comprehend the beauty of the earth as you have defined it, so much sorrow could be avoided," Eddie said sadly.

Ayden stood up and walked behind Eddie and placed his hands on the back of his chair. "There is a palace, Eddie, a palace of love, securely fastened in a rock. Souls that have reached the true meaning of love will enter that palace. It is love that links the higher with the lower. Love lifts everything to a level where all become one." Ayden walked back to his chair, put his foot on the seat, and continued in earnest. "You see, every soul is composed of a male and a female before coming into this world. When each soul enters the world, it is separated and placed into different bodies. Then, through the act of intercourse, the souls reunite. I also believe, Eddie, that when two males, or two females couple in passion, that their souls do not actually join as one, but rather that they draw strength from one another, making each male more intelligent and each female more spiritual. You see, son, when God created the souls, some were good and some were evil. But God decides which soul goes into what body. We have no choice in the matter. All that we learn here on earth, we already knew before coming here. All we must do to obtain this vast storehouse of knowledge of understanding is to remove our thoughts from our bodies and let our souls soar outward to meet the higher level. Then God takes over. But, meanwhile, God has spoken to me on several occasions and has instructed me to take his place here on earth. It is so important that you follow my instructions since, while they come from me, they were first spoken by God."

Looking over the photos once again, Ayden said, "You must leave tomorrow." He was quiet for several minutes. Finally, he said, "I caution you, my friend; it is imperative that you get into and out of the city without being seen. This won't be easy. When I called Jenson earlier today, I made it perfectly clear to him that he had to meet you on Harbor Island at precisely 10 p.m. By that time, the area will be relatively desolate." He paused once again. "Count the money before you give him these two pictures and the negatives," Ayden instructed Eddie, as he placed the items into a large manila envelope.

"Are these the right negatives?" Eddie questioned as he held them up to the light.

Ayden's eyes sparkled as he slowly responded, "No, they are not."

"You mean—?"

"Look, it is going to be pitch-black on the island. Jenson will be in a hurry to get back to the city streets. He surely won't want anyone to see him near a place that's a known pickup spot for homosexuals," Ayden explained. "He tried to get me to pick another spot for the exchange, but I stood my ground."

When Eddie heard Ayden's reference to homosexuals, the hair on the back of Eddie's head stood up. He and Ayden had been lovers for some time now, so perhaps Eddie just mistook his tone. In fact, Ayden has been a lover to all cult members with the exception of Willie. *Why not Willie*, Eddie wondered?

"What's wrong, my beautiful friend?" Ayden asked warmheartedly.

Eddie hesitated. "Why, ah…nothing, Ayden, nothing at all. Are you sure Jenson will be there with the money? Could he bring the police along with him?"

"He'll be there—that's for certain. He won't bring any cops. You can rest assured of that. Mary has made arrangements for a boat to be at Devil's Landing. No one will see you—it's about a ten-minute row to the island. Go to the top floor of the observation tower, and from there you'll be able to see anyone who may be walking or bicycling over the foot bridge that Jenson will be using. If you see anyone coming with him, or immediately after him, who looks suspicious in any way, you get out of there. Just make certain that he doesn't get a look at the negatives while you're there. By the time he gets to examine them in the light, it will be too late for him to do anything about the transaction. Jenson's family is wealthy—they own a large horse farm in Maryland. They will be more than willing to provide the money to protect their image."

Ayden watched the young man carefully. He needed him to complete this task correctly. Then, very softly, he said, "We need the money, Eddie. Mary sold her pearl necklace and the last of her rare coins right before we left Ohio. But I have connections in California, where we'll be able to live our lives the way we wish. Money—we really need money to travel and to set up new living quarters. We have a lot of mouths to feed, Eddie. But we can do it. The Lord is on our side."

CHAPTER 19

(October, 1978)

Pete didn't know what to expect. The caller wouldn't give his name and Pete hadn't recognized the voice. All the man had said was that Pete should meet him at City Pub if he wanted some information about the whereabouts of Ayden Ash.

Pete made his way down the darkened street. He normally spent as little time as possible in this section of New Valley. But the thought of finally getting something new on Ayden made his heart race so fast that he felt that it was going to pop out of his chest. The row homes he passed were in bad shape. The once-proud residences now seemed to pull themselves back into the dark recesses of the alleyways, ashamed to be found there. Many windows had been boarded up and few panes of glass had managed to escape the wrath of gangs that roamed the streets, aimlessly looking for trouble—and usually finding it.

The lights of the small pub were a welcome sight as Pete pulled his jacket around him. He was shaking. He had convinced himself that it was not fear that was making his body tremble, but rather the chill of the early October night.

The floor of the barroom was almost completely covered with peanut shells. Pete made his way carefully to the only vacant table and slid his tall frame into a rickety chair that had probably been part of the pub's décor since it had opened about seventy years ago. He tried to appear casual as he glanced around the dirty saloon even though he had no idea who he was looking for. A heavy-set woman, whose low-cut blouse exposed her saggy breasts, sauntered over to his table. She tried in vain to present a provocative smile. However, all Pete could observe were teeth that had obviously never seen a toothbrush, nor had they apparently ever been taken for a visit to a dentist.

"Hi, there, sweetie, what can I get for you?" the waitress asked as she leaned in very close to Pete.

Pete leaned further back in his chair to put some additional space between the garish woman and himself. Bleached blonde hair, badly in need of a good shampoo, clung to the side of her face like a spider. Her neck was covered with scab-crusted marks. The loose skin on the bottom of her arms jiggled even worse than her ample breasts. Dark red nail polish on her stubby fingers was the only part of her that shone.

"Just a beer please," Pete managed to get out.

"Look, honey, don't take this the wrong way, but I really—"

"Get your ass out of here and get us two beers, you old slut," said a man who had joined Pete at the table. "Don't mind Mabel—she used to be a classy whore but time has taken its toll. Now, she gives two dollar hand jobs in the back alley."

Pete looked over the newcomer guardedly. He was a large man with a weather-beaten look. Dark black hair, tinged with gray, spilled across a broad forehead, forming tight little curls that reminded Pete of the perms his mother used to give herself with those slick little do-it-yourself kits. Heavy black eyebrows formed a shelf just above large, sad eyes—eyes that projected an abyss of unhappiness. This mysterious companion had ample muscular arms, jutting smoothly into an extremely wide neck, which Pete would later find out was the result of long hours spent exercising and good body discipline. The man removed his jacket and slung it across the back of his chair like a wrestler throwing his robe over the ropes to get on with a match. But, somehow, in spite of the man's overpowering physical appearance, Pete knew intuitively that he had no reason to fear this man.

"You Pete Forster?" the man said as if he already knew the answer.

"Yeah," Pete replied. "And you?"

"Martin…Martin Culver."

Pete hesitated a moment and said, "I'm sorry, but I don't think I have the slightest idea how you're linked to Ayden Ash."

Just then Mabel returned with two, large mugs of beer and a small basket filled with freshly roasted peanuts. She slammed them down on the table, spilling some of the frothy brew, and stomped away.

"I'm gonna tell you a few things about that bastard, but I want your promise that you won't tell a damned soul where you got this information. I want revenge on the sonofabitch. I can tell you where he's at, but you got to give me your word that you'll keep me out of this fucking mess," Martin said with a tremor in his voice. "I've had enough. I don't want anymore pain."

Pete was astounded. This forceful man, who could probably take on anyone in the bar, was visibly shaken. "Of course, I will keep you out of anything that may happen," Pete said.

Martin took a deep breath and moved his chair closer to Pete. "I read your stuff in the paper. I know that you've been looking for that creep Ash. I know exactly where he is. You see, my wife is with him," Martin said as he put his head down. Slowly, Martin lifted his head and looked at Pete. And, as his eyes welled up with tears, he said in a whisper, "I was his guard when he escaped the first time. I was such a fool. He convinced Mary and me—Mary was, I mean, *is*, my wife—that he had found the answer."

The man stopped. Pete waited for a few seconds and then asked, "The answer to what?"

"To life—to death—the whole fucking mess. God, I wanted to believe in him. I had put all my faith in that man. He had talked as if he knew what so many of us are seeking. We were certain that he knew the way to God." Martin paused once again, looked around the seedy barroom for a few seconds, and then said, "Mary and I had been trying for a long time to find answers to the problems of life. I know it sounds stupid now—dumb. But we had been certain that he could direct us to the true way of the Lord."

Martin took a few sips of his beer. He began running his finger around the top of the mug. Pete was dying inside. He wanted to know more, but he knew that he couldn't rush Martin. As Martin flicked a tear off his cheek, Pete said, "Just take your time."

Martin brought his hands together in front of his chest, gave out a large sigh, and continued. "He asked me to help him get out. He told me that I could learn all he knew and that the two of us would then take the message to others. He explained that the process of taking God out of exile, of bringing God into my life, would mean taking a strong hand, of standing up to authorities and making a platform for God. The worldly things, man-made rules, had to be eradicated in order for the truth to shine through. He convinced us that he had been railroaded by a justice system that didn't understand his philosophy. I believed him. Oh, God forbid, I believed him!"

Pete was captivated. No one else existed in the bar. The noise and stench no longer prevailed. All that Pete was conscious of was Martin and his melancholy voice.

"I let it all happen. Me. But it was Mary who ran away with him. She had known all along where he was going and never told me. When she left me, she took all our money, my coins, and even my mother's pearl necklace—everything that we were saving for years to move away and get a new start. We wanted to get away from the prison, away from the barbed wire, away from the land of Sodom and Gomorrah."

"You...you provided the ladder that he used?" Pete asked incredulously.

Martin shook his head. "No, the ladder was in the workroom. But it was me who made certain that the door remained unlocked, and it was me on the east turret when the bastard crawled across the roof and jumped over the fence. I'm not proud of it. But I truly believed in him. What a fool I've been!" After taking a few more sips of his beer, Martin wiped his mouth and simply looked at Pete for a few minutes. "I tracked him down in Ohio. I just wanted to get Mary to return with me so that we could be together again. I hid in the bushes on the hill behind their house. And...and...oh, God, this is hard." He finished off his drink and remained almost paralyzed until he suddenly began again. "I saw her, Pete, I saw her. Her belly was filled with his child. There she was standing with the rest of them dumb women. They were standing in a circle, performing some type of ritual. I could not believe my eyes, but I knew then that she would never come back to me. I hated her. I hated that unborn kid in her stomach, and I wanted to kill them both. If I could have reached into her womb at that time, I would have pulled that bastard kid out...I would have," Martin said forlornly. "I finally decided that the best punishment for her, for my so-called wife, would be to get that sonofabitch back behind bars. At least, then, he wouldn't be able to touch her again. So, I called the cops and told them where they were."

Martin gazed around the barroom as if he were interested in the other patrons. Then, he turned to Pete again and said, "Then the bastard got out of jail again. I don't know how he did it, but he did. I then quit my job, took what money I had in my retirement and set out to find them again. It was luck—pure luck. I'd like to think that the good Lord helped me, but I'm not sure I believe in a higher being anymore."

"There will always be people like Ash in the world," Pete said. "Those who take the good and twist it into something evil for their own purposes will always be among us. I don't know you, Martin, but don't let vermin like him make you lose your faith. That would mean that he would win once again."

Martin looked at Pete and slowly he shook his head. "I guess you're right. Some time ago I sent you a stupid letter, you know, a kind of crazy letter."

"You mean the one with the quote from Matthew?" Pete replied as he opened his eyes wide.

"Yeah," Martin said, smiling for the very first time. "I tried to be clever and give you some clues, but I realized later that the letter was confusing." Martin shelled a few peanuts, munched on them for awhile, and said, "She sold my mother's pearls, as well as my precious rare coins. She actually sold the pearls that my mom had given her on our wedding day. She sold them for *him*—for a fornicator."

Martin pushed the peanut shells to the floor with a fury that almost sent the beer mugs to the floor as well. "I didn't even know, at first, that she had taken the pearls and coins with her. She had taken every cent I had in the bank, but that hadn't been enough for her, so she took the pearls and the coins I had inherited from my parents. She cleaned me out good."

"Hey, gents. You gonna suck on one beer all night," Mabel asked. "Sweetie," she said looking at Pete, "you interested in any action tonight?"

Martin pushed his chair back in a hurry and stood up. "Get out of here, you damned Jezebel. Go do your dirty work somewhere else and leave us alone."

All eyes were on Martin and Pete as the noise suddenly subsided. The bartender shouted, "Hey, you, shut up and sit down or get your ass out of here."

Pete reached up, gently pulled Martin's arm, and encouraged him to sit down. Martin relented and slowly slouched back down in his chair. Pete leaned over and asked, "Do you really know where Ash is now?"

"You bet I do. You see, the only thing that I had to go on was that sooner or later that bastard would need more money." Martin said. He began shuffling his feet across the wooden floor, making little mounds of peanut shells and then crushing them with his work boots with such a vengeance that little pieces of shells were flying in all directions. He began again, "Well, I started to visit every place that I could find in Ohio to look for my coins. Some guy I met in my travels gave me addresses of shops in the area where Mary might have gone to sell what she had stolen from me. I went into one shop, and, while I was waiting for the owner to finish a transaction, my eye caught sight of a double strand of pearls with a large diamond in the center of the longer strand. Those were my mother's pearls. I just knew they were."

Martin's voice was getting weaker and it was becoming harder for Pete to hear what he was saying. Pete could sense that Martin's discomfort was getting more intense. "Look, would you rather go somewhere else?"

Martin thought for a second before he responded. "Nah, what the hell...what's done is done. My mom always told me that any bed I made I'd have to sleep in and this one's a doozey. Well, anyway, the owner of the pawn shop described the woman who had sold him the pearls and the coins. He said that he rarely purchased jewelry, but thought that the pearls were so unique that he couldn't turn them down. He told me that the woman asked for directions to Masonville, Kentucky. My mom's pearls lay there in that damned case, and I didn't even have enough money to buy them back. It was Mary," Martin said, "Mary had sold my mom's pearls for him. Can you imagine that? For him—a dirty sex-crazed fiend—for him she had sold the pearls."

Pete wanted desperately to say something to ease Martin's pain, anything to help this man. Martin must have loved his wife very much—a love so powerful that reason didn't exist. Pete was familiar with that type of devotion. He had had such a connection to Estelle and now he was feeling the same way about Jeanette. "Martin, I wish that—"

"No," Martin said firmly. "Don't say it. You can't say anything to make me feel better. Nothing can do that. I've been a fool. Now I must pay. But what you can do for me—what you must do for me—," he said, grabbing onto the lapel of Pete's jacket, "is to get him. If I go, I might kill them both—I don't want to do that. As much as I hate her at this moment—I cannot kill her."

"Do you have an exact address?"

Martin dug into his jacket pocket and extracted a business card. "On the back—the address is on the back. Pete, I had the gun and everything. I had it all planned. I was gonna kill them both—Ash and Mary." He covered his face with his hands. "But I couldn't do it. I drove straight back here to meet with you. "Pete, get him. That guy is dangerous. For God's sake, get him before he ruins any more lives."

As Pete raised himself up, he shook Martin's hand and said, "I will, Martin and…" But before he could finish, Martin withdrew his hand and fled.

Pete looked at the address on the card. He could almost feel the vibrations. If he hurried, and luck was with him, he could make it there by tomorrow night.

CHAPTER 20

(Two days later)

Ayden was pacing the floor. He was restless. Eddie had left two days ago, and he should have been back by now. The plan had to go right—they needed the money. A strange feeling was beginning to overwhelm him. It was surrounding him like an invisible vapor—one that was applying pressure to his very soul. He had to regain his strength so he could draw upon the cosmos to give him the clarity he needed.

Mary had often referred to Ayden as her Saint. He had to focus on that. *A saint must be able to receive his sufferings in love because he cannot see them as sufferings. All evil, no matter in what form it may be, is a hidden form of good. The more hidden it is, the higher the good. But the closer one comes to the good, the more limited it is to man's perception. Therefore, sin is a force of good. Why, then, should others want to punish him for following the way of the Lord?*

The house was very quiet. Even Melody and Willie had fallen asleep shortly after the children had settled down. Concentration—he must concentrate on a positive outcome of Eddie's trip to New Valley. Jenson would come across with the money—he must.

When Jenson's money was in his hands, all would be well once again. Ayden would move his little band to California. He would take his beloved first-born son to the promised- land where he would mature and become the next Primate. He thought about the other children: they would be the future of his kingdom. They would carry the message forward to thousands of others. When they got to their new destination, he would make a concerted effort to bring more lost souls—men, women, and children—into his flock.

Suddenly, Mary appeared at his side. "Ayden, I think my time has come. You will soon have another child and Abulafia will have a little sister."

"My dear, let's get you upstairs where your loving sisters will help you bring Baby Beth into the world."

Pete was jammed in between two burly policemen as the black and white raced down the narrow, country dirt road. The unlit houses along the way were silhouetted against the bright moonlight. To Pete they seemed to whiz by like circus animals on a merry-go-round. Clutching his camera between his legs, Pete checked to be certain that he had, indeed, loaded the film. He could not afford to miss this opportunity.

"Are you certain that the man you spotted is Ayden Ash?" asked Sergeant Potter, the driver of the vehicle.

"No doubt about it. It was Ash, all right," Pete responded firmly.

"This guy," asked the cop to his right, "you say that he was convicted of child molestation and had escaped twice from jails? Where the hell did they lock him up, in broom closets?"

"Might as well have—he got out of both of them without having to fire a shot," Pete answered.

"Well, you're dealing with a different kind of law enforcement here, I can guarantee that. He won't be out of our sight until we put him on a plane bound for his home state," Potter stated. "How many people are in the house with him?"

"I think about five or six—oh, and there are some children; I don't know how many."

Pete was trying unsuccessfully to make himself a bit more comfortable but his mind was racing back to his arrival in Masonville a few hours ago. After only one inquiry at a little country store, he had found Ayden's new hiding place easily. After parking his car several hundred feet down the road, and creeping through woods, he had cautiously approached the rear of the house. A single light burned in the living room. But that and the brightness of the moon, was all Pete had to find his way without falling over the boxes stacked helter-skelter around the back door. Crouching below the window sill, he had raised his head slowly and almost lost his balance viewing the scene before him. There was Ayden, seated on a ladder-back chair, with his hands on the head of a woman who was kneeling on the floor in front of him. With disgust, Pete had lowered himself to the ground. As soon as he regained his composure, he got to his feet, retraced his steps to the car, and headed back toward town to find the local authorities.

Potter said, "According to our information, he never carries any weapons. This should be a piece of cake."

Pete was disappointed that Potter was taking this so cavalierly. "Wait a minute—while he didn't fire at anyone, he did point a weapon at the deputy during his last escape."

"You actually saw him getting a blow job?" the cop asked.

"I think that's what was going on."

"I'll never know why some guys go after kids when there are so many women around who'll give you what you want. Hell, go down to Mickey's, or even to the bar in the Comfort Inn—you'll never have to go home to an empty bed," the younger cop said.

"There you go again, always bragging about getting laid. You know what they say about that—men who can do, those who can't, just talk," Potter said. "Okay, guys, shut up. Just follow my instructions. Joe. Mike. You two cover the rear door while Oscar and I go through the front. Pete, you stay out of the way and do not go into the house until I give you permission."

Potter turned off the headlights and brought the cruiser to a halt. As the four policemen slipped out of the car as quietly as possible, Pete was right behind them. He had promised Potter that he wouldn't take any pictures until they led Ayden out of the house. That way, it would look as if Pete had followed the cops instead of being right there in their midst.

It was deathly quiet. Potter inched his way across the porch and tried the knob. To his surprise, the door was not locked. Potter pushed it opened. Suddenly, they were all bathed in the glow of a yellow porch light that had been turned on from the inside.

"Oh, won't you come in, officers" Ayden said as he looked them over. And, as his eyes rested on Pete, he straightened up his shoulders, lifted his head high, and simply said, "Well, Pete, how nice of you to pay me a visit. It isn't often that the betrayer is so willing to face the betrayed."

"Ayden Ash?" Potter asked.

Never taking his eyes off Pete, the cult leader replied, "I am Ayden Ash, Primate of The Church of True Believers. What is the meaning of this?" he asked innocently.

"There's a little matter of two prison escapes, my friend. It appears that you have forgotten to serve the rest of your time," Potter said as he smiled at his newest prize.

"I have been falsely accused, officer. You see, I am the Primate, and as such, I cannot be guilty since my religion supports my actions," Ayden preached.

"Well, there's the rub—the jury pronounced you *guilty.* Look, I'm not here to argue with you. I have a job to do, that's all," Potter said as he pulled his gun out and worked his way farther into the room.

Looking past Ayden, Pete saw that Joe and Mike had already made their way through the back door and were standing at the far end of the parlor. In the opposite corner of the sparsely furnished room, Melody, Sarah and Rebekah were huddled tightly together, making a pathetic sight as they clung to one another. The women were all wearing long, dark cotton skirts and peasant-type blouses, all styled exactly alike. Rows of colorful beads, strung on narrow leather strips, hung down across their chests. Their feet were encased in primitive sandals decorated with the same little beads used in the necklaces.

Ayden looked directly into Pete's face and said, "*The Son of Man is going to be betrayed into human hands.*"

"But you, my friend, are not The Son of Man," Pete replied.

Just then, Pete spied two little faces peeking through the banisters on the staircase. "Daddy," one of them called out. "Daddy, what's wrong?"

Melody said angrily, "See what you've done, you bastards—rednecked-no-good bastards." Rushing to the children, she herded them back upstairs, continuing to berate the interlopers with obscenities.

Sarah took several steps toward Ayden. Her lips quivered and her eyes were filled with fright. Hesitantly, as she looked furtively from one policeman to another, she asked her husband, "What…what…should I do?"

It was obvious to Pete that the woman was still obedient to this snake-oil salesman. Her once-lovely hair had lost its sheen, and she looked as if she had aged twenty years since he had last seen her in the courtroom. Traces of innocence were still there, despite the fear that filled her gaunt face. Her eyes focused on Ayden, shutting out all others. She was waiting for a sign from her husband, looking for instructions on what she was supposed to do for him—just as she had done thousands of times before.

"Nothing," Ayden said as he rejected her. Turning away from his wife abruptly, with an air of nonchalance, as one would dismiss a stranger, he asked Potter, "When will I be permitted to contact my attorney?"

"You can do that down at the station later, Mr. Ash."

Hesitantly, Sarah took a step toward Ayden, but all he did was hold up his hand and she immediately stopped in her tracks. At that moment, Melody ran back down the steps. Pushing Rebekah out of the way, she approached one of the policemen, who was still standing at the rear of the room, and said, "You've got to help. Hurry, it's coming," she screamed as she tugged on Joe's sleeve.

"Hold it," shouted Potter. "What's coming?" he questioned, never taking his eyes off Ayden.

"The baby…Mary's baby—I need help," Melody pleaded. "Something's wrong and I don't know what to do." Melody began sobbing like a frightened child, not at all like the tough woman they had seen just a few moments ago.

Potter, fearing that the whole thing might only be a ruse, ordered, "Joe, upstairs—see what the hell's going on."

As Joe ran up the uncarpeted stairs, Melody followed and continued to plead, "There's no time left to fart around. It's coming now but something is very wrong. Please, someone, help me. I don't know what I can do for her."

"Sergeant," Joe shouted from the upper floor. "You better get Doc here in a hurry."

"Sarah," Ayden said quietly, "Go and help your sisters. I will be all right. The Lord is on my side." And, as he leaned forward to kiss her cheek, he whispered, "Did Willie get out safely?"

Sarah shook her head in an affirmative manner and obediently followed her husband's commands.

"Oscar, go up and help the ladies the best you can," Potter said. "Mike, you go and radio for the Doc." And as his two men disappeared, Potter said mockingly, "Now my little friend, where were we? Oh, that's right, you're under arrest. Your home state is very anxious to get you back." With those words, Ayden's hands were once again confined in steel handcuffs.

While this was going on, Eddie was approaching the house. As soon as he had spotted the police car, he had turned his bike off and pushed it into the woods. He watched as Potter led Ayden to the squad car. Eddie knew that he would have to keep the flock together again until Ayden was able to take over. It would be no easy task, but since he had been successful in getting a tidy sum from Jenson for the photos, at least he would have money to support their needs. But he felt totally inadequate in providing their spiritual needs. He lay flat on the ground for awhile, waiting for the other police to leave the house. He cringed when he heard Mary's screams. Suddenly, the doctor pulled up and ran into the house. Eddie got up on his knees. He kept his eye glued to the front door of the house.

Suddenly, he spotted Melody running out the front door and into the woods. Eddie ran after her. As he approached the hysterical woman, he placed his hands over her mouth and tried to get her to calm down. She drew her breath in sharply when she realized who he was and sank into his arms. With tears streaming down her face, she said quietly, "They're dead—both of them. Mary and Baby Beth are dead."

PART THREE

LOCKDOWN

Bring me out of prison, so that I may give thanks to your name. The righteous will surround me, for you will deal bountifully with me. Psalm 142:7

CHAPTER 21

(November, 1978)

Ayden Ash was once again behind bars. All should be right with the world, but Jeanette was still very uneasy.

Jeanette had spread the newspaper across her dining room table and, once again, began reading Pete's article on Ayden's capture. Pete had handled the episode like the true reporter that he was. The five-column spread was well written and featured an excellent shot of Ayden as he was being led down the steps of the little, weather-worn house. There was also a fabulous shot of the handcuffs behind Ayden's back. But every time that Pete, in his zealousness, had shared the infinitesimal details about the capture with her, Jeanette's apprehension, about the things that she had not shared with him, had grown more poignant.

She was certain that Pete still didn't know about Greg. Logic dictated that Ayden had not recognized her, and that he was unaware that she had attended that asinine séance. Perhaps she could relax, after all, since her hair had been dyed red at that time. Reason would dictate that she had nothing to fear.

But what about Greg; he knew. He also knew about Pete—that had become obvious on their vacation. Before Greg had broken into their hotel room when they were in the islands, she had not seen him since the séance. Now he haunted her thoughts. He invaded her dreams. *Why would Greg want to hurt me now?* Imagination is a powerful tool—it cannot reason or understand logic—it nibbles away at self-confidence. While her past might be safe forever, as far as Greg and Ayden were concerned, she would never be able to escape her guilt until Pete knew the whole, sordid tale.

Perhaps she should just open up and tell him. Let the chips fall where they may. It appeared that that was the only way she could ever regain her sanity. Not talking things out with Pete was like a self-fulfilling prophecy—Frank revisited. She had practiced telling Pete several times, rehearsing the words over and over, but she had been unable to speak those words to the man she loved so desperately.

At first, her relationship with Pete had been merely an attempt to find some type of stability in her life—something meaningful to hang on to. For a long time, that had been all that she needed. But, like a sprig of ivy, growing stealthily, unnoticed at first by the gardener's eye, love grew and had taken over her whole being. It had entwined itself around her heart, her mind, her soul. How could she now confess her stupidity—her shame?

There certainly had to have been other women in Pete's life before he had married Estelle—maybe even during the marriage, since she had been ill for such a long time. *Am I now looking for a way to justify my own behavior?* There were so many faceless, nameless men, who had filled a need for a moment, and then were gone like dissipating fog in the morning, never meaning anything at all. People had horrible names for women who behaved like that.

She wanted to remain special to Pete. She wondered if her need to be so special was some type of magnificent obsession. She had hoped, for a long time now, that somehow, her uniqueness to Pete would eradicate a time in her life that she would rather forget. *Did she really want Pete to place her on a pedestal? Had she been using Frank as a scapegoat, an excuse for avoiding the reality of her own life?* Whatever it was, it had to be faced, not just for Pete but also for her own peace of mind. She had to make a tough decision—one that could have fatal consequences.

As she entered her bedroom, she took one more look at herself in the full-length mirror. After all, it wasn't an every day occasion to be going to a ball at the governor's mansion. Her long, white dress clung to her every curve, showing off her recent dieting efforts. Since she had met Pete, there had been too many high calorie meals, adding some unwanted pounds to her figure.

Pete had been urging her to move in with him, but Jeanette had refused. She didn't want to set a bad example for his young daughter. Besides, Jeanette also needed to let him know about her past—in all fairness, she simply had to do this. Since Pete was going to stay with her tonight, this might be the right moment. The other night, when she had told him that she had decided to take a job in New Valley as head of public relations for the United Telephone Company, he had jumped to the conclusion that she had changed her mind about moving in with him. The new job would be an exciting challenge for her and would allow her to see Pete every day, but she was not ready to live with him.

Just as she was checking her beaded evening bag, she heard the door chime. She opened the door just a crack, peeked out, and said, "I already gave at the office."

"I'm a lonely man and I am checking to see if anyone here is interested in going to the governor's party with me. If not, I'll be on my way," Pete teased.

"God, you're handsome tonight," Jeanette said as she looked him over.

"Well, my little chickadee, can't say you look too bad yourself," Pete said, trying hard to imitate W. C. Fields. He placed his hands on his hips, took a long appreciative look at Jeanette, and let out a slow whistle. "Heavens, my dear, every woman at the party is going to hate you on sight."

Jeanette turned around slowly, enjoying the warm, sensuous feeling moving through her body. "Thank you, kind sir."

Pete handed her a small package.

"What's this?"

"Something for the most beautiful woman I know," Pete said.

As Jeanette began to open the gift, Pete put his arm around her waist and held her close.

Jeanette's heart began to race. She hoped it would not be a ring. She wasn't ready for that—not until all the dirty laundry had been washed. With great trepidation, she lifted the lid of the box and was relieved to find a sparkling pair of diamond earrings. "Oh, Pete, they're lovely. How sweet," she said as she rushed to the mirror.

Pete loved to watch her when she put earrings on—it was such a sexy act. He never ceased to be amazed at how women could put earrings on so quickly. Pete wanted desperately to reach out and touch her hair and pull her down on the sofa—it would be a challenge for him to keep her at bay.

As they drove through the city on their way to the governor's party, their conversation was light. Jeanette was relieved that Pete hadn't mentioned Ayden one time, and her heart was beginning to soar as they neared the lovely brick home where there would be a celebration of the arts. The mansion was lit from top to bottom. As each driver approached the ornate iron gates, young men dressed in tails were helping the occupants alight. The cars were then quickly whisked away to the rear parking lot.

As Pete and Jeanette climbed the steps leading to the elaborate front door, Jeanette whispered, "I'm really excited. Like a kid. I've never been to a governor's residence before."

"Well, sweetie, get used to it. You're with a star reporter now. I'll probably receive hundreds of these kinds of invitations and if, and only if, you play your cards right, just maybe I'll take you along," Pete teased.

As they entered the hallway, Jeanette was astounded at the beauty of the small but elegant ballroom. The ceiling was a miniature replica of the beautiful dome in the main capital building. Tiny, gold rosettes and small, light blue stars outlined exquisite murals depicting historical events in the state's history. The walls were lined with paintings of famous politicians, all seemingly smiling upon the tastefully dressed crowd moving through the reception line. Lovely crystal chandeliers reflected beams of light that danced gleefully throughout the room.

"You mean that I have to shake hands with all those people," Jeanette said quietly.

"Either that, or I'll have to hide you under my jacket, and you're much too beautiful not to be seen."

One by one, the guests paid their respects to the VIPs in a polite, but amiable manner. Greetings were exchanged warmly and an air of genuine excitement filled the room. Jeanette was particularly impressed with Governor Toth and his wife. Despite the rush of guests, they seemed at ease with everyone. Mrs. Toth was a charming woman of about fifty with the remarkably smooth complexion of a much younger woman. She was smartly dressed in a pale blue ball gown and her hair was expertly groomed. Complimenting the governor extremely well, the First Lady knew just how to greet her guests with a graciousness that made all feel welcome.

"Hey, babe," Pete whispered to Jeanette. "get a load of the governor's wife's earrings. They're four times the size of yours."

Jeanette leaned forward and smiled. "Well," she whispered back, "after you become rich and famous, I'll expect you to trade these in for a pair like those."

Pete stopped in front of the governor and his wife. "Good evening, Governor and Mrs. Toth. I would like you to meet Jeanette Logan."

"How nice to see you," the governor responded, shaking Pete's hand with a well-practiced firm handshake. "That was quite a remarkable story you wrote—my congratulations on a fine job. Our citizens will rest easier now that that scoundrel has been caught and will be eventually confined to Hunter Prison. My sources tell me that you played a key role in his capture. We appreciate your efforts," the governor said as he hung on to Pete's hand and gave the reporter a pat on his back.

"Thank you, Governor. Let's hope that this time we can keep him where he belongs."

"Miss Logan," Mrs. Toth said, "I remember the piece you wrote some time ago on child care facilities, and I want you to know that your article was the force behind the formation of our task force to examine the problem across the state. We're grateful that you brought this situation to light. Thank you so very much."

Jeanette smiled and replied, "I'm pleased to hear that."

"You certainly got my wife's attention," the governor said, as he shook Jeanette's hand. "The task force has been charged with identifying what needs to be done as well as developing a comprehensive plan to address the issues involved in our state. Perhaps you would be interested in helping us. Your reporting has long been admired by my wife."

"Thank you, Governor. I must tell you that I'm no longer a reporter. I'm now working for the United Telephone Company as Public Relations Director. However, if there are no conflict of interest issues involved, I would be delighted to help in any way," Jeanette managed to get out.

After all the amenities were taken care of, Pete steered Jeanette around the room, showing her the various artifacts and providing little vignettes about the pieces of art on display from the state museum. "You've got to admit, this is one top-drawer affair. You see, I not only take you to the worst of places, but every once in awhile I take you to a place like this."

As the crowd began to move out to the dance floor, Jeanette took Pete's hand and said, "Shall we?"

As the lovers began moving their bodies in sync to the music, Pete pulled Jeanette closer to him, and said, "See, I was right."

"About what?"

"Look around," Pete said, as he motioned to the other dancers, "all the women despise you and all the men envy me."

"Oh, Pete," Jeanette said softly as she nestled contentedly in his arms.

When the music stopped, Pete began to usher Jeanette around the ballroom. He introduced her to several politicians that she had previously known only from sitting in the visitors' balcony in the Senate during legislative sessions. They appeared to be so different than they were when she had watched them debate issues on the Senate floor—when their politeness would occasionally manifest itself in cutting remarks. She had often heard them say "*my learned colleague from...*" when they really had meant something like "*you dumb ass.*" But here, in the governor's mansion, they shook hands, smiled at one another, and followed the rudiments of good behavior to the limit.

Jeanette found herself dancing with the Speaker of the House, a large man who was surprisingly light on his feet. He was a wonderful conversationalist, and she was thoroughly enchanted with this huge man, whom she had once taken to task in one of her columns. She was grateful that he hadn't mentioned the article, even though she would have taken the same position today. But tonight, she didn't want to talk politics or legislative issues or, heaven forbid, the state budget.

Pete led Jeanette to the dance floor once again, but their escape to the music was ended abruptly when Dr. Jenson tapped Pete on the shoulder and said, "Hey, Pete, great job on the Ash story—too bad though about Culver."

Pete swung around and placed his hand on Jenson's arm and inquired, "What about Culver?"

Jenson registered surprise. "You mean you haven't heard the news?"

"What news?"

"Culver wrote a note blaming himself for his wife's death, and then he jumped from the tenth floor of the New Valley Hotel. I heard it on the radio coming over here. His body was splattered all over the sidewalk."

CHAPTER 22

(The morning after the governor's party)

Jeanette knew that it was now or never—she had to tell Pete everything. If their relationship had any chance at all, she had to clear the slate. She had told herself, over and over again, that if Pete rejected her, she would still be able move on. But way down deep, into her very essence, she didn't believe that at all.

She could hear Pete as he moved about in the bathroom. Swallowing hard, she tied her bathrobe around her and took a seat on the edge of the bed. This was confession time—this is where she had to go, but she really didn't want to. After all, what could he do? He couldn't change her past—but he could certainly radically change her future, one way or the other.

"Good morning, gorgeous," Pete said as he opened the bathroom door. "It seems that I know who you are—now young lady—what did you tell me your name was?" Pete teased as he leaned down and kissed her on the cheek.

"Pete, sit down, please. We must talk."

Pete took notice of her serious tone and immediately did as she had instructed. "Wow, this sounds really bad. Sweetie, do I really want to hear this?"

"I doubt it, but you must. You see, there are things about me that you must know—things that may make you change your mind about me," Jeanette said as she tried to avoid looking directly at Pete.

"I have no idea what you could possibly tell me that would make me change my mind about you, unless, of course, you're really an ax-murderer."

"That might be easier for you to take. Let me talk until I am finished and then you can respond. Just don't interrupt, or I may lose my courage." She reached over and took his hand in hers. "You know, my late husband, Frank, was killed by an angry patron. But you don't know what had occurred before, or what happened after his death. God, this is really hard," Jeanette said. Taking a few more breaths, she continued. "One day, I happened to drop in on Frank at his office, and I found him and his secretary going at it on the floor. I backed away and I never told him what I had seen. It was that incident that started me out on a path of self-destruction. I felt lost and confused. I had been certain that he had loved me as much as I had loved him. The betrayal was overwhelming. I felt stupid and used—worthless."

"Baby, look here," Pete said as he tried to get her to look at him.

"No, Pete, please. I must finish. I started running around like crazy—I even ran away and went to Woodstock with Greg, an old boyfriend of mine. I was there with the crowd and went nuts when I heard Arlo Guthrie, Santana and the others play. I ran around with *Grateful Dead* fans. I didn't care who I made love with at any time. I dressed like the others—Bohemian style. Greg had given me a necklace that had a metal peace symbol attached to a leather strap." Jeanette stood up, took the necklace out of her dresser drawer and handed it to Pete.

"It was Greg who broke into our hotel room when we were in the islands. I knew who it was. I didn't tell you. I've been sorry ever since. After you ran out the door, I discovered that Greg had put that damned necklace in my straw bag. I don't know why he did that. Greg didn't have an ugly bone in his body—so I don't know why that incident scared me so much. I realize now, that it was not Greg who scared me—it was my own guilty conscience."

Pete now had the necklace in his hand. He put his hand through the loop of leather and let the peace symbol swing back and forth. Without saying anything, he gathered the necklace together and laid it on the top of the dresser.

"Now, here comes the really difficult part," Jeanette said, as she took Pete's hand in hers. "I was at a séance."

Pete's head shot up. He had an incredulous expression on his face. "Where?"

"At Ash's church."

"You knew him? You were in his church?"

"I didn't know Ayden before Greg took me there, but I was there. We were served some kind of punch that really made us all relax. Then, Ayden put on an act that he claimed would prove that he could communicate with the dead." Jeanette swallowed hard and began breathing heavily. "After his silly act was over, he invited everyone to…people were encouraged to undress and have sex with anyone they wanted. He even offered his wife and other women to help his guests fulfill their fantasies." Jeanette's voice began to get softer. Closing her eyes, she continued, "I started to undress. But my stomach turned and I couldn't go through with it. I grabbed my clothes and ran out of there as fast as I could. But I was there. I have never told anyone about the whole damned thing. I don't know if I should have told the District Attorney's office about it, but, selfishly, I wanted to protect what good reputation I might have left. God, Pete, you're free to leave if you want."

Pete sat perfectly still for a few minutes. He turned to her and said, "Jeanette, when I told you that I loved you, I meant it—love is all-forgiving."

"I haven't seen him since. Oh, I wish I had never met him at all. I'm so very sorry Pete," Jeanette said. Through her tears, she said, "Oh, Pete, how I wish that I had never—"

He took her in his arms. "Hush, baby, there's no need to cry. I will always love you. The past is just that—the past. It's what we will do with our future that counts. And, if you want a future with me, you've got it. I still want you to be my wife—no matter what—Frank—Greg—Woodstock—I simply don't care."

"But Pete, there were others and I—"

"Baby, I don't care. Now hush; everything will be fine. I love you and you love me. It's just as simple as that."

They held each other tightly and, when Jeanette finally stopped crying, Pete said, "Now, sweetie, tell me, when are you going to make an honest man out of me by marrying me?"

CHAPTER 23

(December, 1978)

The gray stone building, erected in the 1870s, created an ominous silhouette against the inner-city skyline. Hunter Prison was a foreboding structure, predicting evil with its drab color, its barbed wired fences, and its thirty-foot high walls. The structure was built on an apex where two rivers merged—the Monongahela and the Allegheny, to form the Ohio River. The red glow of man's productivity could be seen, day and night, spewing out of tall smoke stacks of the steel mills just a few miles from the state prison, simply known as The Wall.

A van, belonging to the Department of Corrections, made its way through the winding streets of the city. The occupants—three prisoners—were chained together at their ankles, making it difficult for them to maintain their balance as the van bounced along the pot-holed streets. When the van suddenly stopped, there was a brief exchange between the driver of the van and a prison guard standing outside the gates. The heavy, steel-fortified gates opened and the van crept forward. With the clanging of two more sets of gates, Ayden knew that he was now inside the dreaded penitentiary. The driver turned around and said nonchalantly, "Well, gentlemen, here we are—all out."

As the rear door of the van opened, two armed guards ushered the convicted men from the vehicle into the maximum security prison. Designed to house 900 men, but now holding over 1700, the old prison still remained an unrelenting fortress, presenting an almost unsolvable maze to those inclined to accept the challenge of escape. Ayden was overwhelmed when he looked around and saw the heavy double gates, rolls and rolls of barbed wire, and armed guards everywhere. Bars and chains, chains and bars—this was not going to be easy. But there had to be a way to get out—there always was.

The processing of the prisoners was a demeaning experience for Ayden. As the guards probed and groped his every orifice, he clenched his teeth. Never moving a muscle, he allowed himself to be examined by the guards by withdrawing himself from sensory attachment and confronting the heights of spiritual struggle. As the guards forced him to spread his legs and bend over, he detached himself again from his body until he had disappeared into a bodiless world. The men who were currently searching him were not there at all. Ayden was now a soulless body, allowing the desecration to take place.

The conditions in the prison were dreadful—far worse than Ayden had ever seen. Everywhere there was decay and rot. Ayden would soon learn that the facility would be constantly cold in the winter and unbearably hot in the summer. Because of his previous escapes, Ayden was immediately placed in restricted custody. His cell reeked with human stench that permeated Ayden's nostrils and filled his lungs. It was a disgusting place that had been designed to demoralize the prisoners it held.

The faded blue shirt and trousers they had given him were much too big. Ayden looked almost comical as he struggled to hike the trousers up so that he would not step on them when he walked. The guards seemed to delight in belittling him by making derogatory remarks about Ayden's small stature. He heard them making bets on how long it would take for the other inmates to learn that he was a child molester. He realized that he had to establish his manhood right away or he would become a punk—in The Wall punks were *shes*—treated like slaves. They cleaned for their owner, took care of their owner's wants, and performed any kind of sexual act that their owner desired—a process that, although punishable, was simply overlooked by the guards. Although Ayden had been able to convince people on the outside that he had the ability to rain destruction upon them by spiritual means, he must now get his fellow inmates to believe the same thing. He must establish his dominance in this hell hole as soon as possible or he might be used as a *she*.

During his second week, Ayden became familiar with solitary confinement with amazing speed. As he entered his cell one evening after dinner, Fat Paul, the most hated guard in the prison, had grabbed at Ayden's private parts. Instinctively, Ayden had kicked Fat Paul in the groin. He had instantly regretted his action but had stood his ground defiantly. Ayden had been given three weeks in solitary as his punishment—a smelly, damp hole that had a single light bulb, burning day and night.

After the first few days, he had lost all track of time and had been unable to relate to anything but lunch time. He had been fed only once a day and even that was almost always indigestible. Striped clothes, reserved for those who belonged in solitary, had replaced his faded blue attire. There was nothing in his cell but a steel cot with a lumpy mattress. The cell didn't even have a toilet, just a hole in the floor. Ugly urine stains had formed dark circles around the opening and the smell of human waste was intolerable. But what Ayden had found to be even worse was that he was not permitted to have any books or writing paper. Hours had seemed like days, and days seemed like weeks. Nothing to read—nothing to challenge his intellect—nothing to exercise his mind, but he still had his ability to meditate. Ayden feared that he might lose that ability if he could not bring himself fully under control. Never again would he allow himself to be placed in solitary. He had decided that he would begin to play their game—this time he would win.

After his stint in solitary had been completed, Ayden had been placed in various sections of the prison and was finally housed in a single-man cell. Now his uniform was an ugly, brownish-maroon-colored short-sleeved shirt and trousers. At least these clothes fit him better than the others. Cheap-looking brown shoes, a simple corduroy jacket, and a cap completed his wardrobe. He immediately began to organize his cell. The books that Sarah had sent to him earlier had been returned, and he stacked them neatly on an old metal shelf. And with money that Sarah had deposited in his account, Ayden had been able to purchase writing paper and pencils in the commissary. He had written to Sarah and had given her instructions to inform him about anything that had to do with Pete. Somehow, in some way, Ayden wanted to teach Pete a lesson; a lesson that he would never forget.

Every morning he would make up his bed, tucking the sheets and covers around the edges of a mattress that was covered with blue and gray ticking. He was determined to bring orderliness back into his life. He would then sit down on the metal stool and begin to work on sermons that would be mailed to his little flock. He needed to be certain that they would continue to follow the dogma that he had dictated.

Here, inside The Wall, Ayden's main concern was his safety. Even prisons have social stratum, with child molesters placed on the very bottom rung. Since he was small, almost frail-like, he would need a protector. He needed to find one as quickly as possible.

CHAPTER 24

(June, 1979)

For months, Ayden had been trying, unsuccessfully, to establish friendships among the inmates. When he thought he had made some friends, as soon as they had learned why Ayden had been incarcerated, one by one, they backed away from any contact with him. When he learned that the prisoner, who recently was moved into the cell next to his, worked in the prison kitchen every morning, Ayden began to develop a new plan. If Ayden could get this inmate, a huge black man named Omar, to serve as his protector, Ayden would have nothing to fear from others. In order to get close to Omar, Ayden needed to get assigned to the kitchen at the same time. For several weeks Ayden had been extremely polite to the head guard, Charlie, and it wasn't long before the surprisingly civil man began stopping by Ayden's cell to hold brief conversations.

One evening, when the time was approaching for Charlie to conduct bed check, Ayden positioned himself at the front of his cell. As soon as he spotted Charlie, Ayden called, "Charlie, I have a question for you."

Charlie chuckled, "Don't make it too hard."

"Would it be possible for me to work in the kitchen on the morning shift? I would really like to begin to do something worthwhile around here. You know, I can only read so much before my eyes go wacky. I'm a good worker and I know a little about cooking," Ayden said.

"Well, you haven't had any write-ups for awhile so maybe they might approve that. I'll see what I can do. They might not want to give you too much freedom though, Ash, and you know the reasons for that,"

Charlie said. "I never had an escape from my block and I would like to keep it that way. But, in all fairness, I'll get back to you."

"Thank you, sir. I really appreciate that," Ayden replied very politely.

Within two weeks, when the guards came for Omar for his kitchen duty, they also opened Ayden's cell door and motioned for him to follow. Ayden's hopes began to rise. Omar barely looked at Ayden as they walked side by side to the large kitchen. When they entered the swinging door to the large kitchen, Ayden saw two armed guards sitting at a small table with coffee mugs in their hands. Instantly, Ayden smelled the wonderful aroma of bread baking in the big ovens. Omar moved immediately to the back of the kitchen and Ayden started to follow him.

"Whoa, where do you think you're going?" the one guard said to Ayden.

"I'm sorry, officer, I just assumed that I was to follow Omar—my apologies, sir."

"How about that, a polite one for a change," the guard said. "See that guy over there with the big white hat? He's the boss, Freddie. Check with him; he'll give you an assignment." Freddie spied his newest worker and walked over. "So, you're the new guy. How come you want to work in the kitchen?"

"Well, my neighbor, Omar, seems to like his assignment, so I thought I might like it, too. Maybe we could work together," Ayden replied. "Sure smells good in here."

"I don't always allow the same people to work together, but I'll let you work with Omar today since we're short-handed. The flu seems to be going around the prison and three of my morning shift crew landed in the infirmary. Just go back to Omar. He'll put you to work. Do whatever he says."

"You my new guy?" Omar asked. "Ain't you in the next cell?"

"Yes, Omar, I really want to help you."

"Nobody helps Omar. Omar helps his self."

"Omar, I heard that you're the big man around here."

"Whatcha mean? You better not mess with me. In here, I'm the boss and don't you forget it. I'll do with you what I want when I want—you got that, you little punk."

"Wait a minute, Omar. You and I will get along fine but I'm no punk," Ayden said. He moved closer to Omar and said, "You and I will get along fine. I have friends on the outside—powerful ones. But I only help those who help me. Just you and me. Omar—we can be a team—a team that can get out of this place."

Pulling his bushy, black eyebrows closer together, Omar put his face close to Ayden's. Instantly, Ayden knew that this was going to be a test and that he could not display any sign of fear. He surely didn't want to be in a subservient position with Omar. Staring back at Omar, Ayden said, "Look, with your strength and my brains, we can get out of here. I can guarantee it. I have already escaped from two other prisons."

Omar began opening up large sacks of potatoes and placing them on a conveyor belt, so Ayden started doing the same thing. Ayden watched as Omar pulled down some overhead hoses and locked them into place. Water began to flow over the dirty potatoes. The belt then slowly moved them down to a large vat where they were spun around at a high rate of speed to remove the skins.

"You can get me out?" Omar asked quietly. "If you know what I done, maybe you won't help me."

"I don't care what you did. I can tell that you're a good person. I'll help you like I said, and maybe I can even get some money put into your account. How would you like that, Omar? That means you'll have money to go to the commissary."

"I earns twenty-five cents a day in this here kitchen. I have my own money."

"That's good, Omar, but wouldn't you like even more money to buy stuff like candy and such? All I want is your loyalty and your protection from others. What you did to get in here does not bother me in the least," Ayden said earnestly.

"Maybe after you hear what I done, you'll change your mind," Omar responded.

"Tell me, Omar, tell me."

Omar looked to his right to check on Freddie. He watched as his boss crossed the kitchen and headed to the table where the guards were seated. Omar tapped Ayden on the shoulder and pointed with his head toward the guards. Ayden watched as Freddie placed two large doughnuts in front of the guards. After refilling their cups with hot brewed coffee, Freddie walked away.

"Does that happen every morning?" Ayden whispered.

"It sure do. Every day those screws get treated like hotshots."

After Omar cleaned out the vat filled with potato skins, he said, "She was catting around. I knew it. Then I caught her," Omar said sadly. "There she was, lying in the front seat of the bastard's Cadillac, her head pumping up and down like crazy. I reached in the car, grabbed her by her hair, and pulled her out and she falls onto the street with a loud thud." Omar looked around to check where the other workers were and then he continued. "Then, the guy—the one getting the blow job—starts the car, and his back wheel goes right over her throat. They said that she was already dead from the blow to her head when she fell and they sent me to prison. The damned driver got away free as a bird."

"Hey, you two," Freddie yelled across the room. "stop the yacking. Get to work. Move those trays to the front of the line and do it now."

Omar whispered, "This place is like a damned tomb. You can't get us out of here. I've been here for ten years—ten fucking years. There's no way out—no way."

"I'll tell you what, Omar. If you promise to protect me, keep all the others away from me, I'll teach you what I know about unseen forces—forces that guide me, tell me things that no one else knows. I can help you understand things about life and death."

Omar laughed out loud. "I knows plenty about death. I killed more than once. I can do it with my bare hands. Don't need no gun or no knife. So don't mess with me," Omar warned.

"My friend, I respect you. You're a very special person, Omar, very special. Don't let anyone tell you anything different. You don't deserve to be in here. You know that and now I know that. You're strong—probably the strongest man in this whole damned prison." Omar straighten himself to his full height and flexed his muscles. "And me—well I'm probably the smartest. One on one, these people can get to us, but they will not be able to reach us if we form a team. We can be the driving force in this prison. We can rule this place, Omar. You help me like I want, and you'll be out of here in a few months. So, when I go, you will go with me. Is that a bargain?" Ayden asked as he held out his hand to Omar.

Omar, who towered over Ayden, reached out and took Ayden's hand, shook it forcefully and said, "Okay, now we're friends. But no shitting around, you hear that?"

That's how this odd couple began their partnership. Omar was true to his word. He kept all the other inmates away from Ayden, protecting him from any harm that usually followed those convicted of child molestation. While some tried to make Ayden their punk, Omar did not allow that to happen.

Ayden began teaching Omar simple things about the occult and the spiritual world. He invented symbols that the two of them used to communicate with one another, often arousing the curiosity of others. With a few, simple, mind reading tricks, Ayden had been able to convince Omar that he did, indeed, have mystical powers. And it didn't take long for Omar to convince other inmates that Ayden was a powerful man—a man to be reckoned with.

CHAPTER 25

(December, 1979)

It was a picture-perfect day for a wedding. The sun was shining brightly, the air was crisp and the feeling of Christmas seemed to be everywhere. As far as the eye could see, a line of bright red and green lights, strung down Main Street, added to the holiday ambience. As guests began arriving at Jeanette's lovely new home, they were greeted with a double row of six-foot tall evergreen trees all bathed in little, twinkling white lights like a rain shower of heavenly stars. Large, soft green spotlights shone on the home, and the glow of small electric candles in the windows, created a warm welcome to those arriving in their wedding finery.

Three months ago, Pete had been surprised when Jeanette had accepted his latest proposal of marriage. In fact, he had been so certain that he was going to be rejected once again, he had forgotten to put the ring in his jacket pocket. When she said *yes,* he had found himself standing there empty-handed. Then Jeanette had handed him another surprise; she told him about her net worth—she could be considered *loaded*—throwing him for a loop. He wanted to be the one to take care of his family. Privately, he had wished that her bank account didn't have so many zeros. Pete didn't know that her father had been a wealthy man. Jeanette had been aware that she would be inheriting her father's assets when she turned thirty—an event that happened six months ago.

Jeanette was ready for her new life. She hadn't told Pete about her wealth because she, herself, hadn't realized the inheritance would be so large. The only luxuries that she had allowed herself were her new home and her prized red Porsche. With the help of her favorite uncle Vincent, she invested in several companies, bought some real estate along the Eastern shore, and gave donations to her favorite charities. She sensed that Pete wasn't too happy about her finances so she had her uncle meet with him and, when he offered to serve as their financial advisor, it seemed to ease Pete's uneasiness about the money.

Pete's friend, Jimmy, from the paper, had been chosen as the best man and Cindy, who was now sixteen-years of age, had readily agreed to be Jeanette's only attendant. The wedding and a small reception were going be held in Jeanette's home that had been decorated with flowers in the foyer and on the banister, descending from the second floor to the large living room. Guests would be served drinks from a small bar erected in the foyer and the large dining room table would be used to serve hors d'oeuvres. Jeanette had chosen a simple, pale green silk suit and Cindy had chosen a striking red taffeta dress that couldn't hide the fact that she was rapidly developing into a woman.

Jeanette's bedroom looked as if it had been designed by *House Beautiful.* The canopy of the white poster bed had been draped in ecru-colored silk with white satin tassels hanging from each of the four corners. A beige and gold brocade spread covered the king-size bed and dark brown and gold pillows were stacked in front of the large ornate headboard. A thick plush carpet, in a deeper shade of ecru, covered the large bedroom floor like a sea of fresh sand. A dark brown chaise lounge stood beside a lovely old-fashioned vanity and bench. The room dripped with elegance.

Cindy, clad in a red bra and a half slip, was sitting at the vanity deftly applying eye make-up. "I wish Evelyn were here."

"Who's Evelyn?" Jeanette asked as she started slipping Cindy's dress off a pink satin hanger.

"She's one of my good friends. We met at the theater. She wants to be an actress, too," Cindy replied.

"Too? I thought you wanted to do something with computers," Jeanette teased.

"I changed my mind. I still like computers, but acting's much better. Much more exciting—don't you think?"

"I don't know much about either profession. But listen. You certainly could have invited your friend to the wedding. Why didn't you tell me about her earlier?"

"Oh, she's busy with her stepfather right now. He lives on a farm. He grows something, but I can't remember what. You should see her, Mama Jeanette, she's a knock-out. She has black hair like yours, but hers is really curly, all around her head. Her complexion is smooth like chocolate milk. And, wow, is she built! She doesn't have to stuff her bra. I swear that she's as pretty as Lena Horne. Evelyn wants to hit 'the boards' like I do," Cindy said emphatically.

Jeanette laughed. "*Hit the boards*?"

"Yeah, that's theater talk—it means go on the stage. It's such fun. I can't wait until I get a part. Right now, all they let me do is paint scenery and usher. But soon, I'll be up there on the stage with the rest of them."

Cindy stood up so Jeanette could help her get the dress over her head without messing what the hairdresser had taken two hours to create. "You know, each time I see a show, I picture myself up there. Maybe next year they'll give me some bit part. Will you come to see me?" Cindy asked, her excitement about the prospect of performing on stage coming through loud and clear.

"Wild horses couldn't keep me away. If you had your choice of parts, which one would you choose?" Jeanette questioned.

"Any part?" Cindy thought for a moment and then said, "Well, to be perfectly frank, I'd love to play Juliet. You know, having someone fall so desperately in love with me, and all that tragedy and stuff. But our theater doesn't do any of the classics. I'd like a real meaty part, though—like a tramp. Or maybe even a killer—like a black widow spider. No singing parts, though—that I can't do," Cindy emphasized.

Jeanette laughed. "Somehow I cannot picture you as a black widow spider. You're much too pretty. What about your friend? Has she been on stage yet?"

"Evelyn had a tiny, tiny part in *Guys and Dolls,* but she wants to be a serious actress," Cindy said, as she placed her hand on her forehead, palm forward, trying out her best Clara Bow imitation.

"You're too much!" Jeanette chuckled. "Does Evelyn go to your school?"

"Nah, her parents can't afford the tuition. I haven't met her mother or her stepfather. Her stepsister lives with them and Evelyn says she's pretty but she's involved with some guy in prison. Oh, now I remember, her stepfather works on a Christmas tree farm. But we get together at the theater. She seldom has any money to do anything, but that's okay, I really like her." Cindy began twirling around in front of the full-length mirror. "Gosh, this dress is awfully pretty, don't you think?"

"You look gorgeous. You'll be the prettiest girl at the wedding," Jeanette assured the young girl.

"But I can't compete with you, Mama Jeanette. Look, you have all those curves and I'm still almost flat," Cindy moaned as she ran her hands over her body.

"Be patient, my little one. Before you know it, you'll have those curves, and then you'll spend the rest of your life trying to keep them in the right places."

"Just think. In a little while, you'll really be my mother," Cindy said. She suddenly turned to Jeanette and said, "Is that wicked of me to say that?"

Jeanette put her arms around the young girl and said, "No, it's not wicked to want a mother. I will be Mama Jeanette, but Estelle will always be your mother. She will live in that special place in your heart where no one else can go. You'll feel her often. You will know when she's around and your love for her will continue to grow. Don't be afraid of that, honey. I'll try to do the things for you that she would want me to, but I can never replace her. You have lots of memories, and they'll come flooding back to you now and then. Surprisingly, you will even find the unhappy memories comforting—as a reminder of how much she loved you. No one can ever take your mother's love from you. It's a gift that lasts forever, given unconditionally from a mother to a child."

"I'm glad that you're marrying my dad. I've wanted you to be a part of our family for so long. I was scared that it wouldn't happen," Cindy said.

"Thank you, Cindy. Thank you for letting me into your life. It's the best wedding present I could have imagined."

"All that is left to say now is," Cindy said, "*and they lived happily ever after.*"

CHAPTER 26

(April, 1980)

Since Ayden had successfully indoctrinated Omar, who had been transferred to another cell block, he felt that it was time to move on to another assignment within the prison. Once again, he approached Charlie and asked him to put in a good word for him to work in the library. Emphasizing that he had owned a book store and had been a published author, he felt that he had impressed Charlie. And he was right. Two weeks later, he was on his way to meet Milton Knoblauch, the prison librarian.

Milton was a friendly, dark-haired Jewish man whom Ayden liked instantly. The dedicated librarian was impressed when he learned that Ayden not only loved libraries, but had published several books. He asked Ayden many questions about his publications and the research that had to be conducted in order to complete the manuscripts, especially the historical ones. Ayden also shared his interest in old maps, and Milton was pleasantly surprised at the inmate's knowledge about the arts.

Almost immediately, Ayden had taken over Milton's little work room. He rearranged the items on the desk every time he was there, making sure that Milton knew that he was displeased if the librarian moved things back again. Ayden loved to be around books; but more importantly, he had been relieved of menial chores—duties that he had felt were beneath his elevated intellect. Willingly, Ayden had taken over the challenge of rearranging the entire library. Milton was impressed when he noticed how patient Ayden was with inmates who were conducting research on their cases. Ayden was pleased with the positive reactions he was getting from his fellow inmates as he worked diligently, helping them find the right legal books for use in filing their appeals. Slowly, but surely, he was winning them over.

Thanks to a grant from the State Library, Milton had been able to purchase a set of law books from a retired attorney. When the books had finally arrived, Milton had gently placed them on the shelves, touching the leather bindings of each one, proud that his library now had a distinct look of a good research facility. Of course, after Milton had posted a notice in the mess hall about the law books, he had difficulty allotting enough time for each inmate who wanted to use them. Milton was fussy with the men when they were using the law books. The inmates knew that if they violated Milton's instructions, they would be temporarily banned from using them at all.

At first, Ayden was more than willing to do anything that Milton requested. But little by little, he had been able to steal some time to work on his own writings. Milton turned a blind eye on this practice, unless the library was overcrowded. Then, he would ask Ayden to put his work aside and help the inmates. But in spite of that, Ayden would write long epistles to his little flock, converting English into Greek letters to confuse the guards when they censored the outgoing mail. And, unknown to Omar, he had begun to provide spiritual advice to a group of prisoners known as the White Aryan Brotherhood. Ayden was determined to make as many friends as possible throughout the facility. Privately, he zeroed in on inmates' individual prejudices and hatred—it gave him the status and loyalty he felt he needed. His mysticism had given him prestige and power among those who were the least powerful in society. His fellow inmates respected educated people and, to the residents of The Wall, Ayden was very well-schooled—they seemed to have overlooked that he had been convicted of child molestation.

Ayden spent many hours developing a plan for the creation of his Master Children. Just like Adam and Eve, two of his youngest cult members would unite and bring forth beautiful children to start a new race—a race of people over which he would have total control. People must be engineered properly because the true mysteries of life are not meant for everyone—only a chosen few. If they were allowed to go unguided, it could lead to nihilism and chaos. Ayden would make certain that his students, his Master Children, would understand their own inner beliefs. The idea of legislating personal conduct would not be allowed among his Master Children. They would be cultivated and nurtured to assure a new society—one which would encourage open, free love.

One day, Milton happened to see one of Ayden's writings on Jewish mysticism. "You know, Ayden, some of your arguments in this paper are no longer endorsed by Jews. Your ideas are archaic and out of touch with present religious beliefs. Of course, you're free to believe in whatever religion you want, but I wanted you to know that Jews would be offended by some of the things you say in your writings."

"Thank you, Milton. I appreciate your comments," Ayden said, as he turned and went back to work without another word.

About an hour later, Milton came back to the workroom. "Ayden, when you have a moment, would you please check the map drawers? I've been meaning to do that for some time now, but with your background, it appears that you're the better person to make the necessary decisions. You can decide which maps are historical in nature, especially with your experience in researching blueprints and such, and we'll keep those. If you find any documents of no value—and I'll let that up to your judgment—just toss them out," Milton said.

The steel map cabinet had twelve long drawers and Ayden was extremely eager to dig into the documents. He was shocked to see that none of the drawers had been labeled in any way. How anyone could treat such valuable documents in this manner was foreign to Ayden. Sliding open the first drawer, he spotted recent maps. Being an amateur history buff, he was much more interested in older documents, so he checked the very bottom drawer. As soon as he saw the condition of the maps in that drawer, he knew they were very old. He was exceedingly careful. He touched each document, like a mother touches her baby. He removed the first blueprint and placed it on the library work table. Taking a magnifying glass in his hand, Ayden bent over the 100-year-old drawing and discovered that it was the original layout of the land on which the prison had been built. Immediately, he began thinking about turning these old prints into a book about the history of the prison. That would really give him a project to work on, and, at the same time, allow him more time out of his cell.

After reviewing a few more blueprints and separating those he felt could provide information about the history of the prison, he came across the plans for the library space.

It had originally been designed to be a much smaller space that certainly would not accommodate today's prison population.

"Milton, will you please come here. I found something you may find very interesting," Ayden called out. As Milton entered the room, Ayden said, "Look here. These are the original plans for the library. See how small it was? Perhaps I can find the later drawings that will tell us what additions were made and when."

"Ayden, this is interesting. I never thought of looking through these documents before."

"I have an idea—we can write a book about the prison and use these drawings as the start of our research. What do you think about that?" Ayden asked hopefully. "We can then do more research on how the facility grew. And then determine who the most influential people were and how their contributions shaped the facility."

"I'm impressed, Ayden. You continue your search and later we can review what you have found. But it sounds like a tremendous idea. Oh, I've got to go. There's one inmate out there in the reading room who's misusing one of our law books. I'll be back later."

Ayden found several more blueprints that focused on the library and began stacking them on the table. Then, one drawing, in particular, caught his eye—it provided details for an eight-foot high cistern that stretched from the prison to the apex of the Ohio River. In one of the legends, a drawing indicated that a grate, allowing access to the cistern, had been installed on the first floor to provide workmen access to the cistern. After studying the details for a few minutes, Ayden realized that the grate had been placed under the exact spot where Milton's desk was now located in the library work room. The blueprints also indicated that there was a ladder attached to the wall—apparently placed there for workmen to get access to the cistern. Ayden's heart almost stopped beating. He almost forgot to take a breath. His eyes widened and he checked the drawings several times to make certain that he had not gone mad. He could not believe his luck. He had found it. He had found the way out of The Wall!

CHAPTER 27

(Two days later)

The women reminded the guards of remnants of a sixties love feast parade gone awry as they walked up the metal stairway, awkwardly holding onto their long drab-colored skirts. Stringy unwashed hair, almost covering their ashen faces, and cheap, colored glass beads, clanging against the sides of the railing when they climbed the steps, created a strange spectacle for the guards to behold. The door at the top of the stairway swung open and the three women padded silently across the cold cement floor in their wide-strapped leather sandals. A guard, who was safely stationed behind bullet-proof glass, shoved a clip board toward Melody. In large bold letters, she scrawled Ayden's name across the paper and pushed it back to the surly guard through the small opening in the bottom of the glass panel.

Displaying an inordinate amount of patience, the three forlorn-looking women sat on the hard wooden bench for almost two hours before the guard called out Ayden's name. Walking as almost one body, they moved quietly down the hallway toward the visitors' area. After waiting a few minutes, the solid steel door leading to the cell area opened and closed with a clamor that hurt their ears. Then came the indignity of passing through a metal-detecting machine that was so powerful that even braces on someone's teeth, or a wired bra, could set it off, forcing the guards to search a visitor much more intimately. After the transients were scrutinized, the barred, locked gate to the visiting area room was finally opened. They filed quickly into a rectangular room painted a sickening green color. Two aisles of chairs, arranged back to back, ran through the center of the room. Several small desks and tables, reserved for lawyers and their clients, occupied the far corner and a rostrum-like desk was manned by a single guard. And, in an almost incredible fashion, a tiny fenced off play corner for children of the inmates, was located directly beside Fat Paul, who was holding their fathers captive.

The prisoners, all wearing muddy brown-colored trousers and shirts, were busily engaged in conversations with their visitors. Tears and smiles, laughter and anger, were being displayed throughout the room as if someone had indiscriminately thrown them into a mixing bowl in order to achieve a highly emotional scene. There were people who were well-dressed, business types, as well as a goodly number of those whose mode of dress indicated that they could be counted among the poor. But of all the visitors, none looked stranger than Sarah, Melody and Rebekah.

The women jostled one another as they tried to arrange their chairs in a small semicircle. Each one wanted to be the one in the middle—the one who would sit directly in front of Ayden, their Primate. Even though the women got along fairly well at home, when they came to the prison, they vied constantly for Ayden's attention.

Since Ayden had been incarcerated this last time, the women had established a rather successful craft shop just three miles from the prison. They had been able to get their creations accepted on consignment by several boutiques in the city. Even though they had to work long hours each day filling orders, growing their own food, and taking care of the children, they wanted only to please their Primate. But they had paid a heavy price for their dedication. Their youthful appearance had disappeared and in its place stood three tired-looking women.

Looking more like nineteenth century characters, the women were getting a lot of attention from the other visitors, but they seemed unmindful of the curious glances being cast their way. The women, who were naked under their free-flowing garments, were also not aware that the guards had long ago given them the nickname of "*dirty ankle ladies*."

Omar was at the far end of the room, talking with a skinny white woman dressed in a garish, tight-fitting, red satin dress. He took little notice of Ayden's entourage since he had observed this ritual often and saw nothing unusual about today. The big man used to envy Ayden because his women came so often to visit, while Omar was lucky if his Lilly showed up every couple of weeks. But just today, Lilly had promised to wait for him and be his woman when he got out, for he had assured her that that would be soon. Omar had only two things on his mind lately: escape and fucking Lilly. And Ayden was gonna be his ticket to get both.

As soon as they spotted Ayden entering the visitor's room, the women waved at him, almost as if they were not sure he could find them. Ayden returned their greeting with a smile as he slid into his chair, only inches away from them all. The women began to argue for the right to be the first one to talk with Ayden, but he merely held up his hand and they instantly quieted down.

"I want to know how my first-born son is doing," Ayden said as he looked at Melody.

"Oh, Ayden, he's growing so rapidly. You'll be very proud of him. He's being educated in the manner in which you have dictated. He's truly one of a kind," Melody said proudly.

Sarah pulled her eyebrows together. Then she said, "Aren't you interested in how your daughter, Alice, is doing?"

"Sarah, my Sarah, even when you sit here before me you continue to exhibit your jealous ways. I am interested in all my flock. But you must realize that my first-born son is the most important person in my life—my heir apparent—must be sheltered and protected from harm. Now, I will hear no more of your jealousy. I am certain that when it is your turn to speak, you will update me on Alice."

Then one by one, they obediently took turns and shared little tidbits of their lives with him. Ayden listened patiently, interrupting from time to time with little comments that made them smile.

"Did Eddie understand my note about the way to Nirvana?"

Melody nodded her head and said, "He understands and plans are in the works to get us all to that heavenly place. We'll have a practice run tomorrow and the doorway to heaven, as well as Jacob's ladder, will be verified."

Ayden had researched all the old escape plans. He wanted to make certain that his plan would not fail. Over the years, other attempts had been made to break out of the more than 100-year-old prison. Some had tried digging tunnels, while others hid in crates being shipped out of the prison. But only one inmate had avoided capture. One of the most gruesome prison escape efforts happened when a friend of Omar's climbed into a garbage truck. When the driver put the compactor mechanism into action, the inmate was crushed to death. Ayden was confident that his idea was the only foolproof way to get out of The Wall. He would be known as the only inmate who simply walked out of the facility to freedom.

"Ah, yes, Nirvana. How nice to speak of it," Ayden said, as if he were preaching a sermon. "You must remember, though, Aaron expects all to be ready—down to the final details. The practice run will determine if anything has changed, let's say, in recent years. The way to the truth shall be revealed."

"I must tell you, Ayden, your missives, your wonderful writings, have been duplicated, and we have shared them with hundreds of people. We've had several inquiries into our way of life," Sarah said as she reached out and touched Ayden's hand. "We are ready to follow you."

"That's good news, Sarah. Remember all the documents, photographs, maps, and legal papers in the brown trunk must also be ready. Now go, my children—pray for the strength that you will need for your trip to Nirvana."

CHAPTER 28

(One day later)

For Melody, this was the day that she would be proving her love for Ayden. Even though the skies were beginning to look ominous, she and Willie were getting ready to go into the cistern to verify whether or not it could serve as the escape hatch for Ayden. She stood before the mirror, examining herself. During the past few years, she had discarded her quest for beauty. Instead, she had been focusing on exercising her mind and increasing her intelligence. She figured that, if she wanted to stand at the side of her Primate, she had to prove herself worthy of that status. Ayden had been sending her lists of books to read, and then they would spend all their visiting time discussing the theories and practices offered in those pages. The others had no idea what they were talking about—making Melody feel more powerful than she had ever felt in her life.

She had grown tired of Willie's nonsense. The sex was good but predictable. Willie would do anything that she asked and going into the cistern was just another way to please her. All Melody had to do was ask and Willie was there. But she longed for Ayden. Now that she had been connecting with Ayden on an intellectual level, Willie's days were numbered.

Melody wanted nothing more than to be with Ayden. Worldly possessions meant absolutely nothing to her. She didn't need the things that most women coveted. Her drab peasant-like clothes were easy to make and suited her lifestyle. But today she donned old kaki-colored trousers, a plain knit shirt, a light-weight jacket, and a cheap pair of heavy rubber boots. Long skirts were not the proper attire for someone who would be crawling around in a water-filled cistern. Her taste in jewelry was simple—two copper rings, one wide copper bracelet, and a heavy silver chain holding a large Maltese cross with a tiny diamond in the middle—presents from Willie. She would wear the cross today as a symbol of things to come. Melody had studied Ayden's sketches carefully, scrutinizing all the markings and measurements that her Master had extracted from the blueprints he had found. She would be the one to put Ayden's plan into action. *How grateful he will be!* Willie would do the manual labor, but Melody would use her brains and bring her true love, her Primate, home to her once again. She prayed that she would find no barriers in their way.

With Eddie's help, Willie was busy stuffing a large canvas bag with an odd assortment of tools: crowbars, gloves, ropes, flashlights, a chain winch, two large batteries, and a spool of wire. Today, Melody and he would investigate the tunnel to determine if they could reach the grate beneath the prison library. To Willie, it was like a scavenger hunt, and he was getting as excited as Melody at the thought of having his best friend back. Willie giggled when Eddie handed him two miners' caps, and he was fascinated that they had lights; he knew that this day was going to be lots of fun.

Eddie had reviewed the plan with Melody several times—each time trying to convince her that he should be the one to go along with Willie. But Melody insisted that it was she who could best direct Willie and get him to do whatever had to be done in order to secure Ayden's freedom. Besides, she wasn't afraid of anything. In fact, she had been eager to show off to Sarah that she was the brave one, that she was the one who loved Ayden the most. Sarah wouldn't even go along when they had gone to check where the cistern opening was located. Melody was certain that Sarah was going to rue the day she had decided she could not possibly go through the cistern. *When the praises come from Ayden, and they would, Sarah would regret her faint-heartedness.*

Rebekah and Sarah stood on the steps of their run-down rented home and waved good-by as Melody drove the truck down the bumpy dirt road. "Bye," Willie shouted excitedly.

Willie was busy trying on his miner's cap and playing with the light. "Look Melody, my head lights up."

"Take the hat off now, Willie. Remember, we don't want anyone to see us with this stuff. We've got to be careful now. You want to get Ayden out, don't you?"

"Sure I do. Ayden's my best friend. He shouldn't be in that dumb jail. And I'm gonna get him out. Well, you too, Melody," Willie said as he reluctantly put the miner's hat away.

Melody drove very cautiously, obeying all the stop signs and the speed limits. Keeping one eye on Willie, and the other on the dark clouds that seemed to be moving in rapidly, Melody followed the dirt lane that ended within fifty feet of the sewer. She backed the truck into some heavy brush. When she got out of the truck, she was pleased to see that it was almost completely hidden. And, since the sky was now filled with dark clouds, she was certain that no one would notice that it was there. Willie carried all the equipment to the sewer system opening, and Melody gave him directions regarding how they would proceed. According to Ayden's notes, the main sewer ran under Westhall Street and should intersect at the southeast corner with the line coming out of the prison itself. She couldn't quite understand what was beyond the intersection since the drawing was a little vague at that point, but all she was worried about was getting through the line and beneath the prison library. And, if that wall ladder was still in place, Ayden would be free within a day or two.

The two of them strung wire along the wall as they went in, to provide a guide in case the flashlights failed. Melody wore a small backpack filled with tools, while Willie carried the larger items in a canvas bag. As they trudged along in the three inches of murky water, they laughed and giggled like children exploring a treasure cave. Melody kept checking the diagram and measuring the distance they had traveled, using the markings on the wire. The half-mile-long, 48-inch wide brick storm system was easy to navigate.

Melody suddenly came to an opening where the cistern widened. A heavy steel gate at least six-feet wide prevented them for going any farther. Willie retrieved the larger flash light from his canvas bag, and they both studied the formidable barrier carefully.

“Can we get in there?” Melody asked. “Willie, look, there’s the ladder Ayden talked about—his own Jacob’s ladder—it’s in there,” Melody said excitedly. “All we have to do is figure out a way to open this damned gate.”

Willie, shining the wide beam of light around the perimeter of the grate, answered, “I think we can get in there, Melody, but we’re gonna need more stuff.”

“Wait, shine the light over there, Willie,” Melody urged, pointing to the left. “According to the diagram, there’s some kind of wall or door over there. Let’s take a look. Maybe we can get in that way.”

They trudged another fifty feet or so and discovered what looked to them like a solid steel wall. “Damn, that’s rock-solid,” Melody said.

As they turned away to return to the gate, part of the steel wall suddenly opened and a mass of water, rushing with a tremendous force, surged through the cavity, knocking them to the ground. Unknown to them, this was a diversion wall that opened when the system became filled with too much water. Melody and Willie had been unaware that a heavy rain storm had suddenly moved in and the gates had opened to force the excess water out of the system and into the river.

Melody tried in vain to grab on to Willie, but she was swept away from him quickly. As the water spewed out, she tried to get the pack off her back. The water was forcing her body through the system like a rag doll and her rubber boots bobbed up and down as she tried to maintain some balance. Arms flailing in the air, trying unsuccessfully to find something to cling to, her body continued its way down the tunnel towards the river. The water was picking up speed as the current headed towards the sewer system opening. As she tried to keep her head above the cold harsh water, she found herself flattened against the side of the tunnel with her face only inches away from the top of the subway. She cried out for Ayden just as pressure was being applied to her neck, cutting off her oxygen. Her last realization was that the chain, holding the Maltese cross she was wearing around her neck, had caught on something, tightening itself around her throat, slowly drawing the life’s breath out of her. And, as the frigid water covered her head, claiming her as a victim, she was unaware that Willie’s lifeless body had just rushed past her.

CHAPTER 29

(Later that night)

The rainstorm was one of the worst that Charlie had ever seen. He had just arrived at the prison an hour earlier for the start of his night-shift duty. Hail pounded on the metal roof, bouncing up into the air, and landing in the exercise yard. Lightning streaked across the sky, and the electric flashes almost looked like it could very well be the end of the world. Charlie didn't like thunderstorms, but he had to put on a brave front as he walked around the prison for bed check. Something was wrong. He sensed that all was not right, so he took extra precautions as he peered into each cell, making certain that each inmate was in his cot and accounted for. However, his intuition apparently had been off kilter tonight because he could find nothing out of the ordinary. In fact, after the storm had passed, it had become eerily quiet.

Just an hour before their shift was over, the guards received a signal indicating that there might have been an escape. Before he rushed to his station, Charlie took the time to check Ayden's cell. To his relief, the inmate most skilled at escapes was curled up on his cot fast asleep.

When he entered the briefing room, there was a great deal of noise and the guards were second-guessing one another as to what could have occurred. As the superintendent entered the room, the men quieted down and took their seats.

"Something has happened that might indicate that an inmate may be planning an escape from our facility. At dawn, a tug boat captain spotted two bodies—one male and one female—caught up in heavy debris in the Ohio River, directly opposite the prison cistern. The victims were both wearing rubber boots and were carrying various items on their persons that could be used by spelunkers. Law enforcement has informed us that they believe that the two may have entered the cistern before the storm began and were caught when the extra water was forcefully discharged through the cistern. Police found a truck parked near the entrance of the cistern, and they are currently investigating ownership of the vehicle. Of course, our first suspect is Ayden Ash. We will be interviewing him shortly. However, you are ordered not to discuss this with any of the inmates. If there was a planned escape, we must find out how they knew about the cistern and who was involved in the plan. The media will be all over this in the early news, so we have shut down all television reception and inmate accessible telephones until we have fully questioned Ash. If there was no plan in the works, we don't really want to plant any more ideas in the heads of our guests."

"Sir," Charlie said, "several months ago Ash was assigned duty in the library, and before that he was working with Omar in the kitchen. You may want to speak with both Milton and Freddie before you interview Ash—just a suggestion, sir."

"Good idea. Keep your ears open and your mouths closed about this, and I will brief you again once I have further details to share."

As the guards filed out, Charlie, who had previously been relieved when he had spotted Ayden asleep in his cot, began to worry once more. He was the one who had recommended that Ayden be allowed to work in the kitchen and then in the library. He couldn't make a connection to a prison break with either of these two locations. Both Milton and Freddie were long-time friends of his, as well as faithful prison employees, and he would trust them with his own life. But that damn Ash might have gotten to one of them—but which one?

CHAPTER 30

(Two days later)

The bodies had been removed from the Ohio River and had been lying in the morgue, side by side, in cold steel drawers, for two days. The police had found a battered truck parked near the cistern. At first, they hadn't been able to identify the owner. However, after receiving a telephone tip, they had tracked ownership to a local cult who had denied that any of their people were missing, but after some intense questioning by the police, they had begrudgingly provided the names of the two dead people. They refused to accept any responsibility for taking care of the bodies and had quickly provided the police with the names of Melody's and Willie's parents. When the police deduced what the two were doing in the cistern, they escorted Eddie, Rebekah and Sarah to police headquarters and turned the children over to Child Welfare.

Melody's father arrived at the morgue early in the morning. Mr. Baker was a gentle, gray-haired man, stooped over from working in the coal mines for many years. Hesitantly, he approached the guard and questioned him about a corpse that might be his daughter. In a quivering voice, Mr. Baker probed further, explaining that he had received a phone call that his daughter had been drowned and her body was in the morgue.

"I cannot believe that it could be my little girl," he said. "It cannot be true."

The attendant slowly pulled back the white sheet that covered Melody's body like a transparent vapor. Mr. Baker gasped, closed his eyes tightly, and began weeping softly.

Melody's face was bloated, causing her features to blend into one another, creating a gruesome effect for the frail man to behold.

"Your daughter?" was all the attendant could ask.

Without saying a word, the man nodded his head and wept unashamedly. The attendant recovered the body and began pushing Melody back into the cold, dark cavern, when her father put his hand on the her rigid body and said, "No, please, no. Don't put her back in there, please. Can't you let her out here? I'll get someone to come for her, but please don't put her back in there."

"Certainly, Mr. Baker. We have the body of a man who also drowned. Since he was with your daughter, we thought you might know something about him. Would you mind taking a look?" the burly attendant said in a gentle voice that belied his gruff appearance. "We believe we know who he is, but so far no one has come forward to make a proper identification."

Mr. Baker stood there, watching as the attendant opened the metal door and pulled out another body and turned back the sheet.

"No, I don't know who he is."

"Thank you, sir. The lieutenant wants to speak with you to explain what we believe happened. Then, you can make the necessary arrangements to take care of your daughter."

"Yeah," Mr. Baker said. "My daughter, my only daughter is dead and I don't know why."

Just then Lieutenant McCoy came out of the office and said, "We just got a call from the police that a woman is on her way to see if the man who drowned with Miss Baker is her son. She'll be here sometime this evening." As he approached Mr. Baker, he said, "Sir, come with me, please. I'll explain everything."

McCoy helped Mr. Baker make the calls necessary to remove Melody's body before he began sharing what information he had about her.

"You see, Lieutenant, Melody moved out of my home many years ago. She wanted to go to the big city and find herself. This is the first time I've seen her since then," Mr. Baker recited.

"And you did not recognize the man?"

"No. I don't know who that poor soul was. That's how my daughter will be referred to now, won't she? *Was.* She *was* my daughter," Melody's father said forlornly. "Why was she found in the river?"

"Well, sir, your daughter may have been involved in a small religious cult, located right outside the city. And their leader, Primate, I think they called him, is an inmate at the prison. We believe that your daughter and the man, who we think is an escaped convict from Ohio, were drowned in the sewer, plotting a way to get their leader out of prison."

Mr. Baker stared at the officer with a blank look. Hardly moving at all, appearing to be as cold and stiff as his daughter's dead body, he sat riveted to his chair. His wrinkled, weather-worn skin made him look years older than he really was and his frail body seemed to grow smaller as the conversation continued.

"Melody wasn't religious. I don't know why she would join a cult. She was my only daughter—got three sons—all in the service. Oh, she loved to draw. She was good you know—real good. She'd draw pictures for her younger brother to color and then she'd hang them up on the wall just like they was real important." Mr. Baker suddenly stopped talking and turned around to check on Melody's body. Seeing it there, still covered by the sheet, he asked, "My little girl, did she suffer much?"

Shutting out the image of the bruised and battered girl, McCoy replied, "No, sir, she went quickly."

"I see," said Mr. Baker. "Quickly, you say. I guess that's got to be my comfort. I loved her, you know. She didn't think I did, but I did. She was like a wild flower—not ever wanting to do what others did. She had her own ways, but I loved her and so did her brothers. They used to go down into the caves in our area and..." Mr. Baker stopped, thought for awhile and then said, "Maybe she just went down there to explore like she did with her brothers when they was teen-agers. Maybe she wasn't doing anything bad at all."

Just then the office door opened and the attendant said, "Mr. Baker, the Nelson Funeral Home is here. As soon as you sign these papers, I can release the body."

Melody's father stood up, shook the lieutenant's hand and said, "You know what? I wouldn't want your job for all the tea in China."

McCoy smiled softly. He appreciated the fact that this kind man, even in his sorrow, realized that the lieutenant had to deal with situations like this every day.

"Mr. Baker, your daughter was lucky to have a father like you. You may go now. I wish the best for you, sir."

McCoy sighed and looked at the wall clock. Tonight, another parent would be standing here looking at a dead body. Depression was setting in again. *After fifteen years on the force, I should be handling this part of the job in a much more detached fashion. Detachment hell—that's impossible!*

CHAPTER 31

(December, 1981)

Despite the superintendent's best efforts, word of the drowning and the probable connection to the prison had spread rapidly throughout the prison population. Even before the bodies had been identified as two local cult members, all fingers had been pointed at Ayden. The suspect had been removed from his cell and placed in the restricted housing unit (RHU) unit, where he still resided eight months later. Ayden had been livid that he had been abruptly removed from his cell and physically tossed in the most hated part of the prison. All he was able to see out his new cell was a huge, cement block wall. The other prisoners in the RHU had learned how to throw their voices against the ugly wall so that they could understand one another and actually hold conversations. Inmates in the RHU, who were working on their cases, were allowed to use a tiny cell—about as big as a phone booth—positioned directly beside the guards' station for only two hours a week. They were also given one hour a week to use law books from the library. However, the only time Ayden had been allowed out of his cell was one hour a day and to shower and exercise. His right to use books from the library had been suspended for six months. He steadfastly maintained that he had no knowledge that any cult members had planned to investigate the cistern, but that argument had fallen on deaf ears. Ayden had fired off several irate letters to his attorney, demanding that he file a civil suit against the Department of Corrections. But no such suit was ever processed.

The administration of the prison had conducted a lengthy investigation into the possibility that Ayden might have had help from prison staff. Freddie, the head cook, had been removed from any suspicion very early, but Milton hadn't been so lucky. He had to endure several intense interviews with law enforcement. The mild-mannered librarian had been embarrassed and ashamed when he admitted that he had given Ayden the assignment to clean out the map drawers. The superintendent then examined the drawers that Ayden had been working with and very quickly had found the blueprint of the cistern. Milton felt that if he had done that job himself, the escape attempt would never have happened. Milton had previously won accolades for what he had done for the prison library, and now it was difficult for him to handle being under suspicion. Even though the superintendent had told him that none of the other administrators had been aware of the grate that would allow access to the cistern, Milton hadn't felt any better. The superintendent hadn't accused Milton of any wrongdoing, but the gentle librarian was doing a good job of punishing himself mentally. He was morose for months and, for the first time since he had accepted the position of prison librarian, he began taking sick days.

While Ayden's visitation privileges had been suspended, he still had access to mail. All communications sent to inmates at the prison were automatically opened by staff in the mail room. Any contraband was removed, any inappropriate photographs were destroyed, and anything unusual was reported to the superintendent.

Today, he had received another letter from Sarah. As usual, she droned on and on about how much she missed him and how unjust it was that he had been placed in the RHU. Almost as an addendum, she added that his old friend, Pete, was now the father of a baby girl. It was always hurtful whenever Ayden allowed himself to think about how Pete had abandoned him—never supporting him in any way. When he had first met Pete, Ayden felt that the two of them had developed some type of mutual respect for one another—at least they respected the right of each other to hold dear to his own values and beliefs. Pete had let him down time after time. But Pete had shown his true colors with the biased article that he had written about the drowning. Ayden was angry that Pete had placed the blame on him for Melody and Willie's demise—Melody, at least, should have kept her eyes on the weather—he thought the woman was smarter than that. While Pete had mentioned that Ayden was an author, he never listed the titles of his most popular publications—surely an act of jealousy.

Ayden spitefully decided that as soon as he was allowed to place a commissary order, he would get a card and send it to congratulate the mother and the father of the new baby girl. Down deep, inside his own psyche, Ayden hoped that the card would rattle their peaceful existence. Pete had disrespected him, and now it would be Ayden's turn to get back at the traitor.

Ayden propped his head on a pillow, leaned back, and began to form a plan to get revenge on Pete. Then, silently, like most geniuses, he got the answer. *A baby girl. How nice. Now I have something to use when I get my revenge on my old friend. Be wary, my old comrade. Be careful what you wish for. You never know who will get the last laugh. A baby girl. How delicious!*

PART FOUR

SWEET REVENGE

If this is what you do, I swear I will not stop until I have taken revenge on you. Judges 15:7

CHAPTER 32

(1990)

Darrell Windsor, psychiatrist at the Allegheny State Prison, was sitting in his office, waiting for his next patient with a feeling of great exhilaration. He had finally met someone who could inspire him, someone with whom he could establish a unique relationship. The prisoner that he was expecting any minute had, in just a few short months, changed Darrell's life like no one else ever had, including his wife Vicky. Ayden Ash had shown him the true meaning of life and had provided Darrell with a source of supreme strength, a never-ending font of revelation.

Darrell began to reflect on recent events that had lead to his enlightenment. He had been assigned as Ayden's counselor, but within a relatively short period of time, they had reversed their roles—Ayden becoming the teacher and Darrell the student. Ayden had given him a sense of expectation of what the future could hold. He now understood that in order to eventually reach the silent, unknown dwelling of the infinite, he had to plant his feet firmly on the first and lowest branch of the Tree of Life. And, by using the sexual imagery found in the Jewish Kabbalah, to express his understanding of how the reunion of the male and female aspects of the divine transcends reality, he would, slowly but surely, start his journey up the ladder.

What a knowledgeable man that Ash is. How remarkable that he's been able to interpret the system of esoteric mystical speculation!

Darrell considered himself to be an extremely lucky man. For years he had been searching—searching for the truth which lay hidden beyond men bound by the mundane and archaic rules of society. He had been passed over again and again by institutions that had not found him to be a viable employee. Darrell had only accepted the job within the Department of Corrections because no one else had been able to see his potential. But he had never dreamt that here, in this damned prison, fate would send the all-knowing Master to him. Ayden had taught him that man was created for self-realization, self-investigation and psychological insight meditation. *I always knew that there was more, much more than what I had been taught in college. Out there, in the cosmos—the answers lie out there.*

Last evening, Darrell had had an opportunity to broach the subject of Jewish mysticism with a friend of his, only to hear harsh words of criticism. His friend considered the concept to be a museum piece—a grotesque offshoot from the normative Jewish tree. His friend had scoffed at the idea that anyone in this day and age would place any credence in such an outmoded philosophy. Darrell had held his tongue. He had wanted to tell his friend that he had found the leader, the Primate, of the new religion that would free men from their sexual bondage—a belief that could create peace and happiness. Then, his friend had gone on to preach that real scholars, knowledgeable about the Kabbalah and what it really stood for, would abhor any corruption of the meaning of Jewish mystics. He claimed that those who would dare to attempt such folly would be drawn into a web of decadence. *The fool will regret what he said to me. I will never share the message of truth with him.*

Darrell pulled Ayden's file from the desk drawer and started perusing the reports that it contained. After what the authorities claimed was a botched prison escape, which resulted in two cult members drowning, Ayden had been moved to five different prisons over the years, finally landing at Allegheny. Darrell shook his head in disbelief. The fools who had sentenced him in the first place had not realized that Ayden should not have been tried at all. Darrell rationalized that such behavior was somewhat understandable when one realized that the jurors, who had judged him, had never been exposed to the steps involved in building an egoless behavior. They had never been taught that forbearance, in the face of insult, was a characteristic that only true believers could ever attain. Ayden was teaching Darrell how to achieve complete absence of anger and to display mercy, even to the point of recalling only the good qualities of those who torment. Ayden believed that all humans still had the innocence of their infancy—what an enlightened approach to man's behavior!

The *coup de grace* was that Darrell had been successful in convincing his wife, Vicky, to also join the cult. They had sold their home and had moved in with the remnants of Ayden's little flock. With Ayden's guidance, and his own leadership ability, Darrell was certain that he would be able to increase the number of followers—a gift to his Primate.

Surprisingly, Vicky had accepted their new way of life as if it had always been a part of their marriage. Since sharing a residence with the cult members, Darrell had been able to choose from among the women in the cult whenever he wanted sex. But a secret passion, buried deep within Darrell's heart, had been his desire for sexual bonding with children—something that he had not told Vicky. It was Ayden who had made him realize that this was not a sin at all, but rather an awakening of the true sexual consciousness. Ayden advised him not to reveal his passion to his wife until she was fully aware of the philosophy of true love.

Within the prison, Darrell had become a forceful ally for Ayden. He had access to people who made Ayden's life in prison a bit more bearable. Darrell had a look of innocence about him and a soft, almost feminine-like voice, making him appear to be someone who posed no threat to anyone. In fact, many of his co-workers thought of Darrell as a bit of a *Casper Milquetoast*—lovable, trustworthy, but incapable of taking a strong stand for anything. He had been more than willing to run errands for Ayden—anything that his Primate wanted. Ayden had been granted special privileges within the prison which, ordinarily, would have been denied to anyone who had been involved in prison escapes. It was Darrell's way of repaying his Primate.

Ayden would not be eligible for parole for at least ten more years unless some type of deal could be worked out with the right people. But even if it did take that long, the cult would be there—ready to follow their Primate. Darrell was willing to walk in the footsteps of his

Primate, to serve as well as he could, until such time as Ayden could, once again, take over the reins of leadership. *Out of the dark damp recesses of the Allegheny State Prison, a disciple will arise and lead the people of the world to the Promised Land—of that I'm certain.*

CHAPTER 33

(1990)

Pete was busy setting up the badminton net when his daughter, Anastasia, ran past him and into the house. He smiled broadly. She was going to be the spitting image of her mother. He couldn't believe that Ana was going to be ten years old today. And it was definitely party time. Twelve little girls, from her fifth grade class in school, would soon be filing in, carrying brightly-colored, wrapped presents that would make Ana scream with delight. Not that she needed anything—her mother saw to that. Pete had used what little creative skills he possessed to make a donkey out of heavy cardboard so the children could play *Pin the Tail on the Donkey*. Jeanette had thought that this game was passé, but Ana insisted that she wanted to play it and, after several hours of cutting, snipping and pasting, she made brightly-colored paper tails for the girls to use. Ana had arranged little party packages, filled with goodies and small toys, on both sides of the wooden picnic table. Ana fussed, just like her mother did with most things, to make certain that the little bags were all placed exactly in front of each plate. The birthday cake had been positioned on a side table, which had been covered with a pink tablecloth. All was ready for the guests.

"Hi, Dad," Cindy said as she stepped out onto the patio. "Need any help out here?"

"Don't think so. I never knew there was so much work involved in getting ready to entertain little girls."

"Well, when I was young, you copped out by taking us all out to the arcade at birthday time," Cindy said as she placed a kiss on her dad's cheek.

"How's your little theater group going, honey?" Pete asked.

"I was just going to talk with you about that. We plan to present two plays at Camp Morningside next month, and I want your permission to ask Ana if she wants to be in one of the plays. I think she'd make a perfect princess. What do you think?"

"Are you kidding? She wants to do everything that you do—she loves to act. I can't tell you how many shows she's put on for us. And she always charges us a quarter to attend," Pete said laughingly.

"You do know that it's a religious camp, don't you, Dad? I wasn't sure how you would feel about that."

"Who's sponsoring the camp?"

"I believe that it's a group of four or five churches from the city who have joined together to allow underprivileged children to attend camp for a week. They plan to have it open for only a month."

"How long is she going to be there?" Pete asked.

"Only three days. We'll have rehearsals twice and then we'll put on the shows. I'll keep her with me, Dad. She'll be safe."

When Ana was told about Cindy's invitation, and that she was going to be in one of Cindy's plays, she was ecstatic. "This is the best birthday I have ever had," she declared.

The party was a huge success. Pete had never heard so much giggling and laughing in all of his life, and he had loved every minute of it. The girls hadn't stayed still for any length of time. One minute they were involved in the badminton game and the next they were off chasing one another around the trees.

Later that evening, when Jeanette and he had finally curled up on the sofa with glasses of wine, Pete said, "Woman, do you know how happy you have made this old man?"

"No, why don't you tell me," Jeanette asked.

"How high is a mountain, how high is the..."

"Never mind, sweetie, I get the picture."

"Our two girls really like one another. It looks like we might have another actress in the family. Oh, did you know that Cindy wrote both of the plays that they're going to perform? I guess she gets her talent from her old man," Pete said as he put his arm around Jeanette. "My mom used to tell me *the apple doesn't fall too far from the tree.*"

Pete leaned over to pick up a book from the endtable.

"Pete, before you begin reading, there's something I want to tell you," Jeanette said, as she sat up.

"Oh, this sounds intriguing," Pete said as he leaned over and touched Jeanette's hair.

"I didn't want to tell you this in front of the girls—I saw Greg today."

Pete looked confused. "Greg?"

"You know, the guy that broke into our room on the islands and the one that I went to..."

"Oh, him. Where did you see him?"

"At Walmart. When I was picking up last minute things for Ana's party, I bumped into him—rather he bumped into me. I was shocked, to say the least."

"What did he have to say, and be careful about this, I'm an insanely jealous husband," Pete teased.

"He wanted to know why I dumped him after the séance. I told him I was so embarrassed and humiliated that I had gone there that I couldn't find the courage to face him again."

"Did he say how he found us in the islands?"

"Dumb luck, he told me. And, when I asked him why he just didn't hand me the peace necklace, he said the most touching thing."

"And, what was that?"

"He said that he was on the island working as a bartender. He admitted that he had always carried my necklace in his pocket—sentimental gesture. He felt that it was not a good time to approach me. So, he decided to just sneak into our room and leave it where I would find it. He admitted that it had been a stupid idea. Pete, he apologized profusely—not only for the necklace escapade, but for taking me to the séance," Jeanette said, as she reached up and took Pete's hand.

"Sounds like a nice guy. I would love to hate him, but now I can't."

Jeanette got up on her knees, took Pete's face in her hands, and kissed him. Then she said, "You're so sweet—no wonder I love you."

After Jeanette stood up, Pete reached for the remote and clicked on the eleven o-clock news. "Oh, my God! Jeanette, look—its Ayden Ash."

The close-up of Ayden on the screen made it appear that he was looking directly at Pete.

Jeanette leaned forward to get as close to the TV screen as she could.

The newscaster said, "The wife of Darrell Windsor, a psychiatrist at Allegheny Prison, was found dead in a wooded area from an apparent suicide. A note near her body indicated she had been connected to a small, religious cult headed by Ayden Ash, an inmate at the same prison. Upon further investigation, law enforcement discovered that both she and her husband had been living with the cult for the past few months. The leader of the cult, Ayden Ash, who was Dr. Windsor's patient, had been found guilty of sexual molestation of children in 1973. Prison officials refused to be interviewed for this report."

"The man was a psychiatrist. How could he have fallen for Ayden's theories? A psychiatrist, by God," Jeanette said. "Now his wife's dead. How many more will there be? Do you realize how many people's lives he has ruined? Melody Baker, and Willie—I forget his last name—Martin Culver and his wife and all the children he's molested."

Pete began pacing back and forth in front of the television set. "Will this ever end? He reaches out to people, even from behind bars, and destroys one person after another. Windsor was a college-educated man, yet Ayden had been able to get him to join his cult. But why did his wife kill herself? I bet she knew something—something that she had been unable to handle mentally—but then, maybe we will never know."

Eddie worked as fast as he could, gathering the few items that they could jam into a dilapidated station wagon. The cult was on the move once more. It wasn't Ayden's fault that Vicky had killed herself. The woman had never fully accepted or understood what the rest of them knew to be the truth. When she had walked in on Darrell, who was teaching one of the children how to please him, Vicky had screamed and had run away. Her reaction did not surprise him. From the first day that she had moved in with them, Eddie did not trust her. She was a weak-willed person—someone who had always hung on the edge of the group, watching—watching—never saying much of anything. Eddie was angry with her. Ayden had been depending on Darrell for financial support and for the leadership necessary to allow the group to grow spiritually. Now, because of that stupid bitch, those plans could go up in smoke. He was somewhat relieved when he spotted Darrell driving up the road.

"I'm ready," he said. "I'm ready to join you full-time. I severed my ties with the prison."

"What about Vicky?"

"What about her? She shot herself—plain and simple. She just did not have the intelligence she needed to become one of us. I have made all the arrangements for her, but I no longer have a job at the prison, so I'm ready to move on," Darrell said as he peered into the station wagon to see what Eddie had loaded.

"Money. How about the money we need?" Eddie asked.

"I've got enough and I have a place where we can go. Ayden has passed the gauntlet on to me, if you don't mind," Darrell explained patiently.

"Mind? Hell, no. I'm relieved. Whatever you say, Darrell—from now on, you're the boss."

CHAPTER 34

(November, 1990)

John Murray leaned against his truck and looked down over the hills. He was waiting for his next customers. He loved this place. The trial, which he had tried so hard to wipe from his mind, had occurred about seventeen years ago. Even after all of these years, he was still concerned about Amanda's welfare. Doc Nesbit had been their guardian angel. Not only did he testify at Ayden's trial, he was also by Amanda's side when she lost her baby due to a miscarriage. His concern about Amanda, and her well-being, surfaced once again some time later when he offered John the job of taking care of the Christmas tree farm. Both John and Margaret had hoped that by moving to the countryside and running the farm, Amanda would heal her troubled heart.

But when her mother was killed by a drunk driver, Amanda went deeper and deeper into depression. John would often say to himself '*why not*' when he would think about all the heartaches this precious young woman had suffered. She was only fourteen at the time of the trial and had to face her molester in the courtroom. Then, she had seen her own father, who had abandoned her when she was only five, killed by the police on the steps of the courthouse. Amanda had thought she had found true love when she ran off with Charlie Foreman—but the happiness she was looking for never materialized. When Amanda lost her baby, Charlie had abandoned her. When she finally returned home, teary-eyed and desolate, both he and Margaret had assured her that she would be safe with them. But the media wouldn't let go of her involvement with Ash, and despite John's pleas, they would stalk her, trying to get more seedy details about what had happened in the little church school.

It was a stroke of good luck when Doc Nesbit had approached John and asked him if he would consider managing his Christmas tree farm. He had explained that he would train John and assured him that he would love working on the tree farm—and Nesbit was right—John loved the job. And, since the job came with a rent-free home, it had been a win-win deal for his family. While it was Margaret who looked after Doc's mother, who lived in a big white colonial house, it was Amanda that the old woman took under her wing. Gradually, Amanda had become a polished, well-mannered young lady. Mrs. Nesbit would have tea with Amanda each day promptly at four. Sometimes, John would peek into the large, living room window to watch Amanda and Mrs. Nesbit as they chatted. John would learn later that Mrs. Nesbit had not only helped Amanda with her grammar, but she had also taught her a great deal about art. In fact, Mrs. Nesbit had given Amanda an easel and paints, and John would often see them sitting side by side, painting whatever they saw before their eyes. Amanda had adored Mrs. Nesbit and took it very hard when the old woman passed away at the age of ninety-two. One of Amanda's prized possessions was a painting that Mrs. Nesbit had completed right before her death. The battered-looking easel that Mrs. Nesbit always used still sat in the solarium of the big, colonial home, with her painting of the surrounding hillside perched on its ledge. Amanda treasured the painting, and she loved the room. She began taking art lessons from a local artist, and before John knew it, the young girl was turning out paintings of her own. However, the solarium remained her place of solace.

When he heard the noise of the big tractor-trailer, John knew his next customers were arriving. They had never been here before. John's only contact with them had been by phone when they placed a large order for trees. The men didn't look very honest, so he watched them carefully as they loaded the beautiful evergreen trees. One by one, the trees were placed on the bailer, where they were bundled, trunk end first, creating identical cylindrical-shaped bundles. Each tree was held in place by small paddles between the chain mechanism as they moved slowly down the twenty-five foot elevator and up into the trailer. Unlike unscrupulous growers, who sometimes shoved two undesirable trees into one bundle, John had always made certain that his customers got the best evergreens possible. He could have helped the men, but he stood there, holding his machete at his side, a symbol of his power. He would use it if he had to. No way were they going to get out of here without giving John the money. John had learned how to wield this razor sharp instrument like an expert since starting to work on the tree farm years ago. One false move and one of the men would be minus an arm or a leg. Selling Christmas trees wholesale was a *cash-only* business—no checks and certainly no credit cards—money on the barrel head. Once that truck pulled out, the deal would be completed. John kept his eyes glued on the men. *If they ain't Mafia, I'll eat every one of them trees.*

According to John's count, the men had to load just one hundred more trees and they would be finished. He had worked hard getting this large load ready for pick-up. Each tree had to be cut down and hauled out to the dirt lane. Then, he had to use the wagon and tractor to haul them to the site where the truck would pull in. He had moved a lot of trees out of here this season. That would mean an extra big bonus, just in time to buy holiday presents for his family.

Since John had been living here on the farm, he had never been happier. No dirty streets, no hustle and bustle, just beautiful green trees and serene blue skies. *Well, most of the time anyway.* He loved the work, and since a great deal of the labor was seasonal, he had had lots of time to pursue his hobby of wood carving. Even if John had to say so himself, he was getting better with each new creation. To add to his contentment, John had married. His wife Sue, and her daughter Evelyn, brought stability to the little household.

In a few months, it would be time to plant another 1400 acres of seedlings which would be beautiful scotch-pine trees in ten years. John realized that when it would be time to harvest those seedlings, it would also be time to harvest Ayden Ash. The bastard would be coming up for parole in the year 2000. A long time ago, John had made himself a vow that he would finish the job that Amanda's daddy had been unable to complete. But John's plan would not fail. While he may have to wait ten years or more before that weasel got paroled, that child molester would get his just rewards. How, John was not certain yet, but he had at least ten years to work on his plan. And, by that time, John would be ready.

The two men loading the trees surely did not look as if they were in the tree business. They were both wearing expensive leather jackets and snake skin boots. Their jeans sported designer labels on the pockets, and John could see that one of them was wearing a flashy diamond ring on his pinkie finger.

"Well, that does it," the taller man said as he flung the last tree on the top of the heap. "These trees are headed for New York City, pal. We're gonna get at least a hundred bucks for each one of them. Think of the money we'll be making. Maybe we'll come back for more. Now, we've got to get on the road."

John approached the men slowly, still holding his machete. "All we need now, gents, is the money."

The second man, carrying a small valise, came around the front of the truck and said, "Hey, man, you think we was gonna stick you? We don't do business like that. We got the dough." And, with that, he handed John eight thousand dollars.

John liked the feel of all that money. The most John had ever collected at one time was seven hundred dollars and that was when he had received his income tax refund a couple of years ago.

"Nice doing business with gents like you," John replied as he handed over the bill of sale. "You mind if I ask you a question?"

"That depends on the question," the owner of the diamond ring answered.

"Well, what would happen if you were stopped by the cops and you didn't have that bill of sale?" John asked as he pointed to the slip of yellow paper that the other man was putting into the empty valise.

"Are you kidding? First place, I've never been pulled over. But a friend of mine was and he had been hauling trees which he hadn't bothered to pay for. Get my drift?"

"And what happened?"

The two chuckled. "The dude spent some time in the slammer. It seems that the owner of the trees didn't know nothing about my friend taking them. Are you thinking of setting up a little tree scam with us?"

John scowled. “I was just curious. Doc’s good to me. I don’t intend to spoil what I have here.”

“If you do, look us up,” the driver shouted as he gunned the engine and slowly pulled the big red tractor-trailer out of the driveway, heading down the mountain road.

John watched the truck winding its way down to the interstate. And then it all came to him in a flash—he knew how he could easily dispose of Ayden’s dead body. He would use the bundler to secure Ayden before pushing him into the pond and drowning him. Then he would bury the body in between the scrub trees where no one would ever find it. All John had to do now was to develop a plan to get Ayden to the farm—from there on it would be as easy as taking candy from a baby.

CHAPTER 35

(1995)

Darrell had driven Sarah to the prison for her monthly meeting with Ayden. She was depressed. Just last week Ayden had met with the parole board, and it had denied his request. Sarah had been certain that Ayden would be granted parole, particularly since he had been complying with all the rules and regulations of the prison. This morning Darrell had given her a lecture on how she should behave during her visit with Ayden. She didn't like taking orders from Darrell. He would never take Ayden's place—if it were up to Sarah.

"You must remember, Sarah, that when you visit with Ayden, you set the tone for the two hours that you are there. If you go in with a long face, and he sees that you are depressed, he, too, will be that way. On the other hand, if you are upbeat and hopeful, you will engender that energy in Ayden. He needs to feel that way now more than ever."

She was getting tired of Darrell's psycho-babble and wanted her Primate back in her life. As she entered the prison, she was relieved to see that only one other person was waiting to get into the visitors' room. Sarah sat down on the bench. Suddenly, she became aware that the guards were looking at her and they were whispering to one another. She wanted to stand up and smack their faces—but she knew that she could never do that.

Picking up her purse, Sarah walked over to the row of little, gray metal lockers, opened one of the doors and placed her purse inside. After she locked it, she put the little key in her dress pocket. She carried a small plastic bag that held five dollars in change in her hand. She would use this money to purchase whatever Ayden wanted out of the vending machines—one of the few perks that inmates were allowed.

"We're ready for you now, Mrs. Ash," said the guard.

After she passed through the detector, the guard pressed a button to allow the first gray metal door to open. Sarah stepped into the small space to wait for the inside guard to open the next door. As the second door slammed behind her, Sarah jumped. For all these years, she hated the doors and the noise they made. She saw and heard these doors in some of her dreams and found the very thought of them disconcerting.

The visiting room guard was sitting on a perch that allowed him to view all areas of the room. He nodded to her and then she took a seat. She watched as a young couple, who was seated on the floor with a toddler, played with the child by pushing toy trucks back and forth, belying the fact that they were all behind bars. As Sarah looked at the child, she could see that he was smiling broadly and reaching to be held by his father. That was something that Sarah would never have permitted. None of the children had ever been allowed to enter such an institution—certainly no place for children!

The door at the rear of the room opened and she stood up as she saw Ayden. He walked over to the guard on duty, slid his permission slip across the desk and joined Sarah. They embraced immediately. She wanted to cling to him—never to let him go—but he moved away quickly and sat down.

"Now, tell me all about our little family—everything. Then, I have some unexpected news to tell you."

Sarah's heart almost jumped into her mouth. Maybe the parole board had reversed its decision. She quickly updated Ayden on the new members that had joined their group. And, enthusiastically, she went into detail about the children and how wonderful they all were.

"Your first-born son is doing very well—growing so rapidly that it's hard to keep him in clothes that fit. All the children are doing well with their academic studies, thanks to Rebekah. And, Ayden, you should see how they all pitch in to do household chores," Sarah said excitedly.

"Are you being taken care of financially?" Ayden asked quietly.

"Yes, between what we earn from the sale of our crafts and what some of our members are making on their jobs, along with what Darrell contributes, we're doing fine. Darrell is considering opening a school, but we have not made any final plans about it," Sarah explained. "Ayden, what is your news?"

"First, let me tell you how proud I am that Darrell has been able to enlarge our little flock. Please tell him that. However, you didn't say anything about Eddie—how is he?"

"As usual, he comes and goes. But when he came back two weeks ago, he brought along a friend. I don't like him, though—he seems a bit uppity and orders Eddie around a lot."

"Sarah, my Sarah, I hear jealousy in your voice. That is a sin—one that you seem to have a problem with. You know this is a trait that will deny you access to all that can be achieved through true love. I have spoken with you about this on countless occasions. You must change your ways, Sarah, or you and I will not be united in the hereafter. So, let's move on. But, wait until you hear this—I heard from our Amanda!"

"Amanda Hoffman? The girl who testified against you?"

"Yes, that is the Amanda I mean. Sarah, you seem to have forgotten that it was you who gave the most damning testimony of all. It was you—not Amanda. Why do you always behave like this? Haven't you learned anything after all this time? Amanda may be quite helpful to all of us."

"Just how will that happen?" Sarah quipped.

"She now owns property that could be just the type of place that could prove to be a safe haven for all of us. Think of it, Sarah. In just a few years, I will be out of here. And Amanda might be the answer to our prayers for a stable place to stay."

"When did she come back into the picture, Ayden?"

"She wrote to me. She also sent me a picture—a beauty. She's eager to join us once again. Think of it. Don't always think about yourself. Remember, we're all one. We must move forward; looking back will only cause grief and pain. One cannot grow by looking back. Look toward the eventuality that we will all be together, living the kind of life that we have always wanted."

"Are you sure about her, Ayden? Are her motives pure in heart?"

"Amanda? Of course I am sure about her. I would share her letters with you, but I don't think you are ready for that much information.

I was going to mail them to you so you would have the privilege of reading her heartfelt words. Now you will never see them. I will destroy them. I had hoped that your jealousy would be under control by now. What about Darrell?"

"Darrell—what about him?"

"Does he come to you? Do you receive him?"

Sarah hung her head.

"Look at me, Sarah. Answer my questions." Ayden demanded.

"Yes, I receive him."

"And, you see, I'm not jealous at all. I know that the world is bigger than just the two of us. Our plans, our dreams, include all our members—without them, we will not succeed in changing the world at all," Ayden said. "If you are going to disappoint me like this, then don't bother to visit me again."

Abruptly, Ayden stood up, walked to the back of the room, and signaled the guard that he was ready to go back to his cell.

Sarah sat there for a few minutes. He had turned his back on her and walked away. She looked at the little bag of coins on her lap and wept.

CHAPTER 36

(June, 1995)

Although it would probably be another five years before Ayden could apply again for parole, he was working on his plan. He had read and re-read Amanda's latest letter over and over again. She was contrite. Amanda claimed that her mother had insisted that she testify against him in 1973. She didn't want to do it but had acquiesced to get her mother off her back. Amanda confessed that she had been jealous of Melody. He loved reading this line. Amanda indicated that she wanted to return to the group, but only after Ayden was paroled.

When he learned that her mother had been killed by a drunk driver, he smiled. But the most exciting news was that Amanda had used the proceeds from her lawsuit against the driver to purchase a Christmas tree farm. And, to make amends to Ayden, she wanted the cult to make the farm their permanent residence. *What a turn of good luck! His karma must now be aligning with the grand plan.*

But, in exchange for this harbor of safety, Amanda wanted to be Ayden's number one choice. He surely would not mind meeting her demands. Ayden had hung her picture in his cell with great pride. He decided that he would keep her all to himself—no sharing of this beautiful creature with any of the other cult members. She would be his *Queen*.

Ayden sat down at his small metal table and began to respond to Amanda's letter. He started off with, *My beautiful Amanda*. He didn't want to come on too strong, but he wanted to ensure her that she had always been his first choice. After all, it was he who had taught her all about the sexual experience and exactly how to please him, time after time. He asked her many questions about the Christmas tree farm and how it could protect and nurture the group. Ayden decided that from now on, he would only tell Darrell about his future plans—no one else needed to know until everything had been secured.

The Spirits were truly blessing him. Darrell had come along just in time to stabilize the cult, and his financial backing had allowed the cult to grow in size. Darrell assured him that all the members were adhering to Ayden's philosophy, and they were eagerly anticipating his release from prison. And now, Amanda, beautiful Amanda, had come back into his life. *After all the indignities that I have been through and enduring the lowest of lows, before too long, I will be rewarded—I will experience the highest of highs—with Amanda. I will be living off the proceeds of Margaret's death—what sweet revenge. I will have the money and Amanda. Rest in peace, Margaret.*

CHAPTER 37

(August, 1999)

Pete parked his car outside the red brick church and reached for his coffee cup. He was waiting for the bus that would be bringing Anastasia back from Camp Morningside, where she had been working as a counselor for the past three weeks. Pete was eager to see her once again. The two of them had a special bond that sometimes surprised and amazed Pete. Both enjoyed hiking. They would often spend hours investigating the mountainside around the city. Sometimes they would drive an hour or so away from home, park the car, and then hike new and mysterious trails—talking, laughing, sharing little stories—all the while strengthening the love between them. These treasured occasions had been filed away in his memory bank of favorite things—easily retrievable at a moment's notice.

They both also loved to read. Jeanette would often find them on the back patio, each curled up on a chaise lounge, with their noses buried deeply in books—Pete reading some mystery novel—Ana reading a non-fiction book about nature or animals. From time to time, they would put their books down and share what they had just read with one another. Then, there were those times the books would be resting on their laps while the two of them were content to just sit back and watch the clouds changing shapes. Ana would squeal with delight when Pete would agree with her that a certain cloud formation had formed an animal or a bird.

Around the time that Ana had started going to Camp Morningside during the summers, Pete had noticed a distinct change in her behavior. He was certain that his precious daughter had gone through a metamorphosis. She seemed more content to be alone without appearing to be lonely. While she still had friends coming and going, she started spending more time in her room, writing in her journal or creating poems that she would not share with anyone—not even Pete.

Ana, now nineteen, had been chosen as a camp counselor and her enthusiasm was impressive. She had spent months getting ready for this challenge. Just as her stepsister had done, Ana had written a play for the campers to put on for parents' night. Even Ana's graduation from high school, and the party that had followed, hadn't seemed to excite her as much as her becoming a camp counselor. Besides reading books that Cindy had recommended, Ana had had telephone contacts with several young people who had served as counselors in previous years. She had talked a great deal about a boy called Triple A. When Pete had asked her about the boy's curious name, Ana laughed and said that it was his nick-name and that she just assumed that he really didn't like his real name. But, it was how she had looked when she talked about Triple A that set Pete's mind off in a different direction. He had a sense that this boy was far more important to Ana than she wanted to admit. He knew that this day was coming—in fact, he had expected it sooner—the day when some male—someone he didn't know—would woo her away. He felt a twinge of jealousy raising its head every time Ana mentioned Triple A.

Just as he took his last sip of coffee, Pete spotted the bus rumbling down the street. He could hear the teen-agers singing from almost a block away. As the bus pulled up, it seemed as though there had been an explosion—campers tumbling out the front and the back of the bus, their arms loaded with clothing and sports equipment. Ana was helping the campers retrieve all of their belongings and waved briefly to Pete. As the other parents approached the bus to greet their children, Pete joined them.

"Bye, Miss Forster," one girl said as she gave Ana a big hug. "It was sooooo fun!"

"Miss Forster, are you going to be a counselor next year?" another girl asked.

"Perhaps, we'll see. I don't know if I can take all of you again," she said jokingly, as she hugged each one.

"Are you and Triple A really going steady?" one younger girl asked. "Mary Lou said you were."

Pete noticed that his daughter didn't answer this question. *Steady?* Maybe it's time to find out more about this guy.

On the way home, trying to sound as casual as possible, Pete asked, "Are you going steady?"

"Oh, Dad, you know how kids are. Triple A is a nice person who's about five or six years older than I am. We worked together very well, but no, there's no romance—at least, not yet."

CHAPTER 38

(November, 1999)

John and Amanda were sitting at the kitchen table, working on their plan to kill Ayden Ash. They could not remember exactly when they had decided to kill Ayden—it seemed to have evolved quite naturally—surprising neither one of them. They were almost certain that Ayden would get paroled by next year and they wanted to be ready.

"We have a great deal here to protect, John," Amanda said. "Especially now that we own the land."

"You own the land, Amanda. You purchased it. I'm just the manager. But I fully understand what you're saying," John replied. "You made a wise decision when you bought this property with the money you won from your lawsuit. Your mom would be so proud of you."

"This is really *her* place, John. She loved it here, too. And, if it hadn't been for that damned..."

"Honey, I know. Life's not fair. None of us come with any guarantees. But whatever I do to Ayden, it will be my doings, not yours."

"But, I'm the one who's writing to him—so, that makes me an accomplice. I'll be the one to lure him here to the farm."

"We don't have to do this. Do you want to back out?"

Amanda hesitated. She was filled with hatred for Ayden; but, at the same time, the farm had now given her a reason to move on—to let go of the past. But, John had been so good to her all these years, and he seemed adamant that Ayden had to be killed. She owed John a great deal. "No. He must go. He'll simply go on and on and use other young girls and children to satisfy his lust—he must go. We must plan carefully and make certain that his death cannot be traced to us," Amanda said. Her countenance changed. Then, she looked directly at John and then said, "I did so much lying when I was young—I thought it was a way to get attention. But I kept on lying about some things during the trial. Later, when I realized that those lies had been used in court to cast you in a bad light., I became ashamed of my behavior. For that, John, I am truly sorry. You have been so good to me. I pledge my loyalty to you and I will help you in any way to get rid of Ayden."

When Amanda had first approached John about purchasing the tree farm, John had been ambivalent. While he had wanted desperately to stay on the farm with all his heart, he wasn't sure that it would be the right thing for her. But, when she had told him about her plans for the great house, he knew that she had found her calling. Amanda wanted to turn the great house into an artists' haven—a place where artisans could gather to create, to teach, and to sell their wares. She wanted to create a place of beauty, a place where the lovely things of life would be celebrated.

John had created a new hand-carved sign and had hung it at the entrance to Amanda's property—*Amanda's Tree Farm.* And just from that little sign alone, John had received several orders from local merchants for similar hand-carved signs.

"Does Sue know anything about this? After all, most wives can sense when things are going on," Amanda questioned.

"Absolutely not. This is something that no one else will ever know. I'll make certain of that," John said, as he patted Amanda's hand.

They grew quiet—lost in their own thoughts. Finally, Amanda said, "I hated sending him my picture. Each time that I write to him, I feel sick to my stomach."

"I know, Amanda, but I knew that when he saw what a beauty you are, his ego would kick into high gear. He's probably shown that picture all over that damned prison."

"I don't want people to think badly of me anymore. I have had enough of that—people talking about me behind my back—pointing fingers at me wherever I go. He owes me a lot. He took so much from me. Now, I want to take things from him. What do we do next?"

"In your next letter, make sure you tell him about the great house—that it will be ready to accommodate the cult. How can he resist? You—the great house—and a tree farm—it will appear to be his Nirvana on earth," John said. "Now, don't you worry about how I'll accomplish the final blow. And, after I dispose of him, no one will ever know what happened to him. I won't even tell you."

"I know, but it all sounds so…"

"He won't know what hit him—quick and deadly. I'll make certain that you are not here when I do it. I'll be alone when the deed is done. I plan to trap him first in the tree bundler; that way he won't be able to get away from me. The rest will be quite easy. Now, we must work on a way to get him to the farm as soon as he's released. I've thought of several ways to do this, but I haven't zeroed in on just one, yet."

It was evident that the two trusted and loved one another—the odd couple, who had come together to commit *murder,* never spoke that word.

Amanda got up and said, "John, I'm going over to the big house and browse around a bit. I want some time alone so that I can let my imagination kick in regarding what I want to do with my property. Wow! Do you realize what I just said—*my property.* Who would've ever thought that such a little insignificant woman would own such a charming place?"

"Insignificant? No way! Amanda, you deserve everything you have. Just think how proud Mrs. Nesbit would be of you. Now go, little one, dream a bit. Just remember, I'll always be here for you—no matter what."

Amanda turned the key in the lock of the big house. She really should start to call this house *The Artists' Haven* all the time. She loved the name—she loved the idea even more. First, she went into the solarium with its beautiful stained-glass ceiling. The late fall sun was shining through the windows, creating a picture of happiness and joy. She could almost see artists at their easels, working away on creating scenes from their memories, their hearts, and their experiences—inspiring others to appreciate their beauty, their messages, long after the artists were no longer creating. She walked down the hallway and pushed on the double doors that led to a small, but elegant ballroom, complete with a diminutive stage. She could picture the room with mirrors and a ballet barre stretching along one side of the room. Her imagination allowed her to see little ones, in sparkling pink tutus, getting ready to pirouette across the hardwood floor.

Amanda pictured the large living room as an office and welcome center. Her plans included turning the former dining room into a gift shop, where customers would have the opportunity to purchase the products created on-site. She then climbed the staircase to the second floor, where five large bedrooms would soon accommodate artisans such as jewelry makers, writers, and perhaps sculptors, who not only wanted to create, but teach their crafts to others. Just thinking about the possibilities of such a place gave her chills. Perhaps she would meet with Doc Nesbit again to run some of these ideas by him—he could provide her with financial advice regarding how to get such a huge venture off the ground. She ran down the wide staircase, pretending that she was Scarlet O'Hara on her way to a ball. Dreams—are these just dreams—or could she, little Amanda, make any of them come true?

She sat down on the bottom step and cupped her face with her hands. She could almost see Mrs. Nesbit, her mentor, sitting at the tea table, placing her fine china tea set in just the right order. Amanda loved the way Mrs. Nesbit would crook her little finger as she gently lifted the lovely tea cup to her lips.

Amanda could hear her saying, "Remember, Amanda, never make a noise when you sip your tea. Ladies sip gently, quietly. And never put your elbows on the table."

Mrs. Nesbit had willed Amanda the tea set. Amanda would take it out of the box every so often to admire each piece. Maroon flowers, with a touch of yellow and white circled the teapot. It was the most beautiful possession that Amanda owned.

As she locked the front door, she walked to the edge of the porch where she could hear John as he and his workers were getting the last of the Christmas trees ready for shipment. The farm would be quiet for awhile—at least until planting time. She could see over to the next mountain and was amazed to see that the oaks and maples, which were resplendent with color only a few weeks ago, were now bare. They would soon be faced with another cold winter, but for them, it would only be a short time until their leaves would, once again, burst forth—renewing their crowning glory. Perhaps she could learn a lesson from these trees. If she allowed John's plan to go through, would she ever be able to renew herself? Or, would she, like Ayden, be trapped in a life of regret and hatred? And, what would Mrs. Nesbit say? Amanda wanted to be everything that Mrs. Nesbit wanted her to be—not a murderer.

CHAPTER 39

(March, 2000)

Pete and Jeanette were seated on the large sofa in their living room, when their attention was drawn to the latest news report.

"I can't believe that he's getting out. What the hell are they thinking—letting him out on parole? The court added years to his sentence for his prison breaks and now they are letting him out on parole for his good behavior! Their decision makes no sense" Pete shouted as he heard the latest news about Ayden.

"That's the way the system works. I bet the neighbors around his church aren't too happy about this," Jeanette said.

"They have every right to be angry. He'll start up again—you know that. He's like a moth drawn to a flame."

"Maybe he won't come back to New Valley. After all, his cult is living somewhere. Maybe he'll go there," Jeanette said.

"That would be fine for the people of New Valley. But the bastard has to go somewhere, and there's little anyone can do about that," Pete said disgustedly.

"Hey, you two, are you arguing? There will be no disagreements in this house," Cindy said playfully as she came bouncing into the living room with her friend, Evelyn.

Pete stood up and gathered his daughter into his arms. Cindy and Jeanette then embraced.

"Cindy, what a nice surprise—and Evelyn, it's nice to see you once again. I think it's been over six months since you've been here. How's your mother doing?"

"Just fine, still living on a tree farm and loving it," Evelyn said.

"You both look tremendous. Whatever is going on in your lives, it sure looks as if it agrees with you. Ana will be so disappointed to have missed your visit. Now, catch me up on your comings and goings," Jeanette said as she put her arm around Cindy.

"Big plans, Mama Jeanette, big plans—we're going into partnership with Evelyn's stepsister. Wait till you hear this. Amanda, that's Evie's sister, received a large settlement from a lawsuit that she had filed regarding the death of her mother in a horrible auto accident a few years ago. Well, Amanda purchased the Christmas tree farm where her family had been living for many years. Her stepfather, who manages the tree farm, and Evie's mom, who married Mandy's stepfather, have all lived there for some time. Now, here's the most fantastic part—on this farm is a big old house—I guess you could even call it a mansion—and Amanda wants to use it as an artists' haven. And, surprisingly, she asked Evie and me if we wanted to have space there to teach acting and play writing. I'm so excited that I could split my gut. Amanda plans to include all types of arts—jewelry making, dance, music, and juried crafts. She plans to have a space for her stepfather who is a great wood carver. You should see the beautiful things that he has created. But Mama Jeanette and Daddy, I'll need some cash in order to buy into this place. Any chance I could talk you into investing in us?" Cindy said hopefully.

"Wow, Cindy," Pete said. "Just a minute—her name is Amanda and John is her stepfather—could it be our Amanda?"

"Our Amanda?" asked Cindy.

"Slip of the tongue. Evelyn, is your stepsister the same Amanda who testified at Ayden Ash's trial in 1973?" Pete asked.

"Yes," Evelyn responded hesitantly. "Will that be a problem for you?"

"No, oh my, no—I had no idea what happened to her. I'm delighted to know that she's doing well."

"Dad, wait until you see her—she's beautiful—blonde hair and a slim figure. I could hate her if I didn't like her so much," Cindy said, winking at Evelyn. "I'm sure I'm the *plain Jane* when I stand between Evie and Amanda. Tell me, what do you think about the idea of the haven?"

"This sounds truly wonderful," Jeanette said. "I can understand why you two are thrilled. What a lovely place for an artists' haven—with all those beautiful trees. How's Amanda emotionally, Evelyn? Is she doing okay?"

"Yes and no—while she's working hard on her idea, I've discovered that she's been corresponding with that creep. She's closed-mouth about the whole thing. I cannot get anything out of her about him. That's the only part of her plan that makes me a bit nervous. I thought that she hated him—I know that John does."

"Maybe her writing to him was some kind of therapy—it's a strategy that is often used to help victims heal. Did she ever get counseling?" Jeanette asked.

"I'm not sure about that. Amanda doesn't talk about what happened at the damned school. But, if she lets him back into her life, I'm out of there," Evelyn said firmly. "At last, Amanda seems to be getting better—she's actually happy now. I want to keep her that way. I don't know how to help her, but I surely hope that she is through with Ayden Ash."

Pete had been quiet for some time. Finally, he said, "Evelyn, do you think Amanda would allow me to visit her?"

"I'm not sure, but I could ask."

"What do you have in mind, Pete?" Jeanette asked.

"I'm not sure myself, but I feel that I would really like to talk with her—not as a reporter—but as a friend. Perhaps I could go there as an interested party, since we'll be providing the financial backing for Cindy and Evelyn. She may not even remember me—after all, she was only a teen-ager at the time of the trial. Maybe, with a few interviewing techniques, I might be able to uncover her motives for writing to Ayden."

"Daddy, does that mean you'll provide the money? Do you realize that we'll need about fifty thousand to buy in and renovate our space?" Cindy said as she began to jump up and down with delight.

"Yes, pumpkin, we'll give you the money. Consider it part of your inheritance. No trips to the South of France or anything like that," Pete teased.

"Daddy, you're the greatest!" Cindy said as she hugged her dad and her stepmother.

"Evelyn, how do you think I should approach Amanda?" Pete asked.

"I'll tell her that you're Cindy's dad and that you want to see the place before you give her the backing she needs. That should work."

"Pete, be careful when you talk with her," Jeanette said. "We have no idea how badly she's been hurt through all of this—and, on top of that, losing her mother so tragically has had to make her as fragile as a china doll."

CHAPTER 40

(March, 2000)

Ayden came out of the prison gates clutching two paper bags, one white and one brown, and hustled to get into the battered old van. Darrell was behind the wheel and smiled broadly as he reached for the bags that Ayden was holding in his arms. Sarah was huddled in the corner of the back seat and looked more like a lost puppy dog than the wife of the released prisoner. As Ayden and Darrell greeted one another warmly, Sarah sank deeper into the crevice of the back seat. She appeared to be frightened and didn't even acknowledge her husband.

"Master," Darrell said, "At last, we have you back! Your flock has already been moved to New Valley and they're awaiting your arrival. It will be a joyous time of reawakening."

"And, my first son—is he prepared to complete the task that I have assigned?"

"Yes, he has everything in place. You have taught your son well, Master. He is a true believer."

"My friend," Ayden said, "You too are a true believer. You'll be amply rewarded for your faithfulness. You'll be second-in-command and will reap the rewards you so richly deserve." Then, he turned, looked at Sarah, and said, "Sarah, what is wrong with you? You certainly don't look pleased to see me. Are you going to sulk all the way home?"

"I'm sorry, Ayden, I don't feel very well. Of course, I'm happy to see you. It has been very lonely without you," Sarah said as she reached forward and patted Ayden on his shoulder.

"Darrell, we'll begin our new life in New Valley, but we will not be staying there permanently. As I have shared with you before, Amanda will be inviting all of us to move to her tree farm where we will have full use of the property as well as its resources. She indicated that she'll be in contact with me when all is ready," Ayden said excitedly.

A look of anger came over Sarah's face. While she knew that Amanda was writing to Ayden, she didn't know that they would all be moving in with her. She closed her eyes tightly, trying to shut the whole idea out of her mind.

"Are you certain that she'll come through with her promises? I never met her, but I want to make certain that she is not using you for some other purposes," Darrell said.

"Darrell, I know this woman very well," Ayden said forcefully. "I am an excellent judge of people, and I believe that she's indeed contrite about her appearance in the courtroom and is ready to make amends. As a child, she held me in high esteem, and it appears she still feels that same way. However, my ace in the hole will be these letters that she has written to me," Ayden said as he held up the white paper bag. "If she's not telling me the truth, she certainly wouldn't want them to be seen by anyone."

"Ayden, you old fox, you. I knew that I could depend on you no matter what. You are amazing," Darrell said, as he nodded his approval.

During the two-hour drive to New Valley, neither man paid any attention to Sarah. Darrell shared information about the new members of the cult that Ayden would soon be meeting—their strengths and weaknesses.

"Master, we have grown in your honor," Darrell said proudly. "Your flock now includes six men, nine women, and twelve children. They are all eager to meet you. You will be pleased with the strength of their commitment and the manner in which they demonstrate their loyalty to your tenants."

Then Darrell went into detail about their financial condition, and Ayden was delighted that Darrell had managed to recruit several members who had willingly shared their resources with the group.

Sarah, on the other hand, spent time thinking about Amanda—a young upstart who would probably be getting all of Ayden's attention.

Sarah vowed to herself that she would not allow this to happen. Uncertain of how she would accomplish this feat, Sarah only knew that she had to get rid of Amanda one way or another. Ayden had warned her many times in the past that jealousy was not an admirable trait. But this was more than that. Sarah was the one who had been faithful to Ayden all these years—she had emotionally saved herself for him—a gift to the man she loved with all her heart. Amanda was not going to have him—no way. Amanda was a traitor and she would always be one.

"Just five minutes more, Ayden, and you'll be home. Properties around the church haven't changed much. There is one building, however, on the opposite side of your place that is now a large apartment house. I think it will provide access to possible recruits for our group," Darrell said as he gave Ayden a wink.

"Ah, my friend, you and I will be able to work wonders together. You are exactly what I needed for a long time. How fortunate that we two were able to unite. And then…"

Ayden stopped talking when he spotted a group of about twenty people walking up and down the sidewalk, carrying placards. "What the hell?" Ayden said.

Sarah poked her head up and her mouth fell open when she read the placards. *Sinner. You are not wanted here.*

Darrell said, "Ayden, don't react—that's what they want you to do. Let's just get out of the van and get into the building. Don't even look at them."

Ayden was following Darrell's advice, when he suddenly spotted Pete, standing on the corner, with his camera aimed directly at him. While the shouting continued, Pete and Ayden locked eyes.

Smiling broadly, Ayden said loudly, "Pete, my long-lost friend. You have disrespected me for the last time. Your sweet reward has already been planned." Ayden then hurried into the church building, paying no attention to Sarah, who was still huddled in the van with a blanket over her head.

Later, after Darrell had introduced Ayden to the new cult members, they all sat down to a celebration meal. Eventually, Ayden excused himself and disappeared upstairs. First, he looked around his private office. Nothing had been disturbed—it was exactly the way he had left it after he was so wrongly convicted He was holding the bags that he had carried out of the prison and began looking for a safe place to put his treasures. He tucked the brown bag, filled with writings and epistles that he had created while in prison, into the bottom drawer of his desk—these would be the beginnings of his next book. They would also provide the basis for his planned lawsuits against the Department of Corrections. Ayden felt that he had been discriminated against in several ways, and that the prison had been charging outrageous fees for items sold in the commissary and for mailing and copying services. However, he was far more concerned about the bag that held the few letters that Amanda had sent him. He didn't know where she lived since she had used a post office box for her address. But, she had promised that she would contact him at the church. And, when that day arrived, he would also take her for his bride.

Ayden lowered the steps that provided access to the attic that he used for storage of old books and maps. Apparently, it too had not been disturbed since he had been sentenced. He wanted to make certain that none of his flock would find these precious letters. In case Amanda was not being honest with him—which he doubted—he would use them against her. Ayden had learned early on in his life to always have a back-up plan—just another technique to assure that he obtained the things that he wanted—and he wanted Amanda.

Ayden lifted himself into the small area and removed the letters from the bag. He touched each letter tenderly. Opening a small leather valise, Ayden gently placed the letters inside. But, the picture of Amanda, the one that had hung in his cell was far too precious to be tucked away out of sight. He would put this vision of loveliness in a frame, and place it on his desk—no matter what Sarah would say. In fact, he began to relish the idea of Sarah finding Amanda's likeness in such a special place of honor.

CHAPTER 41

(April, 2000)

Amanda watched as Pete got out of his car and approached the big white house. And, much to her relief, he was a pleasant-looking fellow who didn't appear to be threatening. Evie, her stepsister, had told her that Pete was Cindy's dad and that he would provide the funding for their space in *The Artists' Haven.* She had been surprised when Evie revealed that Pete was one of the reporters who had covered Ayden's trial so many years ago—making Amanda a bit apprehensive. She had tried so hard to forget about the trial, but, like a thief in the night, memories of the courtroom would come crashing back into her life every so often—invading her space—taking away her peace.

This visit from Pete might change the plans that she had made with John. Maybe that was just wishful thinking. For some time, Amanda had wanted to tell John that she no longer wanted to harm Ayden. If they went through with their plans, she would probably be one of the people under suspicion. She thought about those letters—maybe they had been a huge mistake. If he saved them, and he probably had, the authorities could use them against her in some way. She was already a tainted woman—as some people had called her twenty-seven years ago. What would Mrs. Nesbit say if she knew about the plans that she was making with John?

"Amanda, make sure that you get him to sit on the gold sofa. I'll be behind the divider screen. I want to be certain that you'll be in no danger," John said, as he quickly took his hiding place.

Pete walked up the wide steps and pulled on the old, brass door knocker. Amanda opened the door, and with a weak voice said, "Hello, Mr. Forster, welcome to *The Artists' Haven.*

"Hello, Amanda," Pete said, looking over the entrance way. "My, I can see why Cindy is in love with this home. It has so much charm. My wife would go wild in here. She loves traditional houses and she loves to decorate."

"Thank you. I love it, too. Before we discuss what Cindy and Evie want to do as part of *The Artists' Haven,* I'd like to show you the rest of the home. Let's begin by going upstairs."

After Amanda cast a sideways glance at the place where John was secluded, she guided Pete up the lovely curved stairway to the second floor. He listened intently, only interrupting her presentation one time. Pete was impressed. The home was even lovelier than he had imagined. But, what surprised him the most was that the skinny little teen-ager, who had sat on the witness stand so many years ago, had blossomed into this refined, intelligent woman. Amanda patiently pointed out architectural details in each room and explained how she pictured what would be needed to help the artists teach their crafts and sell their wares.

"I think of Scarlet O'Hara whenever I come down these steps," Amanda said.

"I can understand that," Pete said. "You just won't find many homes like this, especially in the North."

Later, after Amanda had shown Pete all the rooms downstairs, she encouraged Pete to make himself comfortable on the old-fashioned love seat, positioned at the right angle to allow guests to view the gardens.

"Before too long, the gardens will be in full bloom. I know nothing about gardening, but John, my stepdad, has already made arrangements with a local man who will take care of all that for me. I believe that we could also offer to perform weddings here—picture the bride and groom, surrounded by flowers—taking their vows," Amanda said rather proudly. "My favorite room, however, is the solarium. It's the perfect environment for artists. I'm just starting to fool around with landscape painting, and while I've taken a few lessons, I can't wait until a real artist is here to teach me."

"Amanda, I'm amazed. You're such a charming woman. Your enthusiasm is really catching. I couldn't agree with you more. I really believe that you have a winner on your hands. How do you feel about managing all this?"

"Scared—unbelievably scared—so much, in fact, that at times I think that I might be out of my mind. I really don't have the education, or the know-how, to do all of this. But Doc Nesbit has agreed to be my business advisor—that kind of takes some of the scariness away."

"Amanda, how do you feel about Ayden Ash getting out of prison? Do you feel safe?" Pete asked tenderly.

Amanda avoided looking at Pete for awhile. After staring at the floor for several minutes, she lifted her head and said, "Mixed—my emotions are mixed. I have hated him for so long that I cannot ever remember not hating him. To be honest, I've wanted him dead. And I would kill him in a second if I thought I could get away with it."

"Let's talk about that. If you would—harm him in some way, Amanda—then you would become just like him. Not caring about how your actions would affect others. Think of it, Amanda. You could lose this place. You could lose your freedom. But, most of all, you could lose yourself to darkness and evil. That's what Ayden has done his entire life."

A little tear streamed down Amanda's face. "I know—I know. But how can I release myself from wanting revenge? I lost my father—and then my mother. I lost my childhood innocence. And when I thought I was going to become a mother, I lost my baby. How much more can I lose? How can I ever get them back?"

"You can't. When bad things happen to good people, we look for reasons—why such things happen. But we never get the answers we're seeking. Look around you. You never expected to own all this property. Your ideas for using this property will have a lasting impact on the teachers and students of the arts. The beautiful things that they will create—the paintings that will hang on walls of homes, the plays that audiences will enjoy, and the beautiful crafts that will brighten their lives—all this will make your heart soar. You will be bringing beauty into not only your own life, but into the lives of others. Think of it, Amanda. You can counteract Ayden's evilness, his egotistical, maniacal behavior, by allowing artists to create beauty in various forms. What a legacy you will be able to leave!"

Just then, John stepped out from behind the screen. Startled by John's presence, Pete immediately stood up. He watched as John took Amanda into his arms. "He's right, Amanda, he's right. I was so caught up in my own desire for revenge that I almost ruined your future. I'm so sorry."

Amanda nestled in John's arms and wept.

"The letters, John, they could destroy us if we change our plans. How can we get them back?" Amanda asked through her tears.

CHAPTER 42

(One day later)

When Sarah walked into Ayden's office, she immediately spotted the framed picture. There, in the middle of Ayden's desk, in a silver frame, was a picture of a beautiful smiling Amanda. Sarah's photograph, which used to reside on the desk, was gone. Her stomach churned and anger filled her very soul. *How could he do this to me?*

She had overheard Ayden telling Darrell about Amanda's letters. She needed to find where he had hidden them. After rummaging through his desk, she came up empty-handed. She looked around the room that was filled almost floor to ceiling with books. She wondered if he could have possibly hidden his precious letters in one of those books—if so—it would take her days to look through all of them. Then, she realized that the panel, leading to the forbidden storage space, was not closed properly.

Sarah used a side chair to get high enough to pull the rope that was attached to the storage opening. She was surprised when the ladder came down so quickly, almost knocking her off the chair. After climbing the few steps, she positioned herself so she could look around the area. At first, nothing seemed to be out-of-place. There were several cartons, all labeled *Department of Education*, and little stacks of books tied with white cord. Then, taking another look, she saw Ayden's leather briefcase sitting in an upright position. Grasping the handle, she pushed it over to the edge and snapped it open. There they were—the letters—the letters that were going to destroy her life. After closing the briefcase, she climbed back down the steps while balancing the brief case in her arms.

She placed the brief case on Ayden's desk and opened it once again. Picking up one of the letters, she sat down in Ayden's desk chair and began reading. *How dare she? How dare she say such things to my husband.* She tossed the letters into a metal wastebasket. Next, she picked up the picture of Amanda and broke open the frame. After ripping the picture into tiny pieces, she threw them on top of the letters. Looking around for matches, she walked over to the little altar on the far side of the office. A box of candles had been stored on a little shelf under the altar. When she opened the box she found them—the matches needed to get rid of Amanda.

Her hands began shaking. She had a difficult time trying to get the match to ignite. The first match crumbled in her hands. However, the next match ignited immediately. The flames coming out of the wastebasket were glorious. Sarah was smiling now.

Suddenly, the office door opened and Ayden stood in the doorway. When he saw the flames, he shouted, "Sarah, what are you doing?"

"I got rid of her. I got rid of her face and her letters. I hate her," Sarah said woodenly as she moved over to the ladder.

"You—what?" Ayden yelled as he took a rug and tried to expunge the flames. "So help me, I will kill you!"

Sarah realized that she was trapped between the ladder and the doorway and would be unable to get past Ayden. She turned and scurried up the ladder and pulled herself back into the storage area. Ayden was right behind her. As she attempted to close the opening, he was already pulling himself into the space. "You bitch, you fucking bitch," Ayden yelled. "I will strangle you!"

Sarah leaned back and positioned her feet on Ayden's chest and pushed with all her might. It worked—he fell backwards—hitting his head on the corner of the desk. He landed on the office floor with a thud. She looked down at her husband, lying motionless along side the smoking wastebasket.

"Ayden…Ayden…" a panicky Sarah said as she climbed down the ladder.

She picked up his lifeless hand. It was then that she saw the blood gushing out of his skull and on to the carpet. Sarah opened the door and began screaming.

Darrell rushed up the stairway and, when he saw Ayden lying on the floor, he shouted, "Sarah, what did you do?"

"I didn't do it. He fell. I didn't do it. He was angry with me. I burned the harlot's stuff!" Sarah said frantically.

As Eddie rushed up the stairs, Darrell said, "Get her out of here. And then wait downstairs for my instructions."

Darrell leaned over Ayden. He could not believe his eyes. His Master, his Primate—was dead. Now, it was going to be up to him to save Ayden's little community. He knelt by Ayden's body for a few minutes and unashamedly wept. He had lost his hope—his future—and he didn't know what he was going to do now. He leaned over the motionless body and planted a kiss on Ayden's forehead.

Ten minutes later, Darrell went down the steps to the living room. Eddie had assembled the cult members, and they were seated obediently around the perimeter of the room—their faces drained of color. A sense of dread filled the air. They were frightened and were looking for direction from Darrell.

"Our Master is dead," Darrell said quietly.

Sarah, who had hidden herself in a darkened corner of the room, would not make eye contact with anyone.

"What happened?" Eddie asked.

"Now, all of you—listen to me. I must call 911, but first I need your assistance. If we are to keep our group together, if we intend to live our lives the way our Master instructed us, we must all tell the same story; so listen very carefully: Ayden went to his office, and when he did not respond to my call to come to dinner—I went upstairs and found him dead on the floor. The steps to the storage area had been pulled down and I believe that Ayden fell off the ladder and hit his head. That is all you need to know. Sarah, did you hear what I just said?" Darrell questioned in a firm voice.

Sarah finally raised her head. "Yes, I heard you."

Darrell then made two calls—one to 911 and the other to Ayden's son.

CHAPTER 43

(May, 2000)

Carrying the Sunday paper in one hand, while balancing a mug of coffee with the other, Jeanette made her way to the brick-lined patio. Jeanette was looking forward to reading the supplement that Pete had written about the life and death of Ayden Ash. It had only been two weeks since Ayden had died after a fall in his own office. She looked at all the pictures first, admiring the shots that Pete had taken throughout the years of Ayden's life, which represented the unbelievable series of events that had surrounded this evil man. She was very impressed with how well Pete had summarized the abnormal happenings involving Ayden and his cult members. She noticed that Pete hadn't mentioned Amanda by name, but merely an *under-age girl.*

This man, an abomination of a human being, had been part of their lives for a long, long period of time. She thought about the times when Pete had wrestled with the strange appeal this man had on others who blindly followed him and, in doing so, they had crossed over to darkness. If only Ayden had started out on the right path. What a wonderful preacher he might have been. He could have made a positive impact on society instead of leaving a legacy of evil.

"Hey, sweetie, how did you like my piece?" Pete said as he pulled a chair alongside Jeanette.

"You did a great job, Pete. I loved the photos you included."

"Well, they were taken by a crack photographer, you know," he said, as he snatched the paper out of her hands.

"I'm still having a hard time believing that Ayden is really dead. To think that he spent so many years in jail, avoiding foul play, only to stumble and fall to his death in his own office, is surreal."

"I'm not certain that we've heard the last of this. His death hasn't been ruled an accident as yet by the coroner."

"You think one of them killed him?" Jeanette asked incredulously.

"It's a possibility. However, that'll be hard to prove given that the cult members all had the same story," Pete said. "The gash in his head was certainly enough to kill him. But, was it really a result of a fall from the ladder, or was it something else?"

"You know, Pete, when I read your article, I couldn't help but recall the threat that Ayden made on his way out of the courtroom after he had been sentenced. Revenge—that's what he focused on—in fact, I think he used the words *sweet revenge.* While I don't believe in dead people being able to ravage revenge on others, he was such a strange, mystical person, that it makes me wonder if such powers do exist," Jeanette said.

"On the day that Ayden returned to New Valley, when he stepped out of the van, he shouted at me. And, once again, he used the words *sweet revenge,*" Pete added.

Picking up the paper, Pete riffled through the pages, and said, "You know what I think—I think the bastard had enough time for debauchery—his time for hurting and destroying the lives of others is over—now he has a Higher Authority to answer to. I hope that Amanda followed my suggestion not to read the paper at all. When I called her yesterday, she seemed to be in a very positive mood, and I believe that she's on the road to recovery. I didn't want her to begin to relive her ordeal one more time. I hope she tossed the paper away," Pete said. "One thing for certain, his time for *sweet revenge* is over. So we can toss that idea out of our minds."

"I wish we could have just tossed Ayden away," Jeanette said. "He always gave me the creeps. His evilness seemed endless."

The two settled back in their chairs. The sun was streaming down and the spring flowers were in bloom "It's so lovely out here. Whenever I have time to spend lounging around like a lazy old housewife, I realize just how lucky I've been."

"Well, Sweet Stuff, maybe you are lazy, but an old housewife you are not. Babe, it's such a gorgeous day. Let's go out for a Sunday brunch, drive around the mountains for awhile, and then, well, maybe, we can come back here for a little nap."

Jeanette looked at Pete out of the corner of her eye. "Nap, you say? Are you sure it's a nap you want?"

"I'm surprised you question my motives. I have nothing but your best interests at heart. Yes, a nap, or whatever."

"Oh, whatever—well, we'll see."

"Oh, before I forget, what about Ana?" Pete asked. "When she left the other day, I was under the assumption that she would be back yesterday. How long does it take to get trained to be a camp counselor, for God's sake? She's been doing this for the past few years—now she needs training—for what?"

"Pete, our daughter is almost twenty-one. She's a big girl now, who's totally capable of running her own life," Jeanette responded. "But I'm surprised that she hasn't returned or at least called us. Wait here, I'll call the church secretary and perhaps she'll put our minds at ease," Jeanette said as she went back into the house.

Pete settled back in his chair. He then reached for the supplement and re-read what he had written. It was good. In fact, he thought it was probably the best piece he had ever written. In his heart of hearts, Pete was hoping that this piece would be considered for a special award.

"Something's wrong, Pete," Jeanette said as she came out the door once more. "No training sessions for counselors at Camp Morningside have been held since last year. That means Ana lied to us. Pete, where could she be?" Jeanette asked, as she put her hands over her face. "She lied—why?"

"Let's not panic. The day is young yet. Maybe in a few hours she'll be home. Let's think about this. Ana is a good kid. I don't understand why she lied to us, but, obviously, something's going on that she didn't want to tell us. Do you think it could involve that young man, Triple A?"

Jeanette thought for a minute or so. Then, she said, "Pete, can you get on Ana's email to check her communications with him? I hate parents who don't trust their kids, but this could be serious."

"I think I can," Pete said. "Let's go upstairs and see what we can find."

After the two of them looked around Ana's room, they discovered that her laptop was gone. "What about the letters she got from him?" Pete asked. "Where would she have put them?"

"In that little box over there—her treasure box," Jeanette said. "Here they are."

They sat crossed-legged on the floor, passing the letters back and forth.

"I feel terrible doing this, Pete. But, in the back of my mind, all I can think about is how often I lied to my parents and how often I got into trouble as a result," Jeanette said, on the verge of tears. As she read Triple A's last letter, she said, "Wow, they are in love—that's for sure," Jeanette said. "Pete, do you think they've run away together?"

"Maybe they eloped," Pete answered.

"No, not my Ana—eloping—that's not what I wanted for her," Jeanette cried.

"Baby, it may well be, but maybe it's what she wanted."

"It's my fault, Pete. When I was her age, I was a wild child—totally irresponsible. I thought Ana was much smarter than I was."

Pete gathered up the letters and returned them to Ana's treasure box. "We don't have to tell her that we violated her privacy. We'll wait for her to tell us about what's going on. But, from what we read, I don't think she's in trouble. I think the lovers are together and, while we are concerned about that, things like this happen every day. Ana will come home—when she's ready."

Later that evening, Jeanette and Pete were seated in the living room, trying to get interested in a television show, when they heard a car door slam. Suddenly, the front door opened and Ana came rushing into the room.

"Mommy, Daddy, I'm back," Ana said joyfully.

Jeanette could see that a young man, with a broad smile on his face, was following Ana through the doorway. Surprisingly, he looked vaguely familiar.

"Ana, where have you been?" Jeanette asked as she tried to keep calm.

Ana held out her left hand. A little gold band was on her ring finger. "Mommy, Daddy, I want you to meet my husband, Triple A."

Pete and Jeanette seemed to be unable to move. They looked at each other, not knowing how to react. Jeanette glanced at Ana and then at Triple A. His smile had disappeared and it had been replaced with an evil sneer.

Finally, Pete said, "Ana, we wish you would have told us this before. And, if this young man is going to be part of our family, don't you think we should know his real name?"

Ana smiled broadly. "Sure, Daddy, this is Adam Aaron Ash."

"No!" Jeanette shouted, as she grabbed Pete's arm.

"Yes, Mrs. Forster, I am Ayden Ash's son."

"Oh, my God! *Sweet revenge.* He did it, Pete. He reached out from the dead," Jeanette said, just before she collapsed on the floor.